The Chinese Chop

The Chinese Chop

Juanita Sheridan

Introduction by Tom & Enid Schantz

Felony & Mayhem Press • New York

Publisher's Note

In this book and in the Lily Wu series, Hawaiian words and names do not include diacritical marks, and text appears as it would have in English-language materials at the time of its original publication, in the 1940s and '50s.

All the characters and events portrayed in this work are fictitious.

THE CHINESE CHOP

A Felony & Mayhem mystery

PRINTING HISTORY
First edition (Doubleday): 1949
Edition with introduction (Rue Morgue): 2000

Felony & Mayhem edition: 2024

Reprinted with the permission of the author's grandson
and literary executor, Alan Hart

Biographical note included with the kind permission
of the Estate of Tom Schantz

Copyright © 1949 by Juanita Sheridan
Biographical note copyright © 2000 by The Rue Morgue Press

ISBN: 978-1-63194-314-0 (paperback)
978-1-63194-315-7 (ebook)

Manufactured in the United States of America

Cataloging-in-Publication information for this book
is available from the Library of Congress.

For Irv, who said: "Johnnie, is Johnnie."

CLASSIC MAYHEM

Devoted to the best traditional mysteries of the 20th century, both Golden Age charmers, written before about 1960, and those from the Silver Age, which shine just as brightly and have much in common with their older cousins. If you love twisty puzzles, witty characterizations, and the art of the civilized crime novel, pull up a chair!

More Classic Mayhem

PAMELA BRANCH

The Wooden Overcoat
and coming soon...
Murder Every Monday
Lion in the Cellar
Murder's Little Sister

JUANITA SHERIDAN

The Chinese Chop
and coming soon...
The Kahuna Killer
The Mamo Murders
The Waikiki Widow

EVELYN E. SMITH

Miss Melville Regrets
and coming soon...
Miss Melville Returns
Miss Melville's Revenge
Miss Melville Rides a Tiger

FELONY & MAYHEM

The Chinese Chop

Introduction

The Many Lives of Juanita Sheridan

Although Janice Cameron refers to Lily Wu as an "Oriental" when she first greets her on the telephone, author Juanita Sheridan was merely using the common civilized parlance of the time (1949), politically incorrect though it may be today. In fact, there's little that's stereotypical about her portrait of Lily, and certainly nothing demeaning. If anything, both Sheridan and Janice Cameron tend to idealize the soft-spoken but self-assured young Chinese woman who can assume whatever demeanor best suits her purposes at the moment. In fact, Lily Wu is one of the earliest and best-realized Asian detectives in the genre. She is certainly not a female version of the movies' Charlie Chan (the Chan of the books was much more fully realized), and if she appears "inscrutable" at times—well, she has her reasons, as the reader and Janice will soon learn. Lily is the spiritual godmother of Leslie Glass's April Woo or S.J. Rozan's Lydia Chin and as original a character as you can hope to meet in mid-twentieth century mystery fiction.

But it would be a mistake to say that Lily was just the first realistic female *Asian* sleuth in the genre because, in many respects, Lily also represents a transition from the female sleuths of the 1930s to the more realistic women characters of

1

the post Marcia Muller period. There's a lot more Sharon McCone in Lily than there is Jane Amanda Edwards.

Sheridan's contemporary critics certainly felt that way. Writing in *The New York Times*, Anthony Boucher (for whom Bouchercon, the World Mystery Convention, is named) commented: "Women make up such a large portion of the best writers and editors of detective stories that it's a pity there aren't more female detectives—women, that is, who star in their own right rather than merely serving as half of a Bright Young Couple." Boucher was grateful for the female sleuths then in vogue, especially Agatha Christie's Miss Marple, F. Tennyson Jesse's Solange Fontaine, Gladys Mitchell's Mrs. Bradley, and Stuart Palmer's Miss Hildegarde Withers.

But of all the female sleuths who had figuratively or actually picked up a magnifying glass up to that point, there was only one of them that Boucher would admit to being in love with—Lily Wu: "the exquisitely blended product of Eastern and Western cultures," explaining that he respected her professional skills while delighting in her personal charms in the same way that characterized his "regard for Barbara del Geddes or Nanette Fabray or Bidù Sayáo." (If you're under fifty and don't understand the comparisons, this might be a good time to call your mother.)

Strictly speaking, Lily wasn't the first female Asian sleuth to grace the pages of a detective novel, although she is generally credited as such. Mountain of Virtue, a beautiful and very intelligent Eurasian, aids a Mexican guerrilla fighter who solves mysteries in war-torn China starting in 1942 with *Murder, Chop Chop* (also reprinted by The Rue Morgue Press) and two subsequent books, *An Inch of Time* and *The Nightwalkers* by James Norman. Nor was Lily even the first Asian female sleuth created by Sheridan, who in 1943 collaborated with her family dentist, Dorothy Dudley (who got coauthor status in return for providing background information as well as—according to a family legend—braces for Sheridan's young son) to produce *What Dark Secret* featuring an Asian reporter-cum-sleuth with an Anglo name, Angie Tudor, who resembles Lily in features and actions.

But Lily is the first fully Asian female detective to be the principal sleuth in a series, and it was a long time before there was to be another one. Although Janice Cameron is often referred to as the chief series character, the promising young novelist actually serves as Lily's sidekick, narrating their adventures and making for a slightly more intelligent Watson than the original, although at times Lily looks at her "like a teacher regarding a deplorably retarded child."

Lily herself was a composite of several of Sheridan's Chinese friends, although she wrote that "she looks like an actress from the Golden Wall theater, who was one of the most ruthless human beings I have ever known."

Lily appeared in four books, starting with the present volume in 1949 which was followed by *The Kahuna Killer* (1951), *The Mamo Murders* (1952), and *The Waikiki Widow* (1953), all of which will be reprinted by The Rue Morgue Press. Some critics consider *The Waikiki Widow* one of the best mystery novels of the immediate postwar period. Although *The Chinese Chop* takes place in New York City, most of the action in the other three books occurs after Janice and Lily move back to Hawaii.

Part of the reason for the bond between Janice and Lily when they meet in New York is that they had both lived in Hawaii, although Lily's family home was located in Manhattan's Chinatown. Having grown up in Hawaii with its large Asian population, Janice is quite familiar with Chinese-Americans and also recognizes, as Lily is quick to see, that many mainland Americans might not be as eager as she to accept a young Chinese girl as a friend.

While much of the charm in *The Chinese Chop* lies in Sheridan's portrait of postwar New York City, where women are struggling with the housing shortage, the difficulty in finding jobs now that the men had returned from war, and the new fashion in longer skirts, the series is at its best after Janice and Lily return to Hawaii, a place where Sheridan lived for seven years with at least one of her eight husbands.

Born Juanita Lorraine Light in Oklahoma on November 15, 1906, Sheridan claimed in a lengthy letter to her editor at the Doubleday, Doran Crime Club that she came by her knack for murder naturally since her maternal grandfather was killed by Pancho Villa in a holdup while her own father may possibly have been poisoned by a political rival.

After her father's death, Sheridan and her mother hit the road, touring the American West. When she was on vacation from boarding school, Sheridan was often put by her mother on a train "with a tag around my neck which told my name and destination. I was never afraid, and never lost."

That self-reliance came in handy years later when at the height of the Depression (ca. 1930) Sheridan, with an infant son in arms, found herself dropped off at the corner of 7th and Broadway in Los Angeles with only two suitcases and five cents to her name. She used the nickel to telephone a friend, who loaned her five dollars, and went out and got a job as a script girl for $20 a week. Her son Ross went to live with a rich Beverly Hills foster family and at about the age of six was legally adopted by his maternal grandmother. After the adoption, Sheridan, who had by then sold a couple of original screenplays, headed for Hawaii to begin her writing career.

Life wasn't all that easy in Hawaii and once again she hit the pawnshops, although, as usual, "the typewriter was the last to go." Sheridan said these tough times taught her that "it isn't the smugly prosperous who offer to help. It's the poor little guys who know what it's like; it's the landlady, worrying over her mortgage, who lets you sleep in her garage when you owe three months' rent. It's the tired counter man, seeing you order black coffee and soup when your neck bones look like coat hangers, who says, 'Why don't you take the roast beef, kid? It's on the house.' It's the shabby girl behind you in line waiting for a job addressing envelopes at $3.50 per day, who catches you when your knees buckle and says, 'Here's a buck, honey. I can spare it. Gotta boy friend.'" No doubt these years of deprivation are why Sheridan filled her books with detailed descriptions of sumptuous surroundings and with characters like Louise in *The Chinese Chop*, who longed for luxury and admitted that the slogan of a popular ad campaign of the time, "because you like nice things," was aimed at her.

Though Lily and Janice are not without money when the series begins, both had known hard times (Janice's description of her early writing career echoes the author's own experiences) and were familiar with the kinds of things a young woman had to put up with when she was on her own. "I once spent a hectic evening being chased around a suite of offices by a boss who was trying to prove that the best position for a woman was horizontal," Sheridan wrote. "It was a difficult situation because I didn't dare lose that job: I was behind on my rent."

To those people, editors included, who thought her plots contained more than a touch of melodrama, Sheridan said she was only writing from life, having been clubbed by a gun, choked into unconsciousness by a man she never saw, and on two occasions "awakened from a sound sleep to find a pair of strange hands reaching for me through the dark…"

And she claimed to know at least one murderer who got away with it. "I know a woman," she said, "who murdered her husband as surely as if she held the gun with which he shot himself. He was a warm-hearted guy with a great talent; what he created is still enjoyed by the movie-going public. She is a sweet-faced, triple-plated bitch. But he's dead and she's thriving."

Sheridan never used much of the material she gleaned from real life, figuring that no one would believe it: "One of my most interesting friends in Hawaii was the madame of a 'house.' She looked like a schoolteacher, wore glasses and spoke New England. She had a record collection and a library. She was twenty-six and her annual net was higher than that of many high-voltage executives. I visited her place occasionally, and after the girls learned to trust me I heard some biographies which can't be printed—no one would believe them."

While in Hawaii, Sheridan began selling short stories. She also married architect Fritz Elliott, at which time she asked that

Ross be allowed to join her in Honolulu. When the boy's grand-mother—and legal guardian—refused, Sheridan came to the mainland, snatched the boy while the older woman was out for a walk and sneaked the two of them on board the *President Hoover* with the steerage passengers, "down where they eat with chopsticks at one big table, the toilets are without doors, and there is no promenade deck." Ross remembers that they embarked on the ship the very day his mother "kidnapped" him but Sheridan claims that she and the boy hid out in San Francisco for a week while the FBI hunted for them.

Sheridan sold several stories, including two mysteries with Asian characters, which won $500 prizes. Ross left Hawaii in May 1941 and went back to live with his grandmother. He was to see his mother again only five more times. Sheridan, with the manuscript to *What Dark Secret* in her hands, left Hawaii in November of the same year, just a couple of weeks before the Japanese attack on Pearl Harbor, landed in San Pedro and headed for New York by car for the next stage of her life.

At some point during this period she settled down (for the time being) in a housing cooperative on a 130-acre farm in Rockland County, New York, where she and her current husband bathed in a stream and slept in a tent while helping to construct their house.

Her mystery novel writing career apparently ended, as it did for so many writers (women, in particular), in 1953, perhaps because television was supplanting books, perhaps because World War II and Korea veterans were demanding books in the Mickey Spillane mode.

Sheridan returned to Hollywood briefly when one of her Lily Wu books was sold to television as the basis for the pilot of a mystery series set in Hawaii. She "left after a couple of sessions with the Hollywood movie types," son Ross reported, because "she couldn't stand the hypocrisy."

Eventually Sheridan settled in Guadalajara, Mexico, with her last husband, Hugh Graham, and found work as a Spanish-English translator. A fall from a horse (she learned to ride while working as a polo horse exerciser in Hollywood in the 1930s) left her with a broken hip. The last time Ross saw her she was in extreme pain and would "lock herself in her room and mix painkillers and alcohol to try to ease the pain."

He never saw her again. In May 1974 he received a post-card informing him of his mother's death. Juanita Sheridan's life was a colorful one, filled with many adventures and the same sort of melodrama she occasionally employed in her writing. She lived through some desperate times and, one hopes, many happy ones as well. Although she is little known today, she made a significant contribution to the mystery genre that ought not be forgotten.

Tom & Enid Schantz
Boulder, Colorado
June 2000

Chapter One

My window at Mrs. Finney's house looked out over one of Manhattan's least publicized views: grimy rooftops, blank courtyards, lines sagging with clothes which flapped forlornly in a bitter winter wind. I finished dressing late that morning and stood surveying my dreary vista, wanting food but reluctant to face the hostile cold street.

As soon as I finished breakfast the day would officially begin, and I dreaded it, for I was engaged in a search more disheartening than that of old Diogenes. I was hunting for a place to live.

As I brooded I heard the slap slap of my landlady's feet in the hall, then her knock. "Miss Cameron, here's that paper you asked for. It just come."

I opened the door and took *The Villager* from her. "Thanks, Mrs. Finney."

"Didn't you say you got an ad in there?"

She inched forward, clutching her mop in one bony hand, and I braced myself for the daily needling. My room was rented to a merchant marine officer, due to arrive momentarily from San Francisco. At first I had wondered why anyone in his right mind would choose to live permanently at Mrs. Finney's; later I decided perhaps he was never in port long enough to give this problem of room hunting the time it actually required. Judging from results I'd had in ten days, a year might do it.

"I cert'ly hope you get an answer to your ad," Mrs. Finney said. "But it ain't likely, with so many looking for rooms. That's why Mr. Bower paid six months in advance. And if he comes in and finds I rented his place…"

She droned on, and I waited, eyeing her with distaste while I reflected that I'd be delighted to get out, happy to see the last of Mrs. Finney and her house.

But first I had to find refuge somewhere. I had long ago given up hope of a desirable apartment. That was why I paid *The Villager* to publish my ad in the "Rooms Wanted" column with a few dozen others phrased in various tones: supplicating, demanding, or pathetically whimsical.

"You know, Miss Cameron," that lugubrious voice reminded me, "I gotta clean in here good today. I was thinkin' perhaps I could set up a cot for you in our front room. That is if you wouldn't mind Yvonne. She's used to sleepin' there; she might want to get on your bed."

Yvonne was a filthy old terrier bitch, obscenely fat, with red eyes and a perpetual snarl. I knew my landlady was trying to be kind, but at the thought of sharing a cot with Yvonne I lost all desire for breakfast. I got rid of Mrs. Finney at last and turned the pages of the little paper to the want ads. Mine was there, three modest lines: Former Secretary Recently Arrived From Hawaii Wants Room or Apt. Will Share if Necessary. And my name and phone number.

If I didn't get an answer to this ad it would be the cot in Mrs. Finney's front room for me. And Yvonne.

I went to the window again. Bleak gray sky, sooty buildings with thousands of human beings penned inside them, living out their days in narrow space, treading endless labyrinths of concrete and steel—it was sordid and depressing.

I thought of home, the old house in Nuuanu Valley where I'd spent my childhood, where my parents had died. In Nuuanu the stream tinkled through a velvet-green lawn where jasmine and yellow ginger grew and the wind blew fresh down from the mountains out to the blue Pacific. For a blissful, deluded year after I met Bob Evans I had dreamed that we'd make a home again of that lonely house; our children would play on the lawn and wade in the little stream. That was to be when Bob got his discharge from the Army Engineers. The first time I saw him wearing civvies he stammered, red-faced and sweating in white linen, as he told me he'd taken a plantation job with Carl Loring. He didn't need to draw a diagram of the rest. The Lorings were related to the Big Five, as Hawaii's economic dictators are called by the press. Their daughter Carolyn wanted a husband. I cried for a week after I told Bob goodbye.

But that was several years ago. And now Hawaii was five thousand miles away.

I left there on wings, literal as well as figurative, my clipper passage purchased from the first solid hunk of money I'd ever earned. Ironic that such triumph should come out of the most humiliating experience a girl can have. After I discovered that what I had mistaken for the whisper of love was actually the Voice of Experience, I retreated into my shell, took a job as secretary at the Ramsey Residence for Women, and spilled my frustration into a novel.

Three years I spent, alternating between the exhilaration of conception and the drudgery of execution, writing that torrid romance of the tropics. Lo, miracle, a publisher bought it! I quit the job, rented my house, and prepared to head for New York.

The office staff gave me a party and presented the customary aloha gift. Not a yellow chiffon nightgown. Not a fitted dressing case. Not half a dozen pairs of nylons. Those pretties we had given to other departing staff members. The aloha gift they chose for me was a guidebook to New York.

Which indicates the kind of impression I gave to others. Nobody suspected that I was a female Walter Mitty. But for a long time there had been a warning tacked over the desk in my room: the only difference between a rut and a grave is in the dimensions. When I was fagged from office routine, when what I craved was to slump with a novel and let the years and the pounds add up, that warning kept me on the nightly grindstone. Then the publisher's check came, and I knew I had one foot out of the rut.

En route to New York I made a Plan. Item number one was to remodel Janice Cameron, that chunky, blond, brown-eyed girl with about as much glamor as a woolen afghan. A base of operations was necessary, preferably a smart modern apartment. Ten days had been enough to reduce my weight by an equal number of pounds and my requirements to one bare essential— simply a place to sleep. Now I stared out at my dismal prospect and shuddered. I hadn't expected my flight to reach a landing like this.

Suddenly New York was frightening and I was a lonely coward, bereft of my fine spirit of adventure. Homesickness hit me like a blow; I wanted to put my head down and howl. I was calling myself a fool for leaving my safe island, for deluding myself that I was equipped with any kind of courage other than imaginary, when those feet came slap slapping along the hall again and I heard a nasal, "Miss Cameron. Oh, Miss Cameron! Telephone."

I didn't know a soul in New York. It must be an answer to the ad. I rushed downstairs to the phone.

"Is this Miss Cameron?" It was a light feminine voice with a strangely familiar cadence which I could not identify.

"Yes, this is she."

"I am calling in response to your notice in *The Villager* regarding a room. It says here"—the voice faded and I heard paper rattling—"that you have recently arrived from Hawaii."

"Yes," I said. Automatically I registered that this was the first time I'd heard that name pronounced correctly since I reached the mainland.

Silence. Someone waited at the other end of the wire for me to add information. "My home is in Honolulu," I explained. "I have been in New York two weeks and expect to stay here indefinitely. I wish to find either an apartment or a room."

Then, for I suddenly realized why the cadence of her voice was familiar, "Am I speaking to an Oriental person?"

I heard a slight tinkle of laughter. "You are. My name is Wu. Lily Wu. I do not have an apartment, but an adequate room, and I need someone to share it with me. Could we meet to discuss this?"

"I'd be delighted."

The address she gave me was on Mott Street in Chinatown. I got out of my taxi there about an hour later and walked slowly along the street looking for the number. I passed grocery stores, their windows filled with produce: Chinese cabbage, ginger root, giant turnips, and meat shops offering dried pork, smoked ducks with varnished red carcasses, while from all sides my nose was assailed by pungent smells: soya, tea, dried fish, seaweed, incense. Here was the window of an herbalist hung with dusty red-satin panels, displaying a bowl of precious ginseng, that root shaped like a man and possessed of marvelous curative properties. Much of this was familiar; I had seen it daily at home. But the people were different, hurried and unsmiling, turning blank faces toward strangers.

I found the number over a recessed doorway which led to a flight of linoleum-covered stairs hemmed in by ugly brown walls. I started up, wondering uneasily what I was walking into. The top landing led to a hall which presented only blank doors. The nearest was painted bright red, and as I paused uncertainly this door opened and a voice said, "Miss Cameron. Come in, please."

The speaker was an Oriental girl, reed-slender, wearing a Chinese dress of coarse blue cotton slit at the sides. She led me through a small foyer painted ivory and vermilion and opened a door. I stopped at the threshold, smothering a gasp of amazement.

The room was magnificent.

The walls were of dark paneling hung with embroidered silks, the deep carpet was peach-colored, the furniture was carved teakwood, there were lamps of rose quartz and jade. The air was slightly overwarm, with the sense-haunting fragrance of sandalwood. A large lacquered screen stood where front windows should have been.

The Chinese girl said, "There are no windows. This house is air-conditioned."

I sank abruptly into the chair she indicated. "Excuse me. I could not help staring. This is so—so—"

"Unexpected," she supplied. When she smiled there was a dimple in her left cheek.

"Yes."

We eyed each other, and I waited for her to begin the conversation, while a sense of recognition began to grow in me. I had met this girl before. But not in surroundings like these. I watched her, trying to remember.

She might have been pretty, I thought, if she were not addicted to such drab clothes. Her hair was glossy black and thick, coiled at the nape of her small neck. Her face was oval, with flawless amber skin, and she wore no makeup. Now if she had worn a page-boy bob, with a gingham dirndl dress and schoolgirlish flat sandals... Suddenly I remembered.

"Aren't you—"

"Weren't you—"

We spoke simultaneously, then stopped. I found myself smiling with relief as I asked, "Aren't you Lily Wu, who used to live at the Ramsey Residence in Honolulu?"

She nodded, dimpling at me. "And you're Miss Cameron from the office there. I never knew your first name."

"It's Janice," I told her.

We regarded each other with mutual pleasure, like old friends reunited in a strange country, although in Hawaii we had been mere acquaintances. I recalled that she had been enrolled at the university and had lived in the Ramsey dormitory. I remembered how much rent she paid and that she had seemed like scores of other Chinese students: quiet, serious, self-effacing. Many of them when out of sight of authority were chattering, giggling, delightful little imps. I wondered if this girl was like that. Probably not; she dressed too soberly.

Our momentary silence was interrupted by the opening of a door at the end of the room. A stout Chinese man entered, bowed in my direction, and seated himself in a chair near Lily Wu. He wore a dark suit of conservative cut, his moon-shaped face was bland, and his eyes sparkled like jet. He turned those keen eyes toward me, and after he finished his inspection I had the feeling that he could have told me the name of my great-grandfather. I tried not to squirm.

He spoke to the girl in Chinese, and she answered rapidly in what I recognized as Mandarin before she said to me, "This is Mr. Char."

"How do you do?" How inane that conventional phrase sounded! This man obviously did as he pleased.

"Welcome to this house, Miss Cameron," he said in unaccented English. "It is pleasant to know that you and Lily have had a previous acquaintanceship." He relapsed into silence regarding me like a complacent, slightly malicious Buddha.

The Chinese girl went to a teakwood desk and picked up a cigarette box of milk jade which she held toward me. "If I were as conventional as the friend whose guest I am," she began more formally, "there would be certain preliminary rituals for us. Bowing ceremonies, tea drinking, polite conversation. But I am not conventional, we are not strangers, and there is also not time. Let us begin to talk."

I nodded rather dazedly and accepted the cigarette she offered.

"I know of a house where there is a room available," she told me. "This house is in Washington Square, a private dwelling which has been remodeled. The room is large; there are twin beds. No doubt privacy would be preferable for both of us, but that is not possible. And regardless of the accommodations—it is necessary that I live there."

It seemed to me that there was urgency in her last words. She added quickly, "The university is just across the Square. It is a most convenient address."

"You are a student there?"

"I am continuing my education in New York."

I began to feel at ease with a familiar situation. It was sheer luck that we had encountered each other, plus, of course, the much-touted power of advertising. She answered my ad because she was also a stranger in New York and because she knew that Islanders liked and respected her people. She might be, I decided, as shy and timid as some other Oriental girls I had known.

"I've been walking the streets for days," I confessed, "hunting for a room. I'm living now in a horrible place near Hudson Street. Compared to my present quarters, Washington Square sounds like heaven. If you're offering me a chance to share that room with you, the offer is accepted."

Her slight body relaxed a little, as if with relief. "You make quick decisions," she said, smiling.

"My landlady is trying to evict me now. When can we move in?"

"Tonight if you wish."

Then the smile vanished, and her voice became crisp and businesslike. "This is what I should like you to do. I will give you the name of the realty company which manages the property. I have already engaged the room and sent a deposit by messenger. I shall appreciate it very much if you will go there this afternoon and pay the balance of the rent in your name and in the name of Lily Wood. If there is any question about my name after we take possession of the room you can say that the clerk misunderstood you."

Oh, I thought, funny business. She wants to use me as a front. I started to bristle, then had a second thought. Easterners don't know Orientals so well as Islanders, who live where the population of Asiatics is very high; a New Yorker might refuse to rent to a Chinese girl. I felt a twinge of sympathy while I thought simultaneously of what good fortune this was for me. During my futile pilgrimage I had wandered through Washington Square without even aspiring to live there, for it was one of the most elegant sections of Greenwich Village.

"The rent is rather high," she told me, and named the amount. "Is that more than you can afford? Because if it is too much—"

Her bright eyes were fixed on me, but her pale little face was expressionless. I understood what was unspoken between us. She was tactfully ignoring the new beaver coat, alligator pumps, other costume details which indicated my economic status. She was giving me a chance to "save face" and back out gracefully. All I had to do was answer yes, it was too expensive, and we would say goodbye and that would be the end of it.

I stood up. "I can afford it. Now if you'll give me the name of that realty office I'll go straight there."

We had agreed that Lily Wu was to pick me up early that evening, and she arrived promptly in a taxi. While the driver carried out my luggage I told Mrs. Finney an unregretful goodbye, then hurried down to join my new companion. The interior of the cab was dark, and all I could discern was that she wore a small fur hat and a fur coat. When I sat beside her I discovered, to my surprise, that she was also wearing Tabac Blond. Nothing modest about that precious stuff.

The somber gray haze of the day had been blotted out by darkness and a fog which seeped in from the ocean and settled over the city like a chill, moist blanket. As we rode toward the Square I saw that bars and cafes had begun to fill; their lights splayed fuzzily, pinkish or yellow, over damp sidewalks. Excitement began to mount in me as we neared our destination—excitement and a queer sort of nervousness. I was committed to living intimately with a strange girl under strange circumstances. But, I reassured myself, this was not irrevocable; I could move if I didn't like it. It was silly to feel apprehensive; Washington Square was a preeminently respectable section.

The house was in the center of the block, and in the night it loomed dark and indistinguishable from its neighbors. Light was spilling from around curtains at second- and third-floor windows, but the lower part of the building was in darkness. We paid the driver and climbed the steps carefully, avoiding the dripping iron railings. I set down my heavy bags and glanced behind us; in the park across the street gaunt trees were veiled in thick gray mist.

As we paused on the landing some movement at the darkened windows of the basement caught my attention. A curtain was pulled back, and for a brief instant a white face tilted up, peering. Someone watching us. I turned to Lily Wu with a comment, but it died unarticulated. She had been looking down at the window, too; now she averted her eyes.

At that moment I caught an odd telepathic feeling from the girl beside me. She was struggling to repress some emotion; what it was I could not define. She hesitated with her finger over the bell button, and I heard her take a deep breath before she pushed it. We didn't speak. We waited in a strange tense silence.

Chapter Two

It was a long time before the door opened. Then a man said, "Hello. Did you want to see somebody?"

My companion did not speak. "We're moving in," I told him. "We rented a room here today."

He stepped back so that we could enter, and I picked up my bags and walked in, with Lily Wu following. "That's fast work," he told us over his shoulder as he started down the hall. "We didn't expect you until tomorrow; the other girls just left. I'll show you the room."

We were in a dimly lighted hallway containing a wall table with a telephone over which hung an old-fashioned mirrored hatrack. A stairway rose to the right, and before us stretched a long carpeted corridor. Muted symphonic music came from somewhere above. Directly on our left was a living room, vast and shadowy; the gleam of brass by a fireplace caught my eye as we passed.

At the end of the hall our escort threw open a door and preceded us into a spacious room. It was boudoirishly feminine, with walls of faded blue satin and ivory wooden panels. Light came from crystal wall fixtures, the ceiling was high, painted pale blue. There were large windows. Twin beds and two chests of drawers, two good chairs. Space to breathe in. Luxury after my grimy cubicle at Mrs. Finney's.

"You'll find house keys there." Our guide pointed to a night table between the two beds. "Make yourselves at home, girls," he commanded cheerfully.

He was short, about five feet six, and he had a round, semi-bald head fringed with graying hair. His bright blue eyes were slightly bloodshot; he blinked often, as if they were tired. Apparently he had compensated for lack of stature by physical exercise which developed powerful arms and shoulders. He wore maroon corduroy trousers and a blue woolen shirt which was open to expose his tufted barrel chest. He was proud of that chest.

"My name is Bela," he announced. "The last name is Palyi. P-a-l-y-i. To save your asking how it's spelled. I was born in Budapest, which explains this delightfully strange name. And I am an artist—a hack, but a well-paid one which gives me freedom to wear such comfortable clothes as these you see on my magnificent torso. Do not let my height deceive you, girls— it is truly a magnificent torso. I can produce signed testimonials."

I couldn't help laughing. He grinned and blinked at me and said, "What's your name?"

"Janice Cameron."

"Delighted to know you, Janice." He turned to the girl who had been standing quietly behind us. "Then you must be Miss Wood—how how the devil did you ever get a name like that?"

"Like Wu?" she said, showing her dimple.

He gaped and blinked rapidly. I didn't blame him, for I was seeing her in the light for the first time, and she was breath-taking. The pale little creature in drab cotton was gone. This girl was beautiful. She had used makeup skillfully, so that her black eyes looked large and brilliant, and her carmined mouth was startling against that amber skin. I had seen beautiful Chinese girls before, but never one who dressed like this. The coat she wore was sable, her hat was of the same dark, silky fur. In her ears were gold hoops threaded with jade and pearls, and there was a matching clip at the throat of her black woolen dress.

Bela Palyi stopped gaping and recovered the insouciance which apparently was habitual to him. "Welcome to our humble rooming house, Miss Wu," he said with a bow. "If I could paint anything but tired old cab horses and Washington Square I'd love to paint you. Maybe I'll try some day, if you'll let me."

She gave him another smile. "Of course."

He began to chuckle then, as if secretly amused at something. "Before you girls start unpacking you must come and see the rest of the house. I want you to meet our happy family."

He led us to the front of the building and up the stairs, explaining as he climbed. "The lower floor, except the community living room, belongs to the girls—there are five of you altogether. Upstairs we have three apartments occupied by the dominant sex. I assure you that neither of these other men is as handsome, as talented, as irresist—"

His words were suddenly drowned out as the thundering chords of Brahms' First Symphony rolled toward us from an apartment near the head of the stairs. Bela opened the door, and we saw a stout, curly-haired young man standing before a large radio-phonograph. Along the wall on each side of it were cases of record albums; on top of one of these was an open box of Barricini chocolates. The cheeks of the stout man were filled like those of a greedy chipmunk. He was swaying on his feet, waving a baton, his eyes closed in rapture. His absorption was so complete that he didn't know we were in the room until Bela tapped him on the shoulder.

He opened his eyes suddenly, scowling at the interruption. He went to the machine and pushed a button so that the automatic arm lifted. He gulped down his mouthful while he placed the arm tenderly on its rest, then faced us.

Bela ignored his scowl. "Who are you tonight, Jarvis?" he asked. "Mengelburg or Rodzinski?"

"Please, Bela, no jokes," the stout man said petulantly. "I've got to get that damned shop out of my mind somehow. 'L'Amour, Toujours L'Amour!' I wish Lucienne Boyer had been throttled at birth! I sold twelve of those vile records today—twelve! I played it a thousand times. God, what a way to earn a living!"

Bela's tolerant smile indicated that he had heard this lament before. "Cheer up, Professor," he said. "Here's something to brighten the evening. New guests in the house, and they'll be a great improvement over those Tulsa canaries. Janice Cameron and Lily Wu. This is Jarvis Lloyd, girls."

Jarvis barely glanced at us. "How do you do," he mumbled, not cheered up. Obviously he preferred Brahms and Barricini.

"Where is everybody?" Bela asked.

Jarvis ran plump fingers nervously through curly brown hair, displaying an enormous gold ring. One of that kind, I thought. "I met Louise in the hall as I came home," he said. "She was on her way to dinner. Evelyn's at school. And Doris is probably with Henri as usual, correcting manuscript."

"Better tune that thing down a little, or she'll be yapping about the noise again." Bela turned to us. "Come along, girls."

He started out in the lead once more, and we trailed after him to another door down the hall. Lily walked behind us, saying nothing. While we were in Jarvis's room, however, her black eyes had been so alert that I was certain she could have itemized from memory each aspect of his appearance and every record he owned.

At Bela's knock the door was opened by a woman whom I disliked on sight. She was not tall, but her thinness and the rigid posture of her flat-chested body made her seem so. Her mousy hair was tightly waved and restrained by bobby pins, her eyes were pale green, and the tan gabardine dress she wore did nothing to lighten the sallowness of her complexion. She held several sheets of typed manuscript in her hands carefully, as if the words they contained were precious.

"Doris, these young ladies have just moved in. Miss Cameron"—Bela introduced—"and Miss Wu. Doris Manning."

"I thought I heard the doorbell a moment a—" she began, and broke off as she saw Lily. "But there's some mistake!" she said sharply. "I talked with the rental office this afternoon, and the girl distinctly said—"

"Yes, that's what you told us." Bela was grinning. "I didn't know the agency was obliged to report to you, Doris, since you're only a tenant like the rest of us."

She shifted papers to one hand and smoothed gabardine over her narrow flanks with the other. "I happened to telephone them to ask whether they hired a new superintendent for us, and I asked about the room." Her colorless brows drew together in a frown. "I'm positive that clerk said 'Miss Wood.'" She turned accusingly to my companion.

By that time I had moved to Lily's side. The Chinese girl said nothing. She seemed to grow very still as if gathering all her forces, while her exotic little face became completely inscrutable.

Doris Manning might have been matron of a detention home as she addressed Lily in an acid voice. "You two girls are friends?" she asked, as if unable to believe such a thing. "Where have you been staying until now?"

Lily spoke then for the first time. Her voice was smooth, with an undertone of most delicate insolence. "Miss Cameron has recently arrived from Honolulu. I have been living on Long Island with my uncle. But since I have entered the university near here my family considers it more convenient for me to live in this part of the city."

"Your uncle is in business here?"

Lily's red mouth curled slightly, as if she were amused, and her tone was the quintessence of hauteur. "My uncle is in the diplomatic service attached to the United Nations staff."

Doris Manning's thin mouth parted for an indrawn breath, while her gaze raked Lily's features, fastening on the sable coat. Envy flickered in her eyes; her thin hands twitched. When she spoke again, acid had changed to honey. "I hope you will enjoy staying here with us, Miss Wu, and that you will not mind our simple living arrangements. I'll come downstairs and show you around the house."

Lily ignored this and turned to me. "We had better go down now."

"Perhaps I can help you unpack." Doris gushed apology to sable and pearls. She called over her shoulder to some other person. "You don't mind, do you, Henri? We can finish this chapter later."

"But of course not."

The voice came from inside the room, out of our range of vision. The door swung farther open, and we saw a tall, narrow-shouldered man just rising from a paper-strewn desk. His dark hair was receding, he had a black mustache, and horn-rimmed glasses accentuated the gravity of his lean face. His words were accented, and when he was introduced I decided that his mother tongue was French. Henri Ledoux.

"Please do not interrupt your work," Lily said. "We need no assistance." She turned away as she spoke, and I followed her.

Bela was chuckling as we thanked him and started down the stairs. "You must come up to my studio soon," he invited. "Top floor. The attic suite."

When we reached the lower floor I stepped inside the living room and glanced around its darkened interior, but could see only dim masses of furniture. As we walked along the shadowy hallway I wondered uneasily who had been watching us and why that individual did not appear. The basement window might belong to a separate apartment with a private entrance. Many of these old houses contained formerly despised dark cubbyholes which were converted into living quarters.

Lily did not mention the curious face at the window, nor did she comment on the skirmish which had just taken place upstairs. She threw her coat on a bed and stood for a moment in the center of the floor looking around our room. She didn't fit here; insipid pale blue was not the proper frame for her. She belonged in the background from which she had come: teak and rose quartz, vermilion and jade and sandalwood. I shrugged the thought away and opened a bag to unpack my small radio. There was room for it on the night table, and I plugged it in while Lily bent over an alligator dressing case.

When I turned around I saw that she had just finished arranging two framed pictures on her bureau. One was an enlarged snapshot of a shabby wooden house in front of which stood a family group under a palm tree. A tiny Chinese woman in black, a rotund, middle-aged man with a benign face, and four husky boys, one of them still in his early teens. All wore conventional American dress except the Chinese woman.

"My family," Lily explained briefly.

"Do they live in Hawaii?" I asked, because of the palm tree. Families from the other islands often sent children to board in Honolulu while they attended the university.

"No. That house is in Los Angeles."

"That house." She didn't call it home. If her family lived in such poverty, where did she get sables and pearls?

I thought of Mr. Char in that luxurious apartment in the heart of Chinatown. Lily had said she was his guest. Why had she lied about living on Long Island? To impress Doris, so that she wouldn't try to get her evicted from this house? I reminded myself that Lily's wardrobe and her private life were none of my business. I had volunteered no personal information, and she had asked for none. This arrangement between us was strictly from convenience.

I turned to the other picture. It was a reproduction of a Chinese painting, a beggar under a tree. From the appearance of the print the original must have been very old. Lily picked it up, smiling.

"This is the work of an ancestor of mine," she said. "His name was Wu Wei, and he lived a long time ago. I keep it to remind me always—" She broke off, gazing intently at the picture. Then she set it back on the bureau and finished in a changed voice: "—to remind me that art is imperishable and that my ancestors were men of honor."

Her emotion made me feel uncomfortable, since I did not know the reason for it and could say nothing to bridge the distance between us. I went to the radio and switched it on. A voice was saying mechanically, "…now bring you the official forecast of the United States Weather Bureau. There will be a sudden drop in temperature tonight, followed by northerly winds, and a heavy snowfall before morning. The storm which hit Chicago yesterday is now on its way—"

I shivered, snapped it off, and busied myself with unpacking, transferring my scanty lingerie to bureau drawers. I had left most of my clothes in Hawaii. Buying new ones was part of the Plan. Halfway through the job I sat down to rest and discovered that I was hungry. When I mentioned food, Lily said she had already eaten, but would like some cigarettes if I intended to go out for dinner. I took one of the keys from the night table and departed.

Outside the house the fog was thicker, needled with particles of ice, and I pulled my collar around my throat as I hurried toward Waverly Place. There was an Italian restaurant I'd been wanting to visit, and this was the night for it. Some sort of plus gesture was indicated, although I didn't really feel like celebrating good fortune.

Don't be ridiculous, I told myself. You should be delighted that you've found a place to live, instead of questioning its desirability. Stop imagining things, forget those uneasy questions. Concentrate on food: steaming minestrone and veal parmigiana. A glass of chianti too. You're free now. There won't be any Ramsey Residence harpies to report a staff member for imbibing alcohol in public. I ducked into my collar and quickened my steps.

Good food and wine proved to be the proper prescription. I relaxed into contentment. While waiting for dessert I noticed another solitary girl drinking *café espresso* at a corner table. I watched casually, fascinated by her incredibly long eyelashes. She was dark and vivid; she would have been very pretty if her upper front teeth had not been crooked. The waiter gave her a check and said something to which she replied in fluent Italian. I listened enviously, wishing I could understand another language than my own, then remembered with sudden delight that now I had time and money for learning whatever I chose. I made a mental footnote to my Plan.

After dinner I walked to Eighth Street, where I bought two cartons of cigarettes and a new novel, then stopped from force of habit to read the bulletin board of a real-estate agency. They were offering an apartment for rent, and I thought, as no doubt many others have thought before me, when I needed something like this desperately it wasn't to be found. To put it vulgarly, he who has, gets. The rent of the one-room apartment was exorbitant. I mentally thumbed my nose at the agency and started home, warmed with food and a glow of well-being.

Heavy sleet had begun to fall, and I opened the door of the house feeling profoundly grateful to be settled at last in such a comfortable shelter. Even if there were peculiar people in this place, what difference did it make? I didn't have to be intimate with any of them. The only person who really concerned me was my roommate, and she was the sort who would respect my reticences as I respected hers. Lily Wu could be as bizarre as she pleased; she could have a dozen rich lovers; it wouldn't bother me. If she had not asked me to live with her I might be sharing a cot tonight with Yvonne.

The lower floor was still dimly lit. From the room above came the frenzied fiddle-scraping of Stravinsky's "Sacre du Printemps." Apparently Jarvis was still exorcising the memory of "L'Amour, Toujours L'Amour." As I reached the end of the hall the music stopped abruptly in the middle of a measure; the ensuing silence was almost shocking.

I rapped on our door, then hesitated with my hand on the knob, the back of my neck prickling uncomfortably. I heard movement in the room, yet the door did not open, nor did Lily's voice respond. I shrugged away unaccountable reluctance to enter and turned the knob. When I was halfway inside some one rushed in my direction. The door was shoved against me so violently that I reeled backward and dropped my packages. I recovered myself, turned the knob again, and pushed hard. This time I encountered no resistance and stumbled headlong over the threshold.

The lighted room appeared empty. There was no sound, no movement. Yet my heart began to pound with unnameable fright, for the air was filled with a sense of recent human presence.

"Lily!" I called. "Where are you?" The words came out in a squeak. No answer. My legs grew weak, while my hands sprouted sweat. I forced myself to take a few steps forward.

Then I saw Lily Wu.

Apparently she had started to undress, for she wore nothing but a white satin slip and her stockings. Black hair fanned over her bare shoulders. Without the disguise of clothes her body was incredibly small and delicate. She lay crumpled on the floor halfway into the next room, and the only thing about her that moved was the thin line of red which crawled along her temple.

Chapter Three

I crossed the floor and knelt by her side. As I slipped an arm under her shoulders Lily moaned and her eyelids fluttered.

"What happened?" I asked. "Are you badly hurt?"

She opened her eyes. "Someone hit me," she murmured. "I don't know—please look…"

I could find no serious wound; the blood on her temple came from a scalp cut which could have been received when she fell against the doorframe. My shaking knees gave under me, and I sat abruptly, still holding her in my arms. We were in a dressing room, apparently an adjunct to our bedroom, for it was decorated in the same manner. The space was narrow and deep, with a recessed dressing table between two doors at one end and a hanger rod at the other.

Lily drew herself away. "I'm all right," she said in a stronger voice. "Please go and investigate."

I tried the door opposite; it was locked from the other side. I went through our bedroom to the hall. Nothing but shadows. I stood there a moment, took a few uncertain steps, and halted. A door clicked shut somewhere. Silence. Then that frenetic music upstairs burst out again in greater volume than before. I picked up my scattered packages and returned to our room.

Lily was leaning against the dressing table with one hand to her head.

She looked at me with inquiry.

"The hall was empty," I told her. "I heard a door shut, but don't know where. Whoever it was, he could have gone in any direction. Did you see the man?"

"I saw nothing," she answered. "I came in here to hang up clothes. Someone hit me."

Lily's garments were scattered around us. If she had walked into the dressing room carrying clothes high before her, as one does to prevent them from dragging on the floor, anyone hiding there could have attacked her before she had a chance to see him. I bent over her again. "Are you sure you're not hurt?"

She looked at the red smear on her hand, then touched her temple again experimentally. "I fell against something," she said. "It's not serious."

I helped her walk to her bed, but she would not lie down. She sat there, staring into space.

"Do you feel all right now?" I asked. "Because if you don't mind being alone for a minute I'm going to call the police."

She turned quickly. "No!" she said. "Please do not do that."

"But you might have been killed! We can't just sit here and allow—"

"Please," she interrupted. "Don't call anyone. It was probably just a sneak thief."

"All the more reason for calling police. You have valuable furs, jewels."

She glanced indifferently at the sable coat crumpled on the floor. "Everything is insured. It does not matter."

My temper began to rise. "Possibly not to you," I retorted, "but it matters to me. I'm living in this place too."

I stalked into the dressing room to hang up my coat and give myself a chance to calm down. As I reached for a hanger my foot touched a large screwdriver which lay in the far corner. I thought at first it had been used to gain entrance to our room, but when I examined the windows I found them all locked.

The person who attacked Lily had come through the house.

As I stood in the middle of the floor digesting this discovery, Lily watched me. "Janice," she said at last in a soft little voice, "I beg you, tell no one. If my family should hear of this I would have to move from here. And you know how difficult it is to find a room."

Lily's face was pale, her dark eyes were dilated. She looked pathetically tiny and fragile in that white satin slip. At the same time I became suddenly aware that her fragility was completely deceptive. This girl was neither weak nor timid; she was strong as steel. And her spirit was indomitable.

As our eyes met, the recognition in mine must have been apparent, for she dropped her heavy lids like a curtain. She was lying. Her people were in California; there was small chance of their hearing news of Lily's welfare unless she wrote it to them. Mr. Char was not likely to be carrying on a chatty correspondence with the Wu family. Any of those husky Wus would be quite capable of killing one who violated the chastity of this girl. Lily had other reasons, I thought cynically, for avoiding publicity.

But I didn't intend to set the pattern for our relationship by letting her will prevail over mine. I opened my mouth to tell her so. Before I could get the words out someone knocked on our door.

Lily slipped from the bed and hurried toward the dressing room, kicking clothes before her as she went. As she shut the door she looked entreatingly at me again. I glared back at her. Then I crossed the room to admit our visitor.

She was a slight woman with fine white hair rolled in a soft bun on top of her head. She had smoky gray eyes and pink-and-white skin, and she wore a lavender smock over a gray tweed skirt.

"Miss Cameron?" she said.

"Yes."

"I'm Evelyn Sayre."

"How—how do you do?" I stammered. "Won't you come in?"

"Thank you. For just a moment."

Her voice was as gentle as her smile. If she noticed my agitation she gave no sign. "I just stopped by," she said, "to welcome you to the house and to ask if you and Miss Wu would like to join us this evening in the living room."

She glanced around our room, and I knew she was wondering where my companion was. I was on the verge of blurting that we had just received a much ruder welcome than the one she offered when the door of the dressing room opened and Lily appeared. My popeyed reaction would have been comical to any observer—fortunately there was none, for Evelyn was also staring at Lily.

It hadn't been fifteen minutes since I found her lying unconscious on the floor. A short while ago she had been pale and trembling, and I had felt moved to pity by her frailty. Now Lily Wu had changed her personality again. She wore a kimono of scarlet silk; she had painted her mouth the same vivid color. Evelyn Sayre's eyes widened, while I couldn't help feeling a thrill of admiration. Lily's head must have been aching painfully, but the brilliant smile she wore indicated nothing but pleasure at receiving a guest in our room.

As she passed me her eyes met mine briefly, and I gave her a nod by way of reassurance. It was Lily's headache; if she chose not to publicize it she had a right to such decision. I might be foolish, but I would respect that right. I knew how it feels to have intense desire for privacy.

We all sat down, lit cigarettes, and chattered. When Evelyn repeated her invitation I accepted. I needed to get oriented in that strange house. Now I could not remain aloof. I wanted to scrutinize these strangers. One of them had probably just escaped from our room.

"How about you, Miss Wu?" our visitor asked.

Lily produced another brilliant smile. "I have still much unpacking to do," she said sweetly. "I'll come in later, if I may."

"Could you explain the floor arrangement here?" I asked, as Evelyn and I started out. "Which rooms we have access to and so forth. We don't want to intrude on anyone."

"Of course. Let's begin with the kitchen."

The corridor which ran the length of the house was L-shaped, the base of the L leading left to the kitchen. Evelyn opened cupboard doors to show shelves with names on them, where individual food supplies were kept. The large refrigerator held marked packages and food containers.

"We cooperate nicely here," Evelyn told me. "The superintendent cleans house once a week; the rest of the time each does her own cooking and washing up. Once in a while we join efforts for a community meal."

She surveyed the big white-tiled kitchen fondly and patted the electric range with a sort of proprietary affection. "I appreciate such domestic facilities," she explained, looking embarrassed after that involuntary gesture. "Until I came here I lived on a farm upstate where there was neither electricity nor plumbing."

She must be in her late forties, I thought, and I'll bet for years she's been starved for beauty and the amenities of modern living. Her parents probably left her a little money, and she shook that farm dirt from her feet and rushed to New York to gratify a lifelong hunger. I had read stories about people like her, timid middle-aged spinsters emerging starry-eyed from railway terminals with old-fashioned luggage in their hands. Residential hotels always harbored a few of these pathetic pilgrims, who were constantly trotting to art exhibits, slipping unobtrusively into cheap seats at concert halls in their wistful search for "the better things of life."

"I heard someone mention that you go to school," I hinted.

"Not as a student. I'm teaching art in a settlement house." She looked at me shyly and said, almost with apology, "I'm a sort of artist. I write little fairy stories and illustrate them."

Poor thing, I thought tolerantly as I asked, "Do you write under your own name?"

"Oh no!" She seemed alarmed at the thought. "I use just one name, a rather silly one which my publishers suggested. 'Oriole.'"

"Oriole!" I echoed, gaping at her. "Why, Miss Sayre, I've read everything you ever wrote!"

My parents gave me Oriole's books when I was a child, and they brought some of the most enchanted hours I ever spent. Her drawings were exquisite, highly imaginative fantasy. She wrote about trees and flowers and the wonderful invisible people who live in nature, and her writing style was as delicate as the perfect little figures she created.

Impulsively I laid a hand on her arm. "I wish I could tell you how much pleasure your books have given me! There was one—I still have it packed away with my treasures—about the snow-makers who live in the clouds. I remember a drawing of one little fellow floating on a snowflake. The detail was so perfect that I was sure, after I grew old enough to realize it, that you used a microscope to study your subjects."

She stammered, while color stained her cheeks, "Yes, I— nature fascinated me. I used to study leaves and flowers and things like that—" She broke off in embarrassment.

Starved for beauty indeed! I told myself to avoid snap judgments in the future. I'd been wrong about two people today.

"Let's see the rest of the house," I suggested, and she looked relieved.

"Did Bela tell you about all of us?"

I recounted our brief excursion upstairs. "We met Mr. Lloyd and Miss Manning and—I can't remember the name of the other man."

"That's Henri Ledoux, Doris's fiancé. He works for a literary agent as reader. He is also writing a book about his war experiences in France. Doris does his typing."

Doris Manning certainly did not seem the sort of woman who would interest a Frenchman. I reminded myself again: no more snap judgments. There were all kinds of men, each entitled to his own taste. Perhaps Henri Ledoux and his fiancée were completely en rapport intellectually and spiritually—whatever those overused words meant.

In the hall again Evelyn indicated linen and broom closets, then the door to a single room near the kitchen which was occupied by Doris Manning, who needed privacy because she operated her typing service at home.

"Bela said there are five women on this floor," I suggested, and she nodded her white head.

"The one you haven't met is Louise Kane, my roommate. She's a radio actress."

She flung open a door near that of our bedroom. "Here is our special pride. This is the community bath, except that you and Miss Wu have access to it without going into the hall. That door with the mirror on it leads to your dressing room, as you probably know. Isn't this astonishing?"

It was. I had seen luxury bathrooms in the movies but had never lived with one so lavish as this. The walls were tiled in palest rose to the ceiling, which was mirrored. The lavatory and the huge square tub were of pink marble with gold fixtures in the shape of coquettish mermaids. My companion frowned slightly, and I saw that she was looking at some dark smudges on the pink tiled floor.

"That looks like dirty footprints," she said. "The superintendent was supposed to keep this bathroom clean, but he seldom bothered. I hope the new one will be more dependable."

Now I knew how our intruder had made his exit.

I went to the door and tried the crystal knob, turning the key in the lock as I did so. This offered much too easy access to our quarters. I decided to buy a good lock and have it installed on the dressing-room side immediately.

Evelyn was on her knees removing those dirty prints with cleansing tissues. She rose and said, "There. That's better."

"This isn't really a mansion," I commented. "How do you suppose the owner happened to install such a bathroom?"

"I understand there is quite a romantic story attached to the house." She was enjoying my interest. "It belonged to some rich man whose wife was an invalid. Since the stairs were difficult for her, he converted his study—that's your room now—into a boudoir and dressing room, with this lovely bath for her own use."

My sentimental streak was touched by this picture of a devoted husband. "What happened to them?" I wondered aloud.

"I don't know. They probably moved uptown. The Square isn't so fashionable as it used to be; this part of New York is filled with buildings where famous people once lived: Thomas Paine, Walt Whitman, Mark Twain, Edna St. Vincent Millay, Henry James—he was born here and named one of his books after Washington Square. John Masefield lived here too—he once made his living scrubbing floors in a Village saloon. There are fascinating stories connected with this section. You know, some of those trees in the park across the street were used as gallows a long time ago."

I didn't like to think of that. "Who owns this building now?"

"Some trust company, I believe. We pay our rent to the agency."

Piano music began to sound from the front of the house, and she turned her head to one side, listening with a pleased smile. "Debussy," she murmured. "That's Jarvis. When he's in the mood he sometimes plays for hours. Let's go in and listen."

We had traversed almost the length of the hallway when a door I had not noticed before, under the angle of the stairs, opened suddenly. A figure stood silhouetted in light from below.

"Oh!" Evelyn made a startled exclamation.

"Excuse me. I am sorry I frightened you." The man spoke in a low, almost whispering voice. "I am the new superintendent; I arrived today. I found bed linen in my room, but there are no towels. Do you think it would be possible for me to have some?"

"Of course," Evelyn told him. "I'll get them for you. The other superintendent must have cleaned out the place when he left. I must say that's about all the cleaning he did do, poor fellow. He drank too much. Then he simply disappeared without a word."

She started away and then turned back. "Is there anything else you need?"

"Just one thing. I notice there is an electric plate for cooking, but the cord is missing."

"I'll look for it in the broom closet."

"Thank you very much."

His vocabulary and his voice were surprising. I had known schoolteachers whose diction was less meticulous. I eyed him with curiosity while we waited for Evelyn. He wore faded overalls, rather tight on his heavy frame. His face was jowly, his head almost gargoylesque, completely bald, in startling contrast to thick black eyebrows. I noticed his hands as he reached for the towels Evelyn brought. They were the hands of a laborer, work-roughened and calloused, with broken nails.

"I couldn't find the cord," she told him, "but I'll ask Miss Manning about it tomorrow. If you need anything else let us know. It's a relief to have a dependable person here at last, especially with a cold wave predicted for to morrow."

He thanked her again before he started back to the basement; we could hear his steps going down as we turned toward the living room.

The large bay-windowed room had once been richly furnished and was still shabbily elegant. A faded Persian rug lay on the parquetry floor, a massive grand piano of old-fashioned design filled one corner. There were bookcases, big chairs and lamps, and a marble-framed fireplace in which cannel coal was blazing.

Jarvis Lloyd sat at the piano, with Doris and Henri Ledoux standing by. A sofa and a love seat stood diagonally opposite each other near the fire, and Bela slumped in the middle of the sofa, feet on a coffee table before him. He had taken his shoes off, displaying green-and-purple hand-knit socks. He beckoned with his pipe, and we seated ourselves on each side of him. He patted Evelyn's hand when she sat down and whispered something which brought a flush, to her face.

"I love to make her blush," he told me, chuckling—"There's no other woman who does it so becomingly. Now isn't that a perfect color combination? Pink cheeks, gray eyes, platinum hair."

At this her face turned a deeper rose. "You know my hair is gray, Bela," she protested.

"It's platinum. You're my glamor girl, darling."

"You mustn't mind him, Miss Cameron," she said to me. "Bela teases everyone."

"Why don't you call her Janice?" he suggested. "That's her name."

"Please do," I added, and she nodded and smiled. Across the room from us Doris was also smiling, a possessive hand on her companion's arm.

"Henri," she coaxed, "won't you sing for us? Some of those wonderful Maquis songs you know."

He shook his head, looking pained. "No. I am sorry, Doris, but I can not. Seldom can I sing those songs now." Seeing her disappointment, he added, "If Jarvis can accompany, I shall sing for you something more pleasant." He leaned toward Jarvis and hummed. The pianist listened, echoed the melody, then began to play.

"That fellow Jarvis has talent," Bela murmured. "He could make money; he plays anything by ear. But he hates popular music. When the Jones sisters were here they nearly drove the poor guy mad with their harmonizing. Their taste ran to 'My Darling Clementine' or in a real sad mood, 'Tumbling Tumbleweed.'"

I was relaxed at my end of the sofa, enjoying the warmth of the fire and the music. "What happened to them?" I asked, not caring.

"A miracle. It could have been nothing less. Those girls had the stage presence of jackasses and sang like crows. They were torturing the public in a Brooklyn tavern, about to be fired from their miserable jobs. Then their agent tells them some talent scout has spotted their act; they're hired for Lum Char's Shanghai Garden, a big night club in San Francisco. They departed this morning—on two days' notice—still dizzy with their good luck."

As he spoke I stiffened. I covered this by leaning forward to toss my cigarette into the fire. When I leaned back against the cushion, my thoughts were humming. A few pieces of my Chinese puzzle had fallen together. This time I was certain of what had formerly been hazy suspicion.

Lum Char's Shanghai Garden. Lily's "uncle," Mr. Char. My Chinese roommate—Lily Wu of the multiple personality—had not found a room here by good luck or accident. She lied to me when she implied that, as she lied to Doris about living with relatives on Long Island. Possibly she thought up the latter lie quickly when Doris began to question her. I knew where Lily had been living, and I was probably the only one here aware that her residence was the result of a careful plan.

What had she said about this house? "It is necessary that I live there."

Remarkable understatement, that. I wasn't guessing or jumping to conclusions now. *I knew.* It was so necessary that Lily would risk anything—even her life—to accomplish that purpose.

Chapter Four

Lily Wu had been the "guest" of Mr. Char in a magnificent Chinatown apartment. He might be a merchant; certainly with such wealth he was a man of influence known to Chinese businessmen in other parts of the country. Mr. Char could write to a relative or a tong member in San Francisco, for instance, and ask a favor. From another Char, perhaps, who owned a night club.

So the two girls with voices like crows had been beneficiaries of a "miracle" because Lily wanted their room.

An indefinable chill grew in me, a chill which lamps and glowing fire and music couldn't dispel.

Someone else in this house didn't want Lily here. Which one?

At the piano Jarvis played softly, while Henri sang in a nostalgic baritone. Doris's eyes were fixed on that dark, sad face; she listened as if she heard angels. Bela hummed at my side, while Evelyn leaned back with a smile. These were all the residents of the house except one. And while I pondered she arrived.

Henri was beginning a repeat chorus as the front door opened, slammed shut, and a girl in a gray fur coat hurried down the hall. "Louise!" Evelyn called, which brought a frown from Doris. The girl did not stop or answer, and Evelyn rose immediately. "She must be ill again, Bela. I'll find out what's wrong. Excuse me."

After she left Bela turned to me. "What do you think of our refugee?"

"Refugee? You mean Mr. Ledoux?"

He knocked his pipe into his hand irritably, as if he had to hit something, and tossed the dottle toward the hearth. "Yes. Ask Henri to tell you his life story sometime. Prison camp. Escape. Underground. The whole harrowing works. If he won't tell you—he's so sensitive about the past—Doris will. It's her favorite fiction."

Fiction? Bela was smiling, but his tone was sarcastic. I wondered what he implied, or if he were showing some of the spite so erroneously considered to be solely a feminine attribute. Was he jealous?

Bela took my hand and patted it. "No, I'm not, my dear. Not in the least." I jerked my hand away; he was reading my mind.

His good humor returned. "I was born in Hungary, as I told you, but I've been an American for as many years, probably, as you have lived. How old are you, Janice? Thirty?"

"I'm twenty-seven," I said huffily.

He patted my hand again. "Don't be annoyed, dear. You appear older because you're repressed. Quite the opposite of that volatile little friend of yours. Probably that's one reason you two were drawn to each other, eh?"

He was trying to pump me. I said coldly, "Aren't you getting off the subject? We were talking about Henri Ledoux."

"All right," he said with a shrug. "Relax. As I started to say before, no expatriate European gives me the slightest twinge of envy." He glanced toward the singer. "Particularly not this one."

Bela disliked Henri intensely for some reason. I decided that the artist might be the sort who likes only women. To such an individual every male was a potential rival. Both the other men were younger than he.

Evelyn returned then, her soft pink mouth turned down with distress. "Poor Louise," she said. "She has one of those headaches again."

"Then leave her alone. She'll sleep it off eventually." Bela began to yawn. He rose and stretched, throwing his arms back so that his chest swelled impressively. "This fire makes me sleepy; it's almost eleven anyhow. Guess I'll turn in." When he had put on his moccasins he said to Evelyn, "Do you plan to stay up and work tonight?"

Evelyn was looking intently at her skirt where the hem was loose. "Yes, Bela. I'll start as soon as I can."

After he left she explained. "I often stay in here late to write or lay out a drawing; otherwise I'd keep Louise awake. I'd better go and get my work now before she's asleep."

She was considerate and sympathetic as well as talented. Yet she was unmarried. I thought of some of the horse-faced old harridans I'd seen herding their husbands around at Waikiki and wondered why so many undesirable females managed to find men to love them, while this attractive and affectionate woman had not.

Even the unlovable Doris had managed to hook a man. I glanced toward the piano. Jarvis was playing *Claire de Lune,* while Doris and Henri stood together in a listening attitude. Her thin arm lay along the top of the piano, and his hand had pushed the gabardine sleeve back. I watched, fascinated and repelled, as his long fingers caressed that bare flesh, rhythmically, softly. Doris's features were set as in a trance; I doubted that she heard the music.

Then I remembered that they were strangers, that I was alone on the sofa watching an act of intimacy which I had no desire to witness. I said good night and made a quick exit.

I undressed quietly, so as not to disturb the small figure which lay motionless under the covers of Lily's bed. The snapshot of her family had disappeared. Probably she decided that a picture of such a shabby home did not fit with her wardrobe or the story of relatives in the diplomatic service. As I got into bed

I noticed a bottle of aspirin on the night table. Two girls in the house had headaches tonight.

I awakened later with a start, to find light streaming into the room through the open door to the hall, while a figure moved near the window. I sat up and called, "Who is it? What do you want?"

I was sweating; even the sheets were damp. It can't be fever, I thought; I don't feel sick. Then I became aware that the room was stiflingly hot. The woman near the window answered, "It is I, Doris. I came to see if your radiator is on. The house is like an oven."

At that I switched on the light. The small mound in the bed opposite did not stir. Evelyn appeared in the doorway, fully dressed, carrying a sketch pad and pencil. "I was in the living room working," she said, "and I heard voices. Is something wrong?"

Doris explained. As she spoke, her eyes darted around our room, fastening on our half-unpacked luggage, on Lily's scarlet kimono and fur-lined embroidered satin slippers. Doris wore a navy woolen robe below which a flannelette nightgown showed. Her hair was twisted on metal curlers, and her long face shone with cold cream. She frowned at her image in the door mirror and turned to Evelyn.

"I'm glad you're dressed," she said. "No one else is, so you'll have to go."

"Go? Where?"

"Downstairs to talk to that super. He must be another drunkard. No one else would stoke a furnace at this hour. Stupid fool, wasting coal like that!"

"Not to mention that the temperature is probably around eighty in here," I put in dryly.

Evelyn looked apprehensive. "Oh dear," she wailed, "I don't want to go down there alone! Can't we call one of the men?"

"And have them see us looking like this?" Doris clutched navy wool to her flat bosom. "You needn't go all the way—just to the head of the stairs where you can talk to him. We'll stand by so you won't feel nervous."

I looked toward Lily's bed and saw no movement. If she chose to pretend sleep, that was her prerogative. I put my robe on and followed Doris and Evelyn to the hall, where Evelyn hesitantly turned the knob of the door to the basement stairs.

"Go on!" Doris urged. "Speak to him!"

Evelyn looked at us with appeal, pulled the door open, and descended a couple of steps, calling, "Super! Oh, super!"

Silence for a moment. Steps crunching across a gritty concrete floor below. Then a voice: "Yes, ma'am?"

"Super, the house is much too warm. We don't need heat at this hour. Can't you do something about it?"

"Sorry, ma'am. The furnace seemed to be out of order. Rememberin' the cold wave, I thought to fix it before mornin'. It'll be okay now."

She drew back a little, relieved. "You mean the heat will go off?"

"Yes, ma'am. Just open your window for a bit to let the hot air out."

"Very well, thank you."

When she rejoined us Doris clutched her arm. "Is he drunk?"

A look of distaste showed briefly on Evelyn's face as she moved out of Doris's grasp. "His voice sounded peculiar," she said, "but I don't know. All I saw was his hand on the railing."

We went back to our rooms. Something about that unseen speaker's voice had been incongruous. But I was sleepy and perhaps stupid from the heat, so my mind wasn't very clear. Maybe fresh air would help.

Raising the window wasn't difficult, and I opened it wide, only to slam it shut again. Sleet and snow were pelting down through the darkness, driven by a strong wind. In that brief, moment my face was plastered with ice. The storm had begun. I sat on my bed and lit a cigarette, "Sorry for the noise, Lily," I said automatically. The bang I made would have awakened the deepest sleeper.

Except one who wasn't there.

I knew it before I finished speaking. It wasn't necessary to pull down the covers, to see the rolled blanket, the little pillbox hat trimmed with silk fringe which was almost as black as Lily's hair. I rearranged things as she had left them, got into my own bed, and doused my cigarette.

After I turned off the light I lay for a while listening to the hiss and scratch of sleet blown against glass. The room gradually grew cooler. The luminous dial of my traveling clock shone weirdly in the darkness. It was 3 a.m.

I awakened at seven, conscious that I was in a strange place, then remembering. The next thing I thought of was the storm. I had never seen a heavy snowfall. I went to the window and found the ledge piled high. Our room overlooked a walled garden which might be very pleasant in summer. Now it was just a flat expanse of white, with a mound in the center which looked like a fountain. I turned from the window and began to dress, shivering, for the room was frigid. When I touched the radiator its coldness hurt my fingers.

I perceived that Lily's bed had a live occupant now, for her feet moved. I wanted to make some comment to her, but she didn't speak. Sleepy, no doubt, after being out all night.

That wasn't my problem. Keeping warm was. Thinking irritably that it was a remarkably poor system to overheat a house in the middle of night and freeze it during the day, I put my fur coat on over a blouse and skirt and stepped into the hall. Doris emerged from her room at that moment, scowling. "That wretched super!" she shrilled. "He's probably sleeping off a hangover while we freeze up here."

She was in full voice as we proceeded along the hall. Before we reached the next door it opened and a dark-haired girl stepped out wearing a red flannel dress and an annoyed frown. "Stop that yelling, Doris," she said. "Have you no consideration for anyone? Evelyn worked late last night, and she's still asleep."

Doris had the grace to look abashed. "Sorry, Louise, I forgot. I have to work myself this morning, and my fingers are so numb that I can't type."

"Don't take it out on us. It's the super's fault."

Doris nodded. "We'll have to get after that man. I'm going down right now to see him." She headed for the basement door.

I had been looking at Louise Kane, first with puzzlement, then with interest. She was the girl I had seen in the restaurant the night before. I would have recognized that throaty voice anywhere, and I could not forget those eyelashes and the crooked teeth. So this was Evelyn's roommate. A radio actress. Suffering recently from severe attacks of migraine. She became conscious of my regard and returned it resentfully.

I smiled with tentative friendliness. "My name is Janice Cameron," I said, "and I moved in yesterday. You're Louise Kane, aren't you?"

If she remembered seeing me in the restaurant she showed no sign of it. "Yes, I am," she snapped. Then she added in a milder tone, "Excuse me for being so irritable. Doris gets under my skin at times. She's so damned officious."

That I agreed with. I made another friendly move. "I feel almost as if we're acquainted already," I offered. "I saw you in the Napoli last night. You speak Italian beautifully."

Her eyes widened; she flashed a look at me that was lethal. "I don't speak Italian!" she said. "And I've never been in the Napoli. I was working last night. We had a rehearsal."

I shrugged. "Sorry. I must have seen someone who resembled you. But there's no need to snap my head off about it."

Her anger died as quickly as it had been aroused, and she made an apologetic gesture. "Don't mind me, please. I've not been feeling well lately. Headaches."

This was safe ground, and I was quick to sympathize. "Yes, Evelyn told me. I hope you're better this morning."

We both turned as Doris came running toward us, her face tight with alarm. She almost bumped into Lily Wu, who at that moment was coming out of our room.

"Please come downstairs!" Doris cried. "I can't awaken that man. I called and called. He's lying there in that dark place, and he doesn't move or answer!"

The three of us followed her down to the furnace room. An unshaded bulb hung near the foot of the steps, and in its harsh light we saw a space in the center of which squatted the furnace, cold as the concrete floor on which we stood.

Doris stopped, hanging on to the stair railing as if for support. "In there!" She pointed to a door.

The room which Lily and I entered had probably once been servants' quarters. Two snow-encrusted windows, high in the wall at street level, let in pallid daylight. The place was furnished with a miscegenation of castoffs: a scarred pine chest, a corner table supporting the cordless electric plate with a shelf for supplies hanging over it, two straight chairs, one placed by the side of an iron bed. The super was lying on this bed with his face turned away from the door. Something about the unnatural rigidity of that figure made me feel queasy. I swallowed and stopped in my tracks.

Doris hadn't followed us; she hung back beyond the door with Louise at her elbow. I waited in the center of the room with my feet rooted to the cold floor, almost as frightened as they.

Not Lily Wu. She went directly to the bed. A rusty iron bridge lamp stood there; she switched on the bulb, and light shone on the man's face. I was close enough to get a good look at him: wide sightless staring eyes, putty colored skin, half-opened mouth. I shuddered and turned away.

Lily switched off the light. She said quietly, "He is dead."

Doris let out a yelp and rushed up the stairs, followed by Louise. I couldn't leave. I watched Lily.

The Chinese girl wasn't frightened, unless her stillness was an indication. She had taken pains this morning to apply a careful layer of pancake makeup which was like a mask on her face. Vivid and artificial in scarlet silk, her mouth curved crimson in a careful maquillage, she stood out in that ugly room like a butterfly over an ash heap.

She didn't seem aware of me. Her eyes swept the room, and I watched curiously in spite of my aversion to remaining so near a corpse. Lily was searching for something. She crossed to a

curtained space on the wall opposite the bed and drew aside the
dirty cretonne curtain which covered it. A man's suit hung
there, carefully draped on a hanger. Very good brown tweed.
From another hanger dangled a tab-collared shirt of fine ecru
linen, with a hand-knit tie flung across it. On the floor was a
Gladstone bag of pigskin.

"Unusual wardrobe for a superintendent, isn't it?" My voice
cracked on the last words.

Lily glanced at me, but I might as well have been trans-
parent, so deep was her concentration. She went to the bed and
switched on the light again to gaze intently at that dead face,
while I averted my eyes. She turned her attention finally to the
chair by the bed. The overalls he had worn the night before
were slung over the back of it. On the chair seat was an ashtray
filled with cigarette butts, a glass with a spoon in it, and beside
that a medicine bottle containing pale greenish liquid.

"Miss Wu?" quavered Doris from the stairs. "Is he really
dead? What are you doing?"

Lily didn't answer. She had picked up the bottle by the
cork and was reading the label. "Ah. I was wondering about
this. Digitalis, and a recent prescription. From Dr. Haynes on
Fifth Avenue. Possibly he died of a heart attack. We had better
call this doctor."

We joined the two other women then, and Lily explained
to them. Doris went to the upper floors to tell the men. Louise
went to her room for a coat. I stood in the hall and waited while
Lily called the doctor.

That was when it came to me, the incongruity which had
teased my mind in the pre-daylight hours following Evelyn's
dialogue with the super. Earlier in the evening he had spoken in
a cultured voice, using excellent English. At three in the morning
both his voice and his vocabulary had been different. The explanation sounded too preposterous even for consideration.

But—there it was. Someone had impersonated the dead
man. Why?

Chapter Five

I stood and waited, shivering and hugging myself for warmth. It was very cold in the house. The chilliness started at the floor, seeped into my feet, and crawled along my spine to congeal in arms and fingers. Stop shaking, I told myself. You'll get warm again eventually. That poor fellow downstairs has a chill no fire can ever thaw.

Lily cradled the phone and turned around just as Louise reappeared, wrapped now in the gray fur coat. "Is the doctor coming?" she asked.

"Immediately. He lives very near here."

"What did he say?"

"He remembered prescribing digitalis for a man from this address yesterday evening," Lily said. "Excuse me. I must dress."

Feet clomped on the stairs and Bela appeared, followed by Doris and the two other men. "What's going on?" Bela demanded. His blue eyes were bright with excitement. He blinked rapidly.

Doris's face was pale, and her teeth chattered. Evidently she had been too hysterical to tell a coherent story. I explained briefly, and there were various exclamations and comments. Jarvis seemed jittery; he stood twisting the belt of his maroon flannel robe tight over his round paunch, looking from one face to another as if waiting for a cue.

Henri's eyes were somber. He moved to Doris and put one arm around her shoulders, apparently feeling more concern over her welfare than distress at hearing of a corpse in the basement. Probably during the war he grew used to dead men, I decided. Anyone who fought with the Underground slept with Death holding his hand every night.

"You are chilled, *chérie*," he murmured to Doris. "This has been a shock. Why do you not go to your room?"

"She won't get warm there," Louise pointed out, "unless she goes back to bed. Why don't one of you men do something helpful and start a fire in the furnace? It can't do any harm, and we'd all be more comfortable."

Jarvis seemed horrified at mention of manual labor. He looked at his soft, plump hands and winced as if he already felt that rough shovel in them. Henri glanced vaguely toward the basement door and tightened his arm around Doris. He seemed to consider that he was doing enough warming up in his own bailiwick. Bela looked at both men with disgust, snorted, and headed for the stairs. We followed him.

"Where's the super?" Bela asked, and I pointed to the room. He glanced inside and closed the door. There was a pile of coal in the basement beneath a side window through which fuel deliveries were made. Bela nodded toward it, took off his corduroy jacket, and handed it to Louise.

He gathered kindling wood from a box beside the furnace and tossed it into the cold monster. He poured kerosene over the wood and added some chunks of cannel coal. When he struck a match the furnace came to life with a roar and a crackle. Bela picked up a shovel from the coal pile and filled it. The muscles of his arms stood out; he bent to the job with easy familiarity. "Hold that furnace door back," he ordered. "Whichever of you men feels strong enough."

Jarvis's mouth set in a pout, but he held the door without a word. We all watched absorbedly while Bela shoveled coal onto the fire, then moved nearer the furnace to catch the first welcome waves of heat. As he wiped his hands on his trousers Bela said, looking at Henri, "You ought to be good at this kind of job, *mon vieux*. After living in caves with the Maquis you're probably much tougher than you look."

Henri made no answer. It was Doris who turned angrily on Bela. "You know why Henri can't do heavy work. I'm tired of hearing you say such things to him. Where were you during the war while he was lying in a miserable French hospital ward?"

Bela said quietly, "I was working in a miserable American hospital ward, my dear, teaching occupational therapy."

This unpleasant dialogue was broken by the ring of the doorbell, and Doris went up to admit the doctor. Dr. Haynes was a big, handsome man with iron-gray hair and an air of pomposity. He looked sleepy and annoyed at being called out so early on a stormy day. He nodded toward our little group huddled around the warming furnace and said, "Where is the patient?"

No one made a move. I had been the only person besides Lily who had gone near the dead man. Now they all looked at me, as if meaning that once exposed to a corpse I could stand it again. I led the doctor into the room.

He switched on the light and bent over the figure on the bed, at which I turned away again. While he made his examination I looked out the windows toward the street. The iron railings which had dripped moisture when we climbed those steps several hours ago were now covered with inches of smooth white snow. When we stood there last night waiting for the door to open someone down here in the basement had peered out at us. The picture was wrong, though, and it was a few minutes before I realized why. Then it came to me with a shock of surprise.

These windows were under the steps. The face I saw had been staring from a window on the other side of the house beneath the living room. I looked for a door which would indicate that the super's quarters consisted of more than one room.

There was no door. Maybe the other part of the basement really was a separate apartment. Strange that no one had mentioned it.

The doctor had finished. He dropped some instruments into his bag and announced briskly, "This man has died from cardiac failure."

I went almost limp with relief. What had I been expecting to hear? I couldn't define it. I knew only that some vague dread was lifted.

In the furnace room the doctor repeated his pronouncement. "The man came to my office last night," he said. "When I examined him I found serious organic weakness, and I warned him against exertion of any kind. He told me then that he had been ill for several years."

Someone in the group sighed deeply. Was it the same relief I had felt or just emotional strain being released?

Henri asked, "What is to be done now?"

The doctor looked at his watch. "I can sign a death certificate," he in formed us, "since I examined the patient less than twelve hours ago. Then someone must notify his family so the body can be removed."

"But we don't know the man," Doris protested.

"Who hired him for this job? He must have given references."

"The realty office. They will know."

Bela had been peering into the room. Now he spoke from the doorway. "Why don't we go through his clothes? He'll have papers of some kind."

"One of you men do it," Doris begged. "I'm afraid of de—I don't want to go in there."

Henri and Bela and the doctor went into the room. Through the open door we watched them: Bela opening and shutting drawers, Henri examining the man's clothes and his luggage, and the doctor bending over the scarred pine chest to fill out the death certificate.

"Nothing in here," Bela announced.

"I find nothing," Henri said. "The pockets of his clothes are empty. The bag contains only personal garments."

"Let's make sure," Bela said. He carried the bag over to a lighter part of the room and set it on a chair near the door, while the rest of us craned to see what it contained.

"You're right, Henri. Nothing but underwear and a couple of shirts. Unless—here's a pocket." He pulled a zipper and straightened with something in his hand. "Looks like a photograph. A family portrait of some kind," he said curiously.

He held it toward us, a large photograph in a frame of blue leather. A handsome man with a slightly arrogant face dominated by dark bushy eye brows. A slim, lovely woman with golden hair. A child in a white dress.

Someone behind us let out a long, shuddering gasp. We all turned toward the sound. Doris was staring at the photograph in Bela's hand with eyes which seemed about to leave their sockets. As we looked, she swayed on her feet. There was a thump as her body landed on the concrete floor.

Bela and Henri got her up the stairs and laid her on the sofa in the living room. Lily and Evelyn were there, sitting before the fireplace, where coal was blazing. They jumped up from the sofa to make room for Doris's body. Dr. Haynes produced a stimulant, and after a while Doris recovered consciousness. She looked ill: her face was ashen, and her eyes were glazed with shock. Henri bent over her. "You are all right now, Doris. Lie quietly and rest."

She started to sit up, and the doctor said, "Better stay there awhile, young woman." She ignored him and raised herself so that she leaned against the arm of the sofa, staring blindly into the fire.

Louise voiced the question we were all thinking. "Did you know that man?"

Doris didn't answer for a moment. With returning awareness, several expressions showed on her face: bewilderment, resentment, and finally a sort of angry triumph. "Yes," she said at last, "I know his name. I will arrange for his burial."

She disregarded our curious stares and turned to the doctor with her old air of authority reasserting itself. "Can you recommend a mortician—not expensive—somewhere in this vicinity?"

"Toresco's on Bleecker Street." Dr. Haynes produced the death certificate which he had filled out. "The patient gave his name to my nurse as Charles Collins. Is that correct?"

Doris hesitated, then admitted reluctantly, "No."

He leaned over the piano, filling out a new certificate, and he said, writing rapidly, "What is his correct name?"

Doris glanced at the rest of us. We were all watching, listening. Her mouth tightened, and she pulled herself to her feet. "May I speak to you privately, Doctor?"

He started to protest, shrugged, and walked out of the room. Doris followed him and closed the door. They left a heavy silence behind them. We refrained from looking at one another, and no one spoke. We were straining to hear what was being said in the hall. Not a word was audible. The doctor returned soon, picked up his hat and bag, and departed.

After that our little group scattered. Doris had already disappeared. Bela promised to keep the furnace going until another superintendent could be found and then announced plaintively that he was hungry. Evelyn and Louise offered to cook breakfast and started toward the kitchen. Henri and Jarvis went upstairs, and Lily and I went to our room.

The radiator was warm, but not yet warm enough to dissipate the chill in there. I said to Lily, "Let's get out of here. Let's go for a walk and then have some food."

"That is an excellent idea."

Snow was packed firm on the sidewalks; it squeaked under our feet. It was wonderful relief to be outside and free. The atmosphere seemed bright and fresh after the gloomy chill of that old house we had just left. In the park across the street trees which had been dark skeletons yesterday were now coated with ice; they glittered like crystal in the morning sun.

I looked at their icy branches, and as I did so the sun disappeared, the brightness of the day vanished and left the world ominously gray. Gray like the face of the corpse I had just seen. I wasn't able to get death out of my mind. Which of those old trees had been used as gallows? I thought of dead men swinging

horribly from their branches, necks stretched, heads awry...
Don't turn morbid, I warned myself. What happened to the
man in the basement was a natural thing. We all die from heart
failure in the final diagnosis.

We turned up Fifth Avenue, and Lily said, "I must make a
phone call. Do you mind waiting a moment?"

We went into the corner drugstore. I didn't ask the obvious:
why couldn't she use the house telephone? I stood near the
booth as she dialed the number, listening shamelessly. She might
as well have called from the house, I thought, when she began to
speak; no one could have eavesdropped satisfactorily unless he
understood Chinese.

She was telling someone something, probably recounting
what had happened at the house on Washington Square. No
doubt Mr. Char was concerned about the welfare of his beautiful little protégée. She spoke rapidly, she answered questions,
then finished with a few words which I judged from her tone to
be reassurance. She emerged from the booth so quickly that I
didn't have time to move from my listening position. Lily looked
at me with a bland smile. "Shall we eat now?"

As we relaxed after breakfast over coffee and cigarettes I
asked, "What do you think of Doris?"

Lily said succinctly, "She is not an agreeable person."

"I mean about her knowing that man. Don't you think she
knows more than she is telling?"

Lily stirred sugar into her coffee. She looked at me like a
teacher regarding a deplorably retarded child. "Of course she does."

"What do you think it is?"

She stared into her coffee cup. "I do not know."

I wondered whether she was telling the truth this time.
"Lily," I said confidentially, "do you remember when we first
came to the house? There was someone watching us from the
basement window."

"Yes," she admitted. "I remember."

I told her then of my discovery regarding the windows. "I
thought at first it must have been the super, but apparently

not. Who do you suppose it was? Is there another apartment in the basement?"

"No. I asked Evelyn about that. She said there is only a storage room. It is always locked."

"Whoever attacked you last night might have come from that basement. There were coal-dust prints on the bathroom floor."

She raised delicate brows. "So? That is possible."

The tone of her voice was cold. On her face was that blank expression which indicated that she was on guard, retreating into herself and shutting others out. This time I didn't intend to wonder in silence.

"Now, listen," I said firmly. "That remote act of yours doesn't go over with me. I have no idea what you're up to in that house, but I do know that you have some reason for wanting to live there. I don't care what your reason is—that's not my concern. But please don't think I'm gullible enough to believe that you're a simple schoolgirl who wants to be near the classroom."

Lily sat very still. Her black eyes were fixed on me with a regard so intent and somehow so inimical that I felt almost frightened. I forced myself to continue.

"I'm not interested in your private life, Lily. You may do anything with it that you choose. But whoever came into that room last night invaded my privacy too. I want to know who it was, if that's possible, for the sake of my own safety. If you have any intention of going down to investigate that storage room I'm going with you."

Her small shoulders relaxed. "You are right, Janice," she said very softly. "That is exactly what I am planning to do. If you insist on going I shall be grateful for your company."

She produced a key. "Evelyn told me where to find this. Of course she did not know that I intended to use it so soon. Shall we start now?"

Twenty minutes later we were back in the house again, cautiously descending the stairs toward the basement, where the dead man still lay.

Chapter Six

The room was used for storage, as Evelyn had said. It was crowded with an assortment of old furniture, dusty paper-wrapped bundles, and various pieces of luggage: these things were segregated more or less systematically in different corners, leaving space in the center with a sort of path to each wall. There were two windows curtained by grimy white net through which wan light filtered just strong enough to enable us to see the place clearly.

The first thing evident was that someone had been in the room, and recently.

A large leather armchair had been pulled out from a corner, leaving a track in the dusty floor. A steamer trunk plastered with worn labels—Shanghai, Hong Kong, Ceylon, Singapore, Cairo—was in front of the chair; it had been used as a footrest. Beside the chair arm stood a frail little table of French inlay. It was littered with cigarette butts, and scarred in many places where burning tobacco had been crushed against its surface.

I resented that damage fiercely. It was unmistakable indication of the sort of person who had hidden in this room. There is something more than a little abhorrent about people who show utter disregard for beauty. The table was old, but it was the sort of piece collectors cherish, and it represented the art of a craftsman who had spent long, painstaking hours in its making. It had been wantonly scarred.

As I stood there engrossed in my thoughts Lily touched my arm. "I'm going next door for a moment. I want to look at that photograph again." I nodded, and hardly heard her light steps as she went.

Whoever sat in that storage room had been there for a long time from the number of cigarettes smoked. I noticed then that brown wrapping paper lay behind the chair and that the faded blue velvet curtains it had contained were spread on the floor, apparently as a carpet. One length of velvet led between two stacks of furniture to the wall next to the super's room. I tiptoed across velvet, silent as that voiceless one who lay in the other room, separated from me by only a thin wall. This wall, I discovered, was of beaverboard, evidently built there to divide what had once been larger servants' quarters. The super had occupied the other half of the space.

There were dusty fingerprints on the unpainted beaverboard surface, and when I looked closely I found a torn piece of wrapping paper tacked over a hole in the wall. It was a new hole; bits of fresh beaverboard on the floor showed that recently it had been carefully cut through—and then concealed. There was something else among the shavings on the floor, something which glittered, gold-and-red-striped. I noticed it briefly but didn't pick it up; I was too much absorbed in a larger discovery at that moment.

I turned the paper on the tack which held it and found that I could peer through the opening into the next room. At first I saw only a blur of brown, which I finally identified as the tweed suit belonging to the dead man. By moving over and peering at a sharp angle I could see between the cretonne curtains into the room itself.

Lily was there. She was opening the Gladstone bag. She reached inside and felt around the zippered pocket without even glancing at the photograph. She removed a few garments and explored the lining quickly, thoroughly. She closed the bag and began to search the room. She moved clothes, felt their pockets, and searched the pockets of a shabby overcoat which hung on a nail in the corner. Then she went to the bed and looked through the overalls on the chair. She ran her hand under the pillow, over the mattress, indifferent to the sheeted corpse which lay there.

She must want something very badly, I thought. I wouldn't search that bed for the Kohinoor diamond.

Finally Lily knelt. She lifted the covers and peered under the bed. She bent over a pair of brown shoes which were there, lifting each by its laces. From the toe of one she removed a small white package which she examined hastily, then thrust into the pocket of her dress. She replaced the shoes and started toward the door. I dropped the paper so that it swiveled back into place and returned to the center of the room. When Lily entered she found me reading labels on the steamer trunk.

I glanced at her. "Well, did you find out anything?"

She shook her head and turned to examine the opposite corner of the room. Eventually she would find the peephole in the wall. I tiptoed across blue velvet again and went through motions of discovering it first. "Lily!" I whispered excitedly. "Look here! You can see—"

"Sh-h-h!" Lily said.

She had started toward me. Now she froze where she stood as cautious footsteps sounded on the stairs. I didn't dare move. I waited, my heart thudding, for the door to open, for the voice demanding to know what we were doing there. But the other person did not reach the storage room. The foot steps, stealthy as ours had been, went to the next room. I turned the paper again and peered through to find myself looking almost directly into the eyes of Doris Manning.

She was coming toward me. Hastily I slid the paper back over the opening, hoping she would not notice it because of the darkness of the curtained space where the clothes hung. I heard her move the suit on its hanger; evidently she was also searching for something. When movement of the curtains told me she had dropped them I ventured to peer through again to she what she was doing.

She was at the Gladstone bag, rummaging hastily, her lips pressed tight together. She found the photograph and removed it with an exclamation of satisfaction. Next she went to the bed and pulled the covers off the rigid corpse. She stood looking at him for a long time. Her pale eyes glittered, her features were contorted with rage. She was muttering to herself. Then she did some thing which so astounded me that I gasped aloud. She spat on the dead man's face.

Doris didn't hear my startled gasp. She was spewing out words to the dead man. "I hope you roast in hell forever!" she hissed.

Heavy feet sounded on the wooden stairs. "Down this way, Pete." A man's deep voice.

Doris whirled around, her eyes wild. She slid the photograph inside the navy cardigan sweater she wore and buttoned it hastily. She covered the corpse and crossed the floor. By the time she reached the door she was in control of herself again, and her face wore its usual expression of cold superiority.

"In here," she said, swinging the door open.

Two men in dark suits entered carrying a long wicker basket. I knew who they were. The men from Toresco's, that "cheap" undertaking parlor on Bleecker Street. I dropped the paper over the hole in the wall and made signs to Lily that we should get out of there while we had the chance. The door of the next room was half shut as we fled past, and I hoped that no one saw us.

Our room was warm at last, the radiator clanking with a comfortable, homely noise. When we had closed the door I wilted into the nearest chair, limp with relief. Whatever Lily felt, her expression didn't reveal it. Her delicate face was carefully blank. Only gestures betrayed her. She looked uncertainly around the room, then went to the dressing table and began to repair her makeup, as if trying to regain composure by going through familiar motions. But her hands were unsteady with her lip brush. She tossed it aside and began to pace the floor. I knew that Lily at that moment craved solitude; she had something disturbing on her mind.

And something in her pocket. The little package made a small bulge in the soft black wool of her dress.

Finally she seemed to reach a decision. She dragged a big leather hatbox into the center of the floor and began tossing things out of it—lingerie, stockings, blouses—until she reached the object around which they had been wrapped.

A large Buddha, commonly known as The Laughing One. He is Lo-Han, the god of happiness, prosperity, fecundity, and any other blessing desired by a Chinese household. Sometimes one sees him represented as surrounded by children. Obese and completely bald, with an enormous belly, grinning, complacent, he is a delightful old fellow. Lily's Buddha was a very fine one of blue glazed porcelain.

As she lifted him from the hatbox and polished an invisible speck of dust from his navel I saw that he was not so heavy as he looked, for the figure was hollow. She rose from her knees with the image in her arms and set him carefully on her bureau next to the Wu Wei picture. She took a teakwood platform from the hatbox, then showed her back to me while she carefully fitted the porcelain figure onto it. When she turned around, the bulge in her pocket was gone. I knew then where Lily had secreted the package she took from the dead man's shoe.

I watched without speaking, too numb for conversation or even comment. The impact of what I had so recently witnessed was still with me. I remembered vividly the hateful expression on Doris's face, the venom of her words, the shocking thing she had done. It was like seeing naked a person whom one has supposed to be physically normal and discovering that the exposed body is hideously malformed. I had seen Doris's spirit naked.

I was so absorbed in revisualizing the scene that it was not until I heard my name spoken twice that it penetrated consciousness. Lily had finished unpacking and was sitting on her bed, smoking furiously, watching me. She said, and her voice was puzzled, "Janice, what did you see when you looked through the wall?"

I was startled. Had she been aware of my observation? No, for in that case she would not have bothered with the elaborate maneuver she had just performed with the Buddha. I answered, "I saw Doris."

"What was she doing?"

I thought resentfully, she thinks she can pump me for anything she wants to know without offering a shred of information in exchange. I said, "First things first. Tell me your conclusions about what we found in the storage room." I didn't intend to be pressed with questions until I got some satisfactory answers.

Lily jabbed her cigarette into the ashtray. "Someone was hiding there, probably the person who watched us from the window when we arrived."

"Why was he there? And how did he get into the room? The door was locked."

She ignored the first question. "He must have obtained a key from the same place I did—a hook in the broom closet."

I hadn't expected that. "Then," I said, thinking aloud, "he must be familiar with this house."

"Yes. I found out about the room by asking Evelyn if there was storage space anywhere. When she told me about it she definitely said, 'the key hangs in the broom closet.' She did not say 'keys.' But it would be simple for anyone to have a duplicate made."

"Why do you think he hid there?"

This was dangerous ground. Her voice was guarded as she answered. "I am not sure, but—"

"But it looks as if he was watching the man in the next room, doesn't it? Do you think it was he who attacked you last night?"

This time there was no mask of blankness on Lily's face. "I do not know. But when I recall it now I have the distinct impression—if one can get an impression in such a brief time—that the person in the dressing room was surprised when I walked in and that the attack on me was more an act of self-protection than aggression."

She clasped slim hands over one knee and looked thoughtful. "You remember we were not expected to move in here so quickly. Bela told us that. Suppose someone had been snooping around this room—"

"In that case it might even have been the super getting the lay of the land."

"Yes. Perhaps he was startled, and afraid he would lose his job if he were caught."

I took it from there. "That could explain the heart attack. From fright, I mean, when you walked into the dressing room unexpectedly and he hit you and ran. When he recovered he went to the doctor for medicine. Later that night he had a second attack, which was fatal."

It sounded so simple at first. Then I grew silent, remembering other unexplained details: the expensive clothes of the man in contrast to his work worn hands, the voice at three in the morning which had not been his voice; the interest shown in him by both Doris and Lily. No casual answers would fit questions which still remained. I waited for Lily to mention some of these, but she did not.

"Well," I said lamely, "I don't intend to leave it so easy for anyone to get in here. I'm going to buy a lock for that bathroom door which will fasten on our side."

Lily looked pleased. "That is an excellent idea!" She abandoned her pose and leaned forward. "Now, Janice. Please tell me, what was Doris Manning doing?"

"She was looking for that photograph. She took it from the bag. Then she went over to the bed and spat on the dead man's face and said she hoped he would roast in hell forever. That was when the undertaker's men came and we got out."

Lily had listened intently. Now she leaned back and sighed, as if she had heard something she already knew.

"You know more about this than you're telling," I accused. "Do you also know who the dead man was and what he meant to Doris?"

Lily said with reluctance, "Yes, I know. He—"

There was a knock on the door, and we both started. I made an exclamation of annoyance, and Lily gave me a glance indicating caution as she went to answer. It was Bela.

"Hi. Evelyn sent me to invite you for a *Kaffeeklatsch* in the kitchen." He breezed past Lily without invitation to enter and sniffed the air.

"Why, Miss Wu," he said, "you disappoint me! No joss sticks! No heathen idols! The other girls at least stayed in character by keeping pandas on their beds."

Lily went through the same metamorphosis I'd seen her achieve before. She dimpled at Bela. She turned soft and feminine, and even managed to convey the impression that she was clinging, figuratively, to his barrel chest.

"Please do not be disappointed," she said prettily, gesturing toward the bureau. "At least I have Lo-Han. And you shall meet Kwan Yin when my trunk arrives."

Bela was delighted with the Buddha. He patted the old fellow's bald head, then bowed elaborately to Lily. "You've restored my faith in human nature. I feel better, my dear." He turned to the bureau again and picked up the Chinese picture. "Ah. Wu Wei. I see, Lily Wu, that you're loyal to the art of your people. Wu—he isn't by any chance a relative a few hundred years back?"

Lily's answer came promptly. "No. I am merely a humble admirer of his art."

Bela was looking closely at the picture. "Excellent reproduction, this. You can see his chop mark clearly."

"Chop mark?" I echoed. "What is that?"

He held the picture so I could see the tiny square ideograph in the upper left corner. "Each Oriental artist has his own chop, his seal, just as some European families use the crest which identifies them." He turned to Lily. "I've been told that many

Chinese use a chop on business documents. In China, for instance, a man's chop is often his legal signature. Right?"

As he spoke, the pretty smile left Lily's face. She said in a toneless voice, "That is correct." She rose abruptly and went to the dressing room. "Excuse me. If we're going to join the others I must improve my appearance." She seated herself on the dressing-table bench and pulled the door shut.

Her hair was smooth and her makeup needed no refreshing, She had left the room to avoid further interrogation. Suddenly I felt depressed again. For a few moments we had joked and laughed, as if everything in this house were normal. Now the feeling of disquiet returned; unease sat on me like a block of stone. Lily had previously been able to maintain her equanimity in spite of lies, hostility, even physical danger.

Why, then, had that simple question from Bela disturbed her so deeply?

Chapter Seven

There was another knock on the door, and Evelyn appeared. "Aren't you coming to have coffee? Everything's ready. Jarvis is fretting because he has to be at work soon."

Lily emerged from the dressing room. "I'm ready." She wore light powder now and had applied pink lipstick. There was a pink ribbon tied on her hair, which fell in waves down her back. She looked about fourteen, and I was sure she knew it.

"Where does Jarvis work?" I asked as we started.

"In a local record shop," Bela said. "He hates it, but he can buy music wholesale there. I believe there are still a few thousand records he wants for his collection. So he sticks to his job."

"And you know, Bela, I've been late once already this week," Jarvis added as we entered.

He sat next to Henri at the table, where places were laid for seven. A bowl of doughnuts sat beside an electric percolator which was burping fragrant steam. Evelyn and Henri had waited for us, but Jarvis was chewing; he gulped down a mouthful and wiped guiltily at powdered sugar on his lips.

Doris was not there, nor was Louise. Henri told us that Doris had gone to bed with a chill. We sat down together, and Evelyn poured coffee with determined cheerfulness.

By unspoken agreement we were all resolved to ignore the events of the early morning and our gruesome discovery in the basement. We were aware, without mentioning it, that the undertaker's men had carried the body away in their basket, and knowledge that death no longer lay in the house lightened the atmosphere considerably.

"Who is the extra cup for?" Lily asked.

"Louise," Evelyn said. "She'll be here soon."

Bela stirred his coffee. "Bet I know"—he lifted the cup and sniffed appreciatively—"where she is."

Evelyn smiled. "You are right. But you shouldn't tease her about it."

At my blank look she explained. "Louise loves that pink marble tub. Bela teases her because she spends so much time in the bathroom."

Jarvis raised his head from his plate and between busy chompings contributed, "I'll bet she's used ten pounds of bath salts in the last three months."

"Louise probably has a bad conscience," Bela announced. "Frequent bathing is a characteristic habit of people with a guilt complex."

"Perhaps," Lily suggested, "she's merely a sybarite."

"Talking about me?"

Louise stood in the doorway, wrapped in a pink satin quilted robe. Her face was rosy and her dark hair curled around her temples. As she entered the kitchen the fragrance of rose geranium competed with the smell of coffee and doughnuts. She sat next to me, and once again I marveled at the length of her eyelashes. She looked very pretty then, until she smiled and showed those crooked teeth. Louise was conscious of this blemish; at my glance she stopped smiling and her face became sullen.

How awful, I thought, to be afraid to be pleasant because a smile spoils your appearance. I felt sorry for her and ashamed of my rudeness.

"Please excuse me for staring," I said. "It's your eyelashes, Louise. They're marvelous."

She brushed at them indifferently; they were still wet and hung together in starry points. "Thanks," she said. No smile. She leaned toward Lily, her voice hostile.

"What do you mean, Miss Wu, by calling me a sybarite?"

"Relax, Louise," Bela said. "That was a compliment, not an insult. Sybaris was an ancient Greek city whose inhabitants were noted for their love of luxury. That's where the word comes from."

Louise looked mollified. "Then you're right," she said. "About my loving luxury, I mean." She reached for the sugar, made a little *moue*, and shoved it away, then sipped her coffee black. "I'm the original girl they wrote those ads for, remember? 'Because you love nice things.' Hand-turned shoes, good furs, real-silk dresses. I have a weakness for luxury. Is there any harm in that?"

"Some people do not consider such taste a weakness," Lily said with a smile. "They call it fastidiousness. I admit I share the same preferences."

"And I," Bela insisted, "call your infatuation with a pink marble tub a guilt-complex manifestation."

Louise sniffed. "You and your psychological jargon! It was a sorry day for us when you discovered Karen Horney. You've been quoting her like a parrot ever since."

Bela took a bite of doughnut and gave her a sugary grin. "I can do more than quote Horney," he boasted. "I can make a pretty fair analysis of anyone in the house—except Janice and Lily, of course. I haven't observed them long enough yet."

"Then tell us about Doris," Louise demanded. "What made her faint when she saw that picture? Why did she offer to pay for the super's funeral?"

"You've got me there, Louise." Bela glanced sideways at Henri, who was frowning at his coffee cup. "Such generosity doesn't fit her pattern. Poor Doris, I had her all figured out before. She suffers from chronic anhedonia."

"From what?" Henri's voice was frigid.

Bela's eyebrows rose. "Do you mean to tell me none of you knows what that word means?" He grinned with satisfaction at his own superior knowledge.

"Anhedonia means inability to enjoy life," Lily supplied.

Bela turned to her with reproach. "You disappoint me, Lily, I thought you were merely beautiful; you spoil it now by having intellect."

Lily dimpled at him. "Not really. My brother majored in psychology. He explained the term to me."

"Then I forgive you."

Jarvis was bored with light talk. "But about Doris," he pursued.

"Please, let's not discuss her when she isn't here!" Evelyn was so distressed by Henri's discomfiture that she was willing to turn the spotlight on herself to avoid it. "Analyze me, Bela. You know me rather well."

Bela lifted her hand and kissed it. "You, my dear, have the talent of a fine artist. But you're inhibited by childish repressions. So you stick to bees and flowers and inhuman figures which won't tempt you to betray any inner yearnings which some stupid parent taught you were shameful."

Evelyn's face turned scarlet. Her gray eyes looked appealingly at Bela, who sent her a satyrish grin. Something was accused and defended in that exchange.

Jarvis, diverted, said, "How about me, Bela?"

"You're easy," Bela told him with pedagogic glibness. "A case of psychic hunger. That's why you stuff yourself all the time, why you collect things. Except in rare cases of glandular unbalance fat people are neurotic. They're hungry, yes, but it isn't food they're starved for. I'd also suspect, from your chronic peevishness, that inside you is a seething volcano of repressed hostility. Both your hunger and hostility have something to do with music."

Jarvis had turned white. The hand which held his cup began to shake; he set the cup down with a crash. "Very clever, aren't you?" He shoved his chair back violently and stomped out of the room.

After his exit Bela shrugged and said smugly, "See? If I hadn't told him the truth he wouldn't have resented it so much." He pointed a doughnut at Louise. "Now you, young lady—"

"Never mind me," she said quickly. "Physician, heal thyself. How about your own self-analysis? You talked us all to death with it for a while, then stopped mentioning the subject."

He blinked at her. "*Touché,* Louise. I'm as vulnerable as any of you. The truth is, I can't go any further with it. I made wonderful progress for a while. It was like tearing down a brick wall and finding another brick wall inside that and so on. I got to the final one, the idealized image, and actually started demolition." He sighed melodramatically. "But where I pulled bricks out of that last inner wall I began to feel such an icy draft coming through to chill my tender little psyche—that I decided to put the bricks back and wait for warmer weather!"

We all laughed heartily. Bela's devastating frankness did not exempt even himself. Louise examined her bright fingernails and said, "I think I'll leave my psyche alone and worry about my career instead. You can have Freud and Horney—I'll stick to Stanislavsky."

She leaned back and put her hands into the pockets of her robe. She felt something, brought one hand out with some bright squares in it, and tossed them on the table. "Here. Somebody take these before I eat more of them and get pimples." She mimicked Bela's melodramatic sigh. "The sacrifices I make to my art!"

The bright squares rolled across the table like gilt-and-scarlet dice. I took one and unwrapped tinfoil from the caramel it covered. I ate the candy, chewing slowly, hardly tasting it, while my fingers smoothed the foil until it lay flat before me. Red-and-gold-striped foil. A puzzling half memory had been struggling for clarity in my mind; now it came sharply into focus.

I drew in my breath, then looked around to see if others had noticed my excitement. Bela and Henri were rising, both saying something about getting back to work. Louise and Evelyn were starting on second cups of coffee. Lily was retrieving her paper napkin from the floor. She pushed back her chair, and as she left the kitchen I followed.

I stood by the window and looked down at the snowy earth, remembering. I had seen that glittering foil before, in the storage room among beaverboard shreds on the floor. I was sure of it, but I had to find proof. Now I was the one with my back turned, wanting solitude, freedom from observation. I heard Lily moving about the room; when I turned I found her dressed for the street. She had tied a scarf around her head, peasant fashion, and was pulling on galoshes.

"I'm going across the Square to see about my registration," she said. "Can I bring you anything when I return?"

"No, thanks. I'll do some more unpacking while you're gone."

I emptied clothes from my largest suitcase onto the bed. I puttered, waiting twenty minutes by the clock. Then I stepped into the hall, suitcase in hand; if anyone questioned me I was putting luggage away. There was water running in the kitchen and the clink of dishes on porcelain. Somewhere a radio was playing; that might be Doris's room. No other sign of activity.

It took all the nerve I could summon to go down the basement stairs again.

It was dim and quiet under the house except for faint stirrings from the furnace. The door of the super's room was ajar; I could see the rumpled bed. My heart began to pound against my ribs as I walked past that room to the door of the other. The key was in the lock where we had left it in our hasty departure. I turned the knob cautiously and stepped inside.

Then I stood there, dumfounded. The room was in order. The armchair was back in its place, blue curtains were no longer on the floor, the little table stood in a far corner with bundles stacked on it. I stepped toward the wall. A gaudy calendar disguised the peephole. The beaverboard shavings were swept into a neat little pile, the broom which had been used to sweep them leaned there against a tower of furniture with the labeled steamer trunk balanced on top. *The broom which had been used…* As I looked it moved slowly back behind the furniture. The broom which was being used… I stood paralyzed and listened to my own harsh breathing. Something icy was crawling up my spine, constricting my lungs, numbing me. The suitcase fell from my hand with a thud.

As if that were the signal, the pile of furniture began to sway. It leaned toward me; the trunk tipped, fell back into place, toppled.

"No!" I gasped. "No!" I raised my arm.

Then it crashed, and I went down.

Chapter Eight

"**J**anice—Janice!" someone was saying. "Janice!"

I opened my eyes. I was lying on the cold floor. Bela knelt beside me, speaking my name. I moaned involuntarily.

"Don't move." He felt my body with quick, exploratory fingers. "Nothing seems to be broken. Can you sit up?"

I nodded, and he slipped an arm under me. His hands were strong; leaning against his arm was like being supported by warm steel cables. When he touched my shoulder, I winced.

"What happened?" he asked.

I was dazed. Had I been knocked out, or had I merely fainted from fright? Was I unconscious long? If not, how had Bela got here so quickly?

I gave the easiest explanation. "I came down to put some luggage away. The trunk fell on me."

I turned my eyes, still sitting half upright against him, clutching my painful shoulder with one hand. The trunk was at my feet. Over my head the pile of furniture still leaned perilously. On top of the pile was a marble-topped table. If that had fallen...I closed my eyes again, feeling sick.

"You lie here a moment," he said. "I'll get one of the girls." I didn't have energy to protest. I lay back and kept my eyes closed. He ran up the stairs. I heard voices in the hall above; then in less than a minute he returned. Lily was with him.

She bent over me. Her coat brushed my cheek; the smell of fur and perfume and stale dust mingled in my nostrils. I looked up into her face. She seemed very concerned.

"Let us help you upstairs, Janice," she said.

"I'll carry her," Bela offered.

"No." I sat up. "I can walk."

This time I looked at the wall behind me. The floor was swept clean; there was no broom. Nothing but bare concrete. "I want to get out of here," I said, and my voice trembled.

In our room I pulled off my dirty blouse and found a large red mark on my shoulder, already beginning to turn blue. The trunk had just missed my head. At this realization I grew weak again.

"You had better lie down for a while," Lily advised. I lay on the bed. She stood at the foot of it and asked, "Why did you go down there alone?"

"I went to—" I looked into her bright eyes searching my face. "I took an empty bag down," I finished. "How did you happen to be here? I thought you were out."

"I was just entering the house when I heard the crash. I thought at first it was Bela at the furnace. When I came in here and found you gone, but with your coat still here, I decided you might have gone to the basement and fallen on the stairs. I started to find you and met Bela."

"Was anybody—didn't anybody else hear the noise?"

"Apparently not. Janice, did you notice that the room had been put in order?"

"Yes." I closed my eyes. I didn't want to talk until I could get my thoughts straightened out.

"How do you feel? Would you like me to call a doctor?"

"No. It's only a bruise. I'll be all right."

I heard her moving around, going into the bathroom. Then she came to the bed again. "Don't be startled. This is only a compress." She laid something wet and aromatic on my shoulder. It stung at first, where skin was broken, then felt infinitely soothing. She pulled a blanket over me, and warmth was welcome. I lay quiet and listened to her soft movements. I must have been weakened by shock, for presently I slept.

When I awakened the room was empty. I moved experimentally and found my shoulder already much less painful. The compress had worked like magic. On a bruised shoulder. But no simple compress would have relieved a fractured skull. It was luck alone that I didn't have a broken head.

I remembered the scarred little table. Some ruthless one had shoved a trunk on me, one who would stop at nothing to prevent discovery of his identity. I sat up and lit a cigarette, while the resolve which had been forming in my mind took solid shape. I was going to get out of that house. Something evil lived there. Too many people, under a façade of amicable companionship, were disguising ugly secrets.

Bela, pretending to be harmlessly outspoken, needled with dislike of Henri. Such enmity must be reciprocated, in spite of the other man's cool reserve. Doris, with viperish hatred of a corpse. Louise—why should she lie about such a simple thing as being in a café and speaking Italian? Jarvis was completely neurotic; it was true that he seethed with hostility.

Lily Wu. The girl I lived with was most incomprehensible of all. Lying, unscrupulously rearranging other lives to suit her hidden purpose. Stealing from the dead. Pretending to be artless and gay when actually she was infinitely complex and deep, obsessed by some secret, inexorable purpose closely connected with this place and the people in it. She had already used me as a front to get into the house. If I stayed, I might find myself involved; I had personal projects of my own which were important enough without adding the problems of anyone else.

I couldn't even be sure Lily had really gone to the university. She might have gone to the basement instead. Anyone in the house had time and opportunity, as far as I knew, to get down to the storage room. One of them had pushed a trunk over on me.

It was time I moved.

I remembered the name of the agency which was offering an apartment. I remembered the notice. One room, kitchenette, fireplace, charming, two hundred dollars a month. Much as I resented that exorbitant cost, it was preferable to staying here and getting my head bashed in.

I got up and put on a fresh blouse, powdered my face, and applied lipstick. My expression in the mirror was grim; rebellion had reached exploding point.

Much of my adult life had been spent under compulsion of doing the distasteful, pursuing conduct unnatural to my temperament merely in order to survive. Now that I had finally achieved personal liberty I was still being prevented from freedom of action. But not for long. I counted my money; there was enough to make a deposit on the apartment until I could get to the bank. I'd call that realtor immediately and tell him I wanted the place. I started to the telephone, feeling the relief which comes with a resolution made and acted upon.

Then, as soon as I reached the end of the hall, I discovered that the right to make any further voluntary decision had been taken from me.

There were voices in the living room, one angry tone rising shrill above the others. I stopped in the doorway to watch and listen.

I saw a tense group of human beings there. Bela and Evelyn occupied the sofa. Louise and Lily Wu sat on the piano bench. Doris was standing in front of the fireplace facing two people: Dr. Haynes and a stocky, square-jawed young man in a dark suit.

Bela seemed interested; he regarded the scene with speculation, as if he were studying some fascinating specimens of humanity. He held Evelyn's hand, patting it absently from time to time. Evelyn looked as if she had received a shock; her face was pale, and her gray eyes were wide with incredulity at something she had just heard.

Lily and Louise were a contrast. Lily wore her smooth blank look, which meant that she was concealing her thoughts with that Oriental inscrutability which she could assume at will. Her impassivity seemed incongruous with the little-girl-wearing-hair-ribbon getup.

Louise, beside her, looked sullen—and frightened. Her well-tended hands were laid carefully over each other in her lap, palms up in a "let us now indicate poise" position. But the inside hand was clenched into a fist.

Doris's face was livid, not from shock, but from temper. Hers was the voice raised in anger, directed at the square-jawed young man. "That's absolutely ridiculous!" she was saying. "I never heard such an insane idea in my life!"

She appealed to Dr. Haynes. "He's making a fool of himself, isn't he, Doctor? You signed the death certificate; you should know."

The doctor was uncomfortable. He had shed his pomposity and seemed to have shrunk so that his expensive gray suit did not fit so smoothly as before. He cleared his throat and started to speak.

Before the doctor could answer, the young man began, apparently resuming an argument: "Look, miss," he said patiently. "I'm not a doctor. I don't sign death certificates. I just prepare the deceased for burial."

Bela snickered. The young man directed a level gaze at him. "Laugh if you want. You may need our services sooner than you think," he said solemnly. "For yourself or for a loved one."

Bela blinked at him, and his hand tightened on Evelyn's. He didn't laugh again.

The young man went on, much as if he were reciting carefully memorized passages from the *Mortician's Manual* to the effect that at a time of bereavement it was his function to bring comfort to the grieving family, to assuage the pain of their loss by arranging that the deceased should be laid to rest with proper solemn rites. So on and so on.

This was the "cheap" undertaker from Bleecker Street. I stood and listened, puzzled at first, straining later to absorb his words, their import was so shocking.

In the middle of this peroration Doris interrupted. "I am not interested in your social contribution, Mr. Toresco"—she sneered—"or the noble ideals of your profession. What I'm concerned about is your effrontery in coming here with such a preposterous suggestion."

The young man set his square jaw more firmly. He couldn't have been much older than twenty-two. I noticed then that he wore a discharge button in his lapel. As he confronted Doris he began to shed his sepulchral dignity and became just an honest, stubborn, angry guy.

"My name is not Toresco, miss. My name is Donahue. I own half the business with my father-in-law. And my 'suggestion,' as you call it, is not preposterous. What I'm telling is facts. When I see a corpse with blisters on his feet, with rope marks on his arms and legs, and burns on his stomach, I don't need no MD to tell me something ain't kosher. Maybe he died of 'cardiac failure,' as the doc here says, but something mighty damned unpleasant happened to the guy to bring on that heart attack. I don't embalm no corpse which ain't become a corpse naturally. That's when the police come in."

"Police!" she yelped. "You cheap little busybody! Don't you dare call the police! Don't you *dare!*" She stepped toward him, both thin hands clawing, as if she intended to scratch his eyes out. He backed away, not in fright, but with disgust.

"I may be cheap in the prices I charge, but I ain't dishonest. I bought into this business on a GI loan, and I ain't fool enough to run chances with my investment. You go ahead and yell if you want, miss. It won't do you no good."

He looked around for a chair, went to the window seat, and settled himself facing us, with the air of one who intends to wait—all day if necessary—for what he knows is coming. As he pulled up his neat dark trousers carefully and crossed his legs, he dropped the bombshell.

"The police have already been notified, Miss Manning. They're on the way here now."

Chapter Nine

All the fight went out of Doris then. She gasped like a fish drowning in air, her face puckered like a tired old woman's, and she collapsed on the love seat and began to cry. I was sorry for her, while at the same time I felt the distaste everyone else must have been feeling at the spectacle she made of herself.

For a while no sound was audible except Doris's sobs. Everyone was silent while the implication of what we had just heard spread like a miasma through the room. The super had not died "naturally." He had been forced to his death in a monstrously cruel manner—torture. I shuddered as actuality finally etched itself into comprehension; my legs grew weak, and I stumbled to the nearest chair.

Heads turned toward me; until then no one had been aware of my presence. Lily looked into my face, her black eyes opaque, her features impassive as a cameo carved in amber. Louise, beside her, seemed distraught with fright. She began to breathe as if the air were thick and her lungs were struggling for oxygen. Finally she put the back of her hand to her mouth and closed her teeth on it to prevent herself from uttering any sound.

Mr. Donahue unwrapped a stick of gum and folded it slowly into his mouth. He began to chew while he looked out the window as though reassuring himself that this was not his world, that he was only a visitor, that soon he'd be out of this unpleasant place.

Lily rose and said with a faint deprecatory smile, "Excuse me for a moment." She avoided my glance of inquiry. I decided that she was probably going to the bathroom.

Evelyn had sagged against Bela with her eyes closed. He put a comforting arm around her, but the gesture was automatic. Bela had managed to regain his former attitude, that of an audience at a highly interesting performance. His alert eyes darted from one of us to the next, examining, speculating. Since he blinked continuously, the effect was that of a double-lensed camera taking multiple candid shots, each blink a frame in the film, to be developed later and studied with care.

Finally he said ruminatively, "So that's why the furnace was working overtime last night. Determined fellow, our murderer. Not ingenious, perhaps, but determined. Hot coals applied to the feet and stomach. No doubt while the writhing victim was effectively bound and gagged. Now why do you suppose—"

Evelyn moaned and hid her face in her hands.

"Bela!" Louise cried, "for the love of heaven shut up!"

Mr. Donahue swiveled his head around from the window to announce, "Here come the police."

My chair was nearest the entrance, so I rose. "I'll let them in."

I came into the hall just in time to see Lily closing the door which led to the basement. She was breathing fast, as if she had run up the stairs, and she started visibly at seeing me, then put her finger to her lips in a gesture commanding silence.

That was too much. I caught her arm and demanded furiously, "What were you doing down there?"

She jerked away from my grasp. "I went to get the key. And to erase your fingerprints from the wall. Or would you rather have the police—"

At that point the doorbell rang.

Lily started into the living room. I hurried to admit a couple of radio-patrol officers, whose coupé was parked at the curb. As I turned to close the door another car drew up in front of the house. Precinct detectives. I had just admitted them when the telephone shrilled, and I answered that bell. It was Dr. Haynes's office nurse. The doctor came out and spoke hurriedly to her. While this conversation was taking place another carload of officials arrived, and from then on the period of time which followed was memorable chiefly for confusion.

We sat in the living room and waited. When an officer from the Homicide Division arrived, he called the doctor into the hall and questioned him. Nothing was audible to our straining ears but their low-pitched voices in a lengthy dialogue. Finally we heard, "Thank you, Doc. We'll get in touch with you later for a signed statement."

Dr. Haynes came into the room with his overcoat on, head up, chest out again. He retrieved his medical bag, nodded to us, and departed.

A man in plain clothes appeared in the doorway. "How many of you live in this house? Is everybody here?"

Bela answered. "Mr. Ledoux is working in his room. Last door at the end of the hall, next floor up. Mr. Lloyd has gone to his job."

"Where does he work?"

"Village Melody Shoppe on Macdougal Street."

"Thanks. Everybody is to stay here. We want to talk to you pretty soon."

Henri came down presently, looking bewildered, like a man not yet able to transfer his mental perspective from the realm of ideas to a world of shocking reality. Doris had stopped crying and was sitting erect, staring into the fireplace and twisting folds of her dress in thin fingers. Henri went directly to her, and she looked up at him apprehensively; whatever she knew about the murdered man Doris dreaded telling Henri. He's sensitive, I thought; he's had more than his share of violence. Perhaps she's afraid of his reaction.

Henri seated himself by Doris, and she began to murmur into his ear. He removed his glasses and polished them with a white linen handkerchief while he listened. His eyes without glasses were dark-circled and somber. As she spoke, his face began to set in lines of rigid sternness, and I thought, Poor Doris.

Lily had left the piano bench to settle in a large chair, where part of her face was turned toward the periphery of light from the lamp near by. She sat with one foot curled under her, the other, childishly small in a flat embroidered slipper, dangling inches from the floor. To the casual observer she might have seemed completely relaxed. But Lily was immobile; not an eyelash fluttered. I recognized her attitude for what it was: the same self-protection as the uncanny stillness of a wild forest creature which knows the stalking enemy is at hand.

The house by then was filled with activity. Down in the super's room police technicians were taking pictures, dusting for fingerprints, examining every square inch of space. Feet tromped up and down the stairs, masculine voices exchanged brief greetings, comments.

"Hi, Mac. Plenty cold, isn't it?"

"Plenty. How's the wife?"

"Fine. She's coming home tomorrow."

"Baby all right?"

"Yeah. Say, he looks like me already."

"Poor little devil. Must be the homeliest kid in five boroughs."

The telephone rang. "Captain Weber speaking. Yes. Okay, Doc. I'll wait. Call me here."

Another ring. "Hello. Miss who? Who's calling? Just a minute."

An officer's head in the doorway. "Miss Kane?"

Louise turned. "Yes?" Her eyes were blank, her voice lifeless.

"Mr. Andrews calling from National Broadcasting."

She started to rise, then sank back apathetically. "Take the message, will you?"

Telephone conversation: "Yes. Yeah. Ten o'clock. I'll tell her. Okay."

She nodded as he delivered the information that rehearsal for the Bartlett show would be held Wednesday morning at ten. She slumped against the keyboard of the piano, started at the noise which issued from it, and sat up right, hands once more posed carefully in her lap. For a few seconds the echo of disharmonious bass notes vibrated strangely in the air.

Jarvis arrived, squawking like a disturbed broody hen as he divested himself of overshoes and coat in the hallway. He bounced into our midst with a shrill question. "What is all this nonsense? Some officer comes in a patrol car and drags me out of the shop—with a customer waiting at the counter and two in the booths!"

"No nonsense, my lad." Bela sent him a malicious grin. "Find a comfortable seat and prepare yourself for a long session."

He waved toward the man in the window seat. "Mr. Donahue over there is the mortician who was going to embalm our defunct superintendent. He found evidence that the unknown was assisted to his last sleep by a very painful method. Hence the police. The cadaver is no doubt in process of official autopsy this very moment. Right, Mr. Donahue?"

Jarvis gasped; his eyes bulged. He dropped heavily into the nearest chair and regarded the square-jawed Mr. Donahue as if he might be carrying a communicable disease. The latter nodded, glanced disinterestedly at Jarvis, then resumed his gazing out the window.

Sounds from the outside world reached us intermittently: rhythmic clanking of chains on passing automobiles, shouts in the park of children who were having a fine time throwing snowballs. I welcomed such evidence of a normal life still going on somewhere. The house in which we were confined was permeated with nightmare abnormality.

At last our waiting was ended by entrance of the man who was to question us. Every eye in the room turned toward him as he appeared, followed by an assistant in plain clothes who carried a notebook. The detective stood surveying the scene for a moment, looking at each of us in turn with deliberate scrutiny.

Captain Weber. He was a big man; ten pounds more would have made him sloppy fat. His lard-colored features looked as if they might have been a sculptor's leftovers slapped together any old how to make a face. He had close-set pale blue eyes, thinning blond hair, and the air of an official who does his job inexorably, without losing sleep over any personal tragedy which might result.

He settled himself in an armchair facing us while his assistant went to the small desk near the window and prepared to write.

"I'll have your names first," Captain Weber said.

Like children answering a schoolroom roll call we identified ourselves while the pencil traveled efficiently over notebook pages. When we had finished, Captain Weber rose. "All right," he said. "You will talk to me one at a time when I call you. I'll take your statements in the kitchen. Miss Manning first."

Jarvis bounced up. "How about taking me first, officer? I *must* get back to work immediately." He put down the ashtray he had been holding.

Captain Weber barely glanced at him. "Sit down. I'll let you know when I want you." Jarvis sat, picking up the ashtray again.

"Now, Miss Manning."

Doris jumped as if she had been jabbed with a needle. Obviously she would rather have faced anything on earth than the interrogation of this lynx-eyed man. "What do you want?" she said.

"I want to ask you some questions."

Her voice grew shriller. "Why single me out for your third degree?" She clutched the love seat with both hands like a runner getting set for a hard sprint.

A bored expression settled over Captain Weber's face. He sat down again. "This is a police investigation, Miss Manning. There will be no third degree. I am calling you first because you knew the dead man. Because you told the doctor you would arrange for his burial. Because you fainted when you saw a photograph which was in his possession, so obviously you recognized some—"

She jerked to her feet and faced him, the last remnants of control gone. "I recognized them all!" she cried. "For most excellent reasons. It was my family! A picture of my mother, and myself as a child, and of *him*. He came back to his own house to die!"

The ashtray dropped from Jarvis's hand, spilling ashes and cigarette butts on the rug. Jarvis didn't look at the mess; he was staring at Doris, his mouth the shape of a large O.

The police stenographer's pencil was racing over the page.

Captain Weber glanced at his assistant briefly, then said, "Now, Miss Manning, if you will kindly save these statements until—"

She glared at him, her mouth twitching. "I'll save nothing. You can all know! The reporters can write the story all over again and bring up every filthy fact which the public might have forgotten. He was my father! And I loathe the very sound of his name!"

She was shrieking now, her eyes raking all of us with hatred. "What's more," she added, "this is my house. You are paying rent to me. And as far as I am concerned you can get out; you can get yourselves out of here, every one of you—tomorrow! My father was a selfish, wicked criminal," she raved. "He ruined my life by the disgrace he brought on me. There was only one decent thing he ever did, and that was to insure himself for thirty thousand dollars. I've scrimped and saved for thirteen years to make the payments on that policy, and now I'm going to collect. I'm delighted that he's dead! Whoever killed him did me a favor. I'm glad he was tortured before he died. And wherever he is now I hope he suffers all the torments of the damned forever!"

With that Doris stopped, her face grew slack, her eyes rolled up horribly under her lids, and she collapsed. Her head struck the coffee table as she went down.

Instantly Henri was on his knees beside her murmuring frantic endearments in French, interspersed with baleful glances toward Captain Weber. *"Canaille!"* He snarled. "Have you no heart! This poor girl was too *agitée* to know what she was saying!"

The captain shifted his weight, looking bored. He spoke to his assistant. "Call Moreno and Klein." He asked Evelyn, "Where's her room?" and Evelyn told him. When two men in uniform appeared he told them to take her there, and they picked Doris up unceremoniously and carried her out. Henri started to follow, but at Captain Weber's terse command he subsided, muttering as he sank back onto the love seat.

The telephone shrilled again. An officer appeared in the door and beckoned to Captain Weber. "M. E.'s office."

We couldn't hear anything more than "yes," "no," and "thanks." When the man returned Bela said, quietly now, "Is it true that the man in the basement was murdered?"

Captain Weber nodded. "We have just received the medical examiner's report. He was first hit on the head by a blunt instrument. He was bound and gagged and then tortured, apparently with live coals, until his heart gave out under the strain. We found burned-out coals under his bed."

His pale eyes swept the room, appraising our reactions. Louise was the one who caught his attention. She shrank back and put her arm against her mouth in a gesture more eloquent than a scream. He looked hard at her for a moment, making note of that, then went on.

"You can all disregard what Miss Manning said about moving. This is a homicide case. No one will leave here until this investigation is completed."

Chapter Ten

Until then, I suppose, I had maintained with fair success my self-delusion that the death of the superintendent—I still couldn't think of him as Doris's father—could not affect me personally. It was shocking, of course. And I was uncomfortably closer to it than one who merely reads of murder in a newspaper. Even while Donahue was making his announcement, and during the scene which followed, some part of my mind had kept reassuring, It's a horrible thing, but you're not really involved. You'll be out of here, safe in another place, very soon.

Now I sat appalled, like everyone else, staring at Captain Weber. I wasn't going to get out. I wasn't going anywhere.

Bela made the first comment. "What if your investigation is never completed, Captain? This might turn out to be one of those unsolved crimes. And there's a limit, you know, to how long we might be willing to—"

His voice died out as Captain Weber gave him a hard stare which indicated that he was not amused. The kind of thing which would make the big man laugh, I decided, would be a close-up of the most subhuman of the Three Stooges beating his brains out with his own fists.

"You'll stay here as long as we want you," Weber said. "Suppose you let us worry over police business. You just answer questions when they're asked."

Bela's brows rose; he shrugged and looked away. Captain Weber spoke to the man on the window seat. "You the undertaker. You can go. I'll talk to you later."

"Okay." Young Donahue swung his legs down from his perch, still chewing gum. He gave us a pitying look, shook his head, and departed.

The detective heaved his bulk up from the chair and spoke to his assistant. "Come on, Fred. We'll take Miss Manning first."

He gave us orders to stay there until we were called for questioning. An officer in uniform came in after he left. He took the chair Captain Weber had vacated and settled himself with a tabloid. Uneasy glances slid around the room, to be withdrawn as eye met eye. We waited.

Presently Bela was called out. At the door he turned. "I'll ask them to carry my broken body to the studio when they've finished," he said cockily. "The rest of you come on up."

All the belligerency was gone from Jarvis. His face had paled. Pasty, epicene, fat thighs straining against the trousers of his tweed suit, he slumped in his seat, thoughts turned inward. Henri had dropped his head in his hands and sat motionless. Louise turned around on the piano bench and began to pick out a tune with one finger; it gave her something to do with her hands. Lily leaned back in her chair and smoked, impassive.

Evelyn looked so forlorn alone on the sofa that I moved to her side. "What is going to happen now?" she whispered.

The officer would report every word we said; that was what he was there for.

"Nothing much," I reassured her. "They just want a statement from each of us about what happened. Anything we saw or heard during the night."

Evelyn clutched my arm. "But I know nothing," she insisted. "I was in here—I was working after the rest of you went to bed. When I work I—I'm oblivious of everything around me. I didn't hear or see anything—"

By the way the policeman's eyes were fixed on the paper he held I knew he wasn't reading. I patted Evelyn's hand exactly as Bela had done. "Don't be nervous. You just tell the truth."

She subsided with a tremulous sigh. I stared into the fire, pondering my own problem which needed quick decision. What should I say when my turn came? I knew more than many suspected. Should I tell it?

I had no wish to confide in Captain Weber; I'm not the confiding type, and, besides, his personality was repellent to me. I judged him to be the sort of official who is completely insensitive to human values. Nothing he heard about his fellow men could surprise him, nor could anything dissolve him into compassion. The idea of playing stool pigeon for this man was utterly abhorrent. Besides, I rationalized, what did I know that was actually pertinent? A few odd facts about strangers, their importance perhaps heightened and colored by a writer's imagination.

Lily. She had used complicated maneuvers and subterfuges to obtain residence in this house. But Lily was subtle, far too clever to jeopardize her much desired tenancy on the first night she became a resident. She had not been in the building during Evelyn's dialogue with the murderer who impersonated his victim. If she had been down there in capacity of accomplice there would have been no need to search the dead man's effects the following day for the package.

Before I said anything to the police about Lily I would ask her where she had been last night.

Captain Weber was interested only in the identity of a murderer; disclosures about our private lives weren't necessary. I had no wish to embarrass Lily and betray her confidence by revealing information which it was her prerogative to withhold. It occurred to me then that Lily's motive for moving into the house might have been to establish contact with someone already living there. Emotional involvement? I played with that idea hopefully, trying to imagine that whatever Lily took from the dead man's shoe was concerned with another man in the house whom perhaps she wished to protect. Either Henri or Bela might be candidates for such a situation; both were sophisticates, Europeans educated without the Fu Manchu bogy about Oriental people.

I recalled the printed comment a newspaper correspondent, married to a Chinese girl, had once made. He would rather have a Chinese wife, he said, than any other. Chinese women were products of a civilization whose written history dated back almost five thousand years, whose people were artists and craftsmen at a period when our Caucasian forbears still lived in caves and solved problems by hitting one another over the head with clubs. The Chinese were industrious, intelligent, and admirably equipped with courage. Chinese women were superior in character to women of younger cultures. They were affectionate, they had a sense of humor, they made wonderful mothers. And their beauty was imperishable.

It was possible that either Henri or Bela might hold the same opinion as that other cosmopolitan.

But Henri was engaged to Doris. And Bela, for all his playfulness, his mercuric humor, seemed to me basically too egocentric to love any other than himself.

Besides, there was Mr. Char. A lover who lavishes sables and jewels isn't to be considered lightly. That again was Lily's affair. Whatever her private life involved, I decided, it did not concern Captain Weber.

I considered Louise. She was behaving like a miserable and terrified girl. Louise was as likely to be implicated as Lily, since the evidence I found indicated that she might have been the one who was secretly interested in the murdered man. Louise could have gone down to remove her traces from the basement while I thought she was still in the kitchen with Evelyn. I tried to recall whether there had been any sign of life in her room early in the morning when we awakened in an overheated house. Evelyn had come from the living room, Evelyn had said that when she worked she was oblivious of her surroundings, so that even though Louise had been active she might not have been aware of it. Had Evelyn gone into their room after that dialogue on the basement stairs? I could not remember. Then I recalled the masculine voice answering Evelyn's questions. Louise might be a liar, she might be an actress—but she wasn't a baritone.

Playing tattletale about the unhappy Louise was too distasteful to consider. Captain Weber had already made a mental note of her agitation. He had said we were to let him handle police business. All right, I'd follow his orders. Let him find the reason for himself. That conclusion gave me a wry sort of satisfaction.

Evelyn rose to put another lump of coal in the grate. We watched as it smoked sulkily for a moment, then burst into fierce flames and cracked apart, Lily came over to the fireplace and tossed her cigarette on the coals, then sat on the arm of the sofa to watch it burn.

Evelyn said, striving valiantly for a casual topic, "You didn't have heating problems in Hawaii, did you?"

Before I could speak Lily surprised me by answering in a chatty, reminiscent tone: "Not at the beach. But in other parts of Honolulu we occasionally needed heat. Janice's house is in Nuuanu Valley, one of the coolest parts of the city. It grows damp and chilly there during winter months, especially in the rainy season. Then we used to burn a light bulb constantly in the clothes closets to prevent mildew."

How the devil did she know my house was in Nuuanu? I tried to recall what I had told her about myself and my background. I had mentioned the house and the fact that it was rented, that was all. And twenty-four hours ago Lily and I were practically strangers.

The only way in which she could have obtained details about me so quickly was by telephoning Honolulu.

She must have put in a call as soon as I left Mr. Char's house; probably they had been busy on a trans-Pacific phone at the very time I was paying our rent. The benevolent, the ubiquitous Mr. Char again! No doubt he had friends in Honolulu also. Or members of his name tong, who did a quick job for him. Compiling a dossier on Janice Cameron.

I tried to visualize how it had been done: a corps of busy Chinese rushing to every source of information in the city—my bank, the Ramsey Residence, the agent who collected rent for me, the people who lived in my house. The efficiency of it awed me.

I started as I realized that Evelyn was asking a question. "…a little confused," she was saying. "Doris said Lily was living with relatives on Long Island, yet I had the impression that you two girls have been friends for a long time."

You take it, Lily, I thought. I'd like to hear the answer you've concocted for this one.

Lily didn't hesitate. "It is confusing, isn't it?" Business of a tinkling little laugh. "We have not been living together recently. But we are both former residents of Honolulu. Janice arrived in New York a short while ago, and we decided to take a room together. So we moved in here."

What she said was of course true, but it implied so much more than the truth about our relationship. Well done! I thought ironically, and raised my eyebrows at Lily. She looked back at me with the serene smile of one secure in a long-established friendship.

I knew now what she intended to tell Captain Weber. She was going to implicate me in her personal life as camouflage for herself. At first I was pricked with resentment, then once again admiration for the icy-steel nerve of her, respect for her cleverness, swung me to her side. Lily was like the cat who walked by himself; she would never have claimed a cherished intimacy with me if she had not so much at stake. She needed protection.

I moved my sore shoulder, remembering the concern she had shown over my "accident," the compress she made. If she had tried to injure me, the natural thing to do would be to get out of that vicinity quickly, instead of coming to my rescue.

I'll give her a break, I decided, and keep my mouth shut. I can disprove her story any time it becomes necessary.

Time crawled past. Jarvis was called to be interviewed. Then Evelyn, then Louise, then Henri. Presently Henri returned and said Captain Weber wished to see me. As I started toward the kitchen he walked with me as far as Doris's room, then went inside. Before he closed the door I caught a glimpse of Doris huddled on her bed. She needed what comfort he could give her.

Captain Weber sprawled in a kitchen chair which was tilted back against the sink. His assistant sat at the table, notebook before him. I noted absently that the dishes we had recently used were racked on the drainboard. Weber had taken one of the saucers for an ashtray. He had a cigar in his mouth; its smoke drifted around his head in pale sunlight which struggled through ice-frosted windows over the sink. He waved his cigar toward a chair at the end of the table, and I sat down.

"All right, Miss Cameron," he began brusquely. "You're the one who lives with that Chinese woman, aren't you?" His tone indicated that in his lexicon this made me a kind of freak. "Let's have your account of what happened here."

If I'd had any intention of confiding in him this treatment would have nipped it in the bud immediately. I looked directly into his hard blue eyes, my spine stiff with resentment. I gave him my most frigid Ramsey Residence manner and said, "Miss Wu and I are friends, if that is what you mean. I know nothing about this distasteful business or anyone involved in it. We moved into this house only last night."

I reported briefly what had happened, leaving out all personal comment or conjecture. When I finished, he asked a few questions, and my answers were terse and haughty. No, I had never met anyone in this house before; such characters, I implied, were far beneath my social level. No, I had never seen the dead man until the events of this morning. After all, I had just arrived in New York. I did not know whether he accepted my act of outraged respectability at face value, but he soon let me go after reminding me that I would be required to sign my statement.

When I rose he asked me to send Lily Wu to him. This time he called her by name. I went to the front of the house and told Lily he wanted to see her, then remembered Bela's invitation. No one had remained on the first floor except Henri. I climbed two flights of stairs to the "attic suite."

It was vast and bare except for a couple of studio couches and some shabby chairs. The floor was covered with paint-spattered linoleum. There were two easels facing a large window which bent up into the roof to admit the maximum amount of light. Canvases were stacked around the room; several hung on the walls. Bela was sitting on a worn leather hassock with a glass in his hand, holding forth to the audience around him. He waved as I entered.

"Welcome! Just in time to join our post-mortem. What will you drink, Janice? Burgundy or sherry? There's plenty of both."

"Sherry, please." He poured from one of the gallon bottles beside him.

I sat on a couch near Louise. She saw my glance at her empty hands and said, "I have a date with my future tonight, and he's a human tank. I don't dare start drinking so early."

"Tell me, darling, is he your future love life or your future income?" Bela asked as he handed me a cheese glass filled with wine.

"Max is a press agent—my future career, I hope. That'll bring the income. I can't afford any love life; that's a luxury for a working girl."

Louise was feeling the stimulus of some inner excitement; if I had not known otherwise I might have thought her slightly drunk. Her dark eyes glittered, and there was tenseness in her posture, and a note of stridency in her voice which normally was kept under excellent control. She had been terrified a short while ago at the prospect of police investigation. Either her interview with Captain Weber had dispelled secret apprehension or she had tapped some inner well of courage and resolved that she didn't give a damn about consequences.

"What did you mean by post-mortem?" I asked Bela.

He took a sip from his glass and set it on the floor. "We were discussing our murder," he said. "Trying to figure out which of us did it."

"I think it was some tramp," Evelyn said. From looks the others gave her I gathered that this wasn't the first time she had expressed that hopeful opinion.

Bela ignored her. "I'm all for indicting Doris. Except that she was too openly delighted at her father's death to have been the instrument of it."

"She pulled that act just for effect!" Jarvis blurted. I turned to him in surprise, for I hadn't expected to see him there, since he raised such a row about getting back to work. Maybe Jarvis decided he'd forfeit a day's pay rather than miss this excitement. He clutched a tumbler of wine in both fat hands, drinking in gulps. His usually pasty face was flushed, and his brow shone with sweat. He started to speak again and then closed his mouth, as if admonishing himself about something. He gulped more wine instead, then sat hunched, twisting the big gold ring on his right hand.

I was torn between two desires. I wanted to stay and hear what was said, and I wanted urgently to talk to Lily Wu alone. There was plenty I needed to find out from both sources. I sat trying to make up my mind which was more important when my dilemma was solved. Lily arrived.

"We're electing a murderer," Bela told her. "You may vote if you wish. Sherry or burgundy?"

"Sherry, please."

"Which of us gets your vote, Lily?" Bela asked.

"Ordinarily," she said, nodding thanks for the drink, "I should choose one of the men in the house. But Evelyn would have seen any of you who came downstairs. That leaves only the women."

She was playing dumb.

Evelyn made a little sound of protest. She said, "It was not a woman. No woman would—would torture another human being like that!"

Bela snorted. "My dear, remember the gentle *Fräuleins* at Auschwitz, the ones who had those chic lampshades—of human flesh? Don't be so childish."

Evelyn shuddered. "It was a man," she insisted. She added with reluctance, "Remember I talked with him."

"Then it must have been an outsider," I contributed. "Doris said her father was a criminal. Perhaps some member of his gang"

"Oh, for God's sake!" Louise cried. She closed her mouth tight over another remark. For some reason she resented that suggestion.

"I want another drink!" Jarvis said loudly. "Nobody cares what I think, but at least I can have another drink."

While Bela poured wine I wandered around the room looking at his pictures. He painted oils of the nostalgic sort: old-fashioned horse-drawn cabs driving off into a misty night, Washington Square Arch in spring rain, Fifth Avenue in a snowstorm. They were almost good.

Bela followed me with Jarvis's glass in his hand. "How do you like my buckeyes? Don't answer. My public is crazy about them. Silly tourists who goggle around the Village are delighted to pay a hundred bucks for stuff I can slap out in one day. That old cabbie, for instance—I adore him, for he practically supports me. I must have a hundred of him hanging in different parts of the country. All originals, I can honestly say, painted by my own little hand."

Evelyn had risen and joined us. "Just a slightly different version of my birds and bees," she murmured. "Bela can paint if he wants to. You should see some of the canvases he—"

"They don't sell," he interrupted, blinking very fast. "Nobody in this country wants art. Americans worship machine products. So I give them over-sized postcards."

He turned on Evelyn waspishly, revenging himself. "For heaven's sake go put on some makeup. You look like a ghost."

Evelyn recoiled at his tone, and her mouth twitched. Then she started obediently for a nearby door. She wasn't carrying any makeup, so I concluded she'd find what she needed in his bathroom. Was it like that with them?

Jarvis finished the wine Bela gave him in two gulps. He got up and poured himself a refill from the bottle on the floor. He sank back in his chair so awkwardly that wine spilled on his knees. He scowled at the stains, shook his head, then raised his eyes with effort.

"Nobody here values my opinion," he announced in a thick voice, "but I still say Doris killed her father. To get his insurance."

He looked around to observe the effect of his words. Desire for the spotlight, stimulated by alcohol, won over previous resolve to be discreet. "I don't blame Doris, y'understand. He should have been killed. I know who he was, and somebody should have killed him."

If he wanted the center of the stage he was gratified. There was a babble of excited questions. Jarvis nodded solemnly and kept saying, "I know. I know. I know who he was."

Finally Bela shook him in exasperation. "For God's sake, man, stop babbling and tell us. Who was he?"

Jarvis's head wobbled as he tried to nod. "Charles Chadwick, that's who. The man who stole my future, wrecked my life. Y'were right, Bela, about my music. See this?" He held up his right hand with the big gold ring on it.

"Georges Enesco gave me this ring. I played for him when he was here in 1936. He said I had talent, he'd be glad to help me if I could get to Europe. Got a scholarship to go, made arrangements with Enesco. Chadwick stole the money my father left us, and I couldn't go. Had to get a job and support my mother. In a box factory!" He looked as if the memory nauseated him. Or maybe it was the wine.

"Dear old Mom!" Bela muttered. "How many of her tender young she has devoured!"

"Don't say that!" Jarvis cried. "I had the most wonderful little mother in the world! Kept house for me, cooked my favorite meals, mended my clothes, waited up every time I went out anywhere, no matter how late I got home—" He broke off with a sob.

Evelyn returned at that point. She had used cosmetics with a light hand and looked less pale, but her eyes were still dark with worry. She sat silently watching, her glass untouched.

"All right, fella, we believe you," Bela soothed the fat man. "She was the best mother a boy ever had. But come on now, who was Chadwick? What crime did he commit?"

"I can perhaps tell you," answered a quiet voice from the door. We all turned. Henri was standing there; he had entered without our notice. He walked toward us hesitantly, as if unsure of his welcome, carrying a large manila envelope.

He stopped with his hand on the back of a straight chair, preparatory to moving it toward our group. "May I join you for a while?" With grave dignity he announced, "There is a most tragic story which I have been asked to relate."

Chapter Eleven

"**J**oin us by all means. Do you want a drink?" Bela didn't sound very hospitable.

Henri pulled the chair over and sat in it. "No, thank you."

He laid the envelope across his knees and removed its contents, a bunch of yellowed newspaper clippings. "Doris requested that I talk to you," he said. "She wishes to apologize for her unfortunate remarks. She asked me to show you these, which will explain her distress. I believe the newspaper accounts of the Chadwick case will provide a more complete explanation than Jarvis might be able to give."

He handed the clippings to Louise, who was nearest him. "Pass them around, please."

They were arranged in order by dates, beginning April 1936. The story they told was not new in the sense that it was unusual, except perhaps to those whom it had affected personally. An account of the defalcations of Charles Chadwick, son of ex-Senator Chadwick, Harvard alumnus, world traveler, bon vivant, and trusted intimate of New York socialites, the financier who organized a Manhattan membership loan association and then embezzled its funds.

Members joined by depositing a hundred dollars and were then permitted to borrow up to five thousand. Those who did not need to borrow—and they were in the majority—deposited large amounts of money and received a high rate of interest. The "membership" setup was a slick way of evading national banking laws. Assets were in the form of negotiable securities held in a bank vault to which Chadwick alone had access. During Roosevelt's administration, when the government began tightening up on banking and loan regulations, investigators examined the books of the company and checked its assets. They found none. The vault contained worthless securities. Chadwick could not or would not explain where the original assets had gone. There was a panic among the investors, which resulted in several bankruptcies and one suicide. He had got away with more than three million dollars.

All of Charles Chadwick's properties, including his wife's jewels, their house in Florida and another at Manhasset, and two custom-built cars were appropriated to satisfy creditors. The family residence in Washington Square was not seized; it had been a gift to Mrs. Chadwick from her father and remained in her name.

The scandal provided a field day for the tabloids. There were pictures of the family: Chadwick, who at that time had a distinctive mane of hair, his wife Lilla, invalided with asthma, and their daughter Doris, seventeen years old and attending school in Switzerland. By the time Doris Chadwick was brought back from Europe her mother had died of an overdose of sleeping tablets and her father was arraigned as an embezzler.

There were accounts of his trial and a huge public hurrah because of the severe sentence he received. Unfortunately for the defendant, one columnist hinted, the judge who presided had once lost money in a similar disaster. Chadwick was indicted on several counts and sentenced to a total of fifteen years. Three years later most of the money was found in a Florida safe-deposit box under another name. But that was too late to save Chadwick. His failure to disclose the whereabouts of his cache proved that he had intended to serve his sentence and then retrieve the money for his own use.

It took us a long time to read the clippings, for we passed them around as we finished. There was no sound except the rustle of paper, an occasional cough, or the heavy breathing of Jarvis, who sat hunched with his glass in his hands, staring at the floor. He would not look at the clippings.

"I've seen them already," he mumbled. "My mother pasted them all in a scrapbook. She used to cry over it."

"But, Jarvis, much of her loss was recovered," I said. "Why didn't you go on then with your musical studies?"

"I'd missed the scholarship. Mother's health broke. We used the money for her care in a rest home."

Henri spoke to him gently. "You came to live here because you knew it was the Chadwick house?"

Jarvis nodded. "When I left the factory I made a step up." He laughed bitterly. "A step up! Got a job as clerk in the music store. I used to walk past here and wonder what it was like inside. After Mother died I applied for the first vacancy. It pleased me to know that while I was living in his comfortable home Chadwick was wearing stripes in a prison cell."

That's how the man got those roughened hands, I realized. The rock pile, or a jute mill, or some such labor.

"Well, now you're alive and he's dead." Louise regarded Jarvis with the special contempt of the fighter for the sniveler. "That ought to be more consolation."

"Consolation!" Jarvis moaned. He stood up, balancing himself with a chair. "Excuse me." He staggered toward the door. "Going to my room now."

Evelyn's eyes followed him. "Poor Jarvis!" she worried. "Do you think he'll be all right?"

Bela gave her a look of affectionate scorn. "Don't be so eternally soft hearted. Jarvis will survive. He'll go fondle his scherzo for a while, and then he'll feel better."

He turned to Henri with the first warmth I'd ever seen him display toward the younger man. "Why don't you relax, *mon vieux,* and have a drink with us? I've got some Noilly Prat, if you prefer that to *vin rouge.*"

Henri looked pathetically pleased at this expression of cordiality. *"Certainement, mon ami. Avec plaisir. Du vin rouge, un peu, s'il vous plaît."*

He sipped the stuff cautiously, then took a heroic swallow with only the faintest shudder of distaste. He regarded us with a grave smile as he said, "I am relieved that you understand now why Doris was so distraught. In the past she has been subjected to many humiliations from the press, and she did not wish to suffer more. For her it is still impossible to discuss these painful things."

He hesitated, then added with apparent reluctance, "But I believe that you will feel for Doris even more sympathy if I tell you just a little of what unhappiness she has endured."

He launched into an account of her personal history which he gave with restraint, leaving us to fill in details which his delicacy omitted. We had seen the photograph of the Chadwick family group. Doris had been the homely child of a handsome father and a beautiful, pampered mother who was too much absorbed in herself to be burdened with such an ill-favored offspring. She spent her formative years in boarding schools, a lonely girl whose only source of pride was family name and money, whose sole emotional outlet was worship of a brilliant and successful father. Since her mother rejected her she had probably hated that mother from babyhood. When the name of Chadwick was disgraced and there was no more money, when the father she adored was exposed as a criminal and her mother died by her own hand, Doris was robbed of every vestige of security.

Her mother's estate consisted only of the house, and in 1936 that was a liability rather than an asset. Doris had refused to sell it to finance a college education. She held on to the property, leased it for years at a rate which barely paid taxes. She obtained a secretarial job and by painful economy managed to make payments on her father's insurance policy. Just before the war she borrowed on the house to convert it into rental units and moved in as a tenant. She had changed her name. She delegated management of the property to a realtor because she did not want anyone to suspect her identity.

"But how could her father obtain such large insurance if he had a bad heart?" Louise wanted to know.

"He did not develop the weakness until a few years ago," Henri explained. "Possibly it resulted from the harshness of prison life."

He sighed, relieved at finishing his long story. He took off his glasses and began to polish them as he said, "Now I bring a message from Doris. She wishes me to tell you that she does not want anyone to move from here, and as soon as she receives payment from the insurance company she will be happy to reduce the rent. Doris believes, as I do, that her father was killed by a stranger. Possibly some unbalanced person who has brooded, like Jarvis, over the disaster suffered long ago. We are certain that the police will bring this murderer to justice. Doris hopes that you will all remain here and that when this unhappy time is forgotten you will be her friends."

He put the glasses back over his somber eyes. He hesitated, then announced shyly, "I should like to add that we expect to be married as soon as we can do so without inviting more publicity. As Doris's fiancé I take the privilege of expressing my friendship and urging that you remain with us here."

He rose, made a formal little bow, and marched out of the room.

We were very quiet for a while after the door closed. Then Louise said, her words dripping sarcasm, "Well, well! I'll have a drink on that, Bela. I need it before I burst into tears."

Evelyn had no sense of humor; she took the words literally. "I keep thinking," she said, "about that miserable old man creeping back to the house he used to live in, asking for a job as janitor. I wonder if he knew his daughter still owned it."

Lily had not moved or spoken for a long time. I looked at her, wondering about her stillness. She sat rigid, holding a lighted cigarette, her brilliant eyes fixed on space with the strained look of one determined to show no emotion. As I watched, she lowered the hand which held the cigarette, her fingers closed over it, and she ground it to shreds. I was aware, for I knew her better than anyone else in the room, that Lily was inwardly shaken. She spread slim fingers fanwise, and shreds of paper and tobacco dropped on the floor. She raised her hand and looked at it thoughtfully, then blew a piece of tobacco from between her fingers. She had deliberately burned herself. As a counterirritant to whatever struggled within her for expression?

Then she said in a remote voice, "I am thinking about the trusting people who lost everything they had or hoped to have because of that 'miserable old man.'"

"Stop it!" Louise yelped. "You're breaking my heart!" She began to laugh so hard that she set her drink down to keep from spilling it.

"You mean your heart is aching after that sad, sad story of Doris's tragic life?" Bela asked. There was a satanic gleam in his eyes.

"Yes. The poor, poor thing! Orphaned with only the family mansion to keep the wolf from the door. She deprives herself for thirteen years—in order to cash in on a thirty-thousand-dollar policy." Louise rocked with laughter. "Isn't it just too generous of her to let us stay on here? And she's even going to reduce the rent—someday."

Evelyn sat up straight, and her cheeks grew pink. "Louise!" she said. "I wish you'd tell me what amuses you so much."

Louise and Bela looked at each other. "Explain to her, somebody"—Louise choked—"in words of one syllable." Both she and Bela by then were so convulsed with mirth that they couldn't talk.

Lily spoke again in that same icy voice. "I think one of the reasons they are laughing is because of the message Henri brought from Doris. You see, we could not move if we wished to. Doris knows that. Since we must stay here, it appears that she has decided to use diplomacy to win our good will."

I put in my contribution. "All that touching business about the clippings was probably calculated too. There are fingerprints of her father on file; and now the police know his identity. Newspapers will rehash the old story. We are more likely to sympathize with Doris if we hear her version first."

"That Frenchman put her up to it," Louise declared, wiping her eyes. "Doris isn't subtle enough." She looked at Bela. "By the way, Michelangelo, why were you so pally with him all of a sudden? I thought you didn't like the guy."

Bela snickered. "I didn't. I still don't. But now I feel sorry for the poor jerk. No man works harder for his money than the man who marries it—and I speak from experience. There'll be no more ivory tower for him, I bet, after he's Mister Doris. That woman loves money too much. He'll write a best seller, or she'll put nettles in his bed. I can see his future production now—the movie of the century, that supercolossal drama of the Underground—in Technicolor." He stopped for breath, then grinned more widely than ever. "But the best joke of all would be if Doris discovered that he couldn't write a word."

He began to laugh again, holding his sides. Bela was a little bit drunk. But there was an acid undertone, a meaning in his words which eluded me.

Evelyn jerked to her feet. Her cheeks were flaming and her gray eyes were bright with anger. "You're both disgusting! You should be ashamed of yourselves!" She slammed the door as she went out.

That was my cue. I looked at Lily. "Shall we go downstairs? We haven't got things completely settled yet."

Lily knew what I meant. "Of course," she agreed quietly. "There is still much unpacking to do."

A policeman was sitting in a chair on the second floor near the head of the stairs. He looked like a man in pain. No wonder, for Shostakovich's Fifth was blaring loud enough to shake the plaster from the walls.

When we were alone together I pulled the pillow from under my spread and put it behind me at the head of the bed. I settled myself comfortably and then hesitated, reluctant to begin the interrogation for which I had been so eager. I couldn't assume at will the cold, impersonal attitude of Captain Weber.

Lily wasn't just "that Chinese woman" to me. She was a girl whom I liked. I hated having to ask prying questions, while at the same time I resented her failure to volunteer information which I was entitled to have. I waited, hoping she would begin the conversation.

Lily went into the bathroom and washed her hands and face. She sat at the dressing table and took off the hair ribbon, brushed her hair quickly and swirled it into a loose knot at the back of her neck. She opened a pancake makeup jar and applied the damp sponge to her perfect skin with care. She smoothed her brows and outlined her mouth with a lipstick brush dipped in crimson. She poured lotion into one palm, massaged it into her hands, then returned, to the bedroom and sat on her bed facing me, like one who has put on armor for the battle.

By the time she had finished this routine I was so exasperated that I was ready to explode. Lily forestalled me. She took a cigarette from a little shagreen box on the table and said as she struck a match, "All right, Janice. What is it that you wish to know?"

This wasn't the resistance, the stubborn secretiveness which I had expected. I'd had a million questions to ask her. Now that she was indicating her willingness to answer I didn't know where to begin. I blurted out the first thing that came to my mind.

"Why did you rush to the basement as soon as you heard that the police were coming?"

Lily laid the match carefully in the ashtray. "I told you. I wiped your fingerprints from the wall. There is no need for us to be involved in this affair. The wall was the only thing we touched when we were there except the door knobs. I cleaned those too. And I brought your bag upstairs."

"Is that all?"

"No. I locked the door and put the key back where it belongs."

She looked so innocent, so defenseless sitting there with a friendly smile on her beautiful face that I felt my animosity beginning to dissolve. I thought, irrationally, that I could understand the helplessness of a man confronted with a fragile, lovely wife. Even when he knows she's basically self-willed and treacherous her beauty must sometimes melt his bones with tenderness.

But I wasn't a man, and I wasn't susceptible to female sex appeal, of any variety.

"Lily," I said firmly, "let's drop that for now and start at the beginning. Please don't try any more evasions with me. I told you before that I have no wish to pry into your affairs. But there is something you're hiding, something I don't know which you must tell me."

Lily was looking at the red mark on her finger where she had burned herself. I stopped and waited. She said nothing.

I went on then, more determined. "If I weren't involved, if you hadn't used me as a cover-up from the time we came here, I wouldn't insist on knowing. But I can't go on pretending a long friendship between us which has no basis in fact, unless I'm convinced you have an excellent reason for this act of yours. The police are here now. We have to swear to those statements we made today. I have a right to know what this masquerade is all about."

Lily's slim body straightened. She looked directly at me and said, "What do you want to know?"

"I want answers to a few pertinent questions. First, where were you last night?"

"I was at Grand Central Station making a phone call. The switchboard operator can verify this." Her mouth quirked up at the corners. "I talked to Honolulu."

"At three in the morning?"

"I waited from twelve-thirty until three. That's 9 p.m. in Honolulu, as you probably know."

"You called for information about me?"

"Yes."

Irritation rose in me again. She had to know all about me. I had taken her on faith, no questions asked. But then I had no reason for extreme caution, no secrets to hide. Again reason soothed my temper.

"All right," I said. "I'll accept that. Now, another question: did you know that man Chadwick?"

"Only as a child knows an adult. I had not seen him since I was twelve."

"Well, you had some reason for coming here, some motive for getting into this house. Was it connected with him?"

She hesitated a fraction of a second. Then, "Yes. It was directly concerned with him."

"In what way?"

"I wanted to see him. I knew he was being released on parole because of ill health. I knew that he would probably come here. And it was urgent that I see him."

"Why?"

"He had something which belongs to my family."

She looked thoughtful for a moment, then seemed to reach a decision. She went to the bureau and lifted the Laughing Buddha. She removed the little package and handed a small box to me.

"Open it."

I opened it curiously. The box wasn't more than three inches long, leather covered, lined with red velvet. Inside was a cylinder of jewel jade of pure, clear green.

"Take it out," she said.

What I held was a piece of jade tipped with gold, like a letter seal. Around the cylinder, carved in detail so meticulous that even his tiny scales seemed animate, his eyes bright with life, writhed a fierce little dragon. Lily took it from me and pressed the gold tip into a small cake of paste at one end of the box. She extended her hand, palm up, then stamped her wrist and showed the result to me. Chinese characters in vermilion ink.

"What is it?" I asked.

Lily sat on the bed, holding the jade. "Do you remember Bela speaking of a Chinese chop?"

"Yes. It's the seal that artists sign their work with, isn't it?"

"Not only artists. A chop is used by Chinese businessmen, families, public officials. This belongs to my family. The Wu chop. It has come down to us from Wu Wei, whose work you see there." She gestured toward the picture on the bureau. "It has been one of our most treasured possessions for many years."

"What does this have to do with Chadwick?"

Lily raised her eyes to mine. Her face was implacable again as she said, "He stole it from my father. I wanted to get it back again."

"Is that what you came here for?"

"Yes."

"How were you sure that Chadwick had the chop or would bring it with him?"

"Because recently my uncle sent an emissary to visit him at the prison, and Mr. Chadwick told him then that he expected to be released soon and that the chop was still in his possession. He was willing to sell it back to us."

"Did you see him or talk to him before he was killed?"

"I was not even aware that he was in the building. I did not expect him to appear in the capacity of servant. You must understand that I do not regret his death or the manner of it. When we found him there I was sorry only that I had not been able to see him alive before it happened. I was afraid then that I might never recover what I had come for. Later, however—"

"You found the chop hidden in one of his shoes under the bed."

She turned her head at an angle, her black eyes widened if she were getting a new perspective on me. "Ah. You watched me through the wall."

"Later I saw you hide the chop inside that old fellow." I pointed to Lo-Han.

"Yet you did not investigate further?"

"No."

Lily smiled. She said softly, "Thank you."

"Tell me, Lily: if the chop is so valuable, why was it not confiscated with the rest of Chadwick's possessions?"

She put the jade back in the leather box and touched it caressingly before she snapped the lid shut. "The value of this is intrinsic. To my family it is priceless. To Charles Chadwick it had value as an instrument only."

"I still don't understand that. Or how he managed to steal the thing."

"He came to our house while my father was away. He used my father's desk on pretext of examining some papers. When he left, he took the chop with him."

"But how did he have access to your home?"

"He was a welcome guest there. My father was his friend. And his victim. Charles Chadwick ruined him."

Chapter Twelve

I remembered a quotation I'd read many times which held no actual meaning for me until now: "The evil that men do lives after them; the good is oft interred with their bones."

What Charles Chadwick had done was being perpetuated in this house; in his neurotic daughter, who sublimated craving for love into money lust; in whining, defeated Jarvis, not possessed of enough stamina to overcome early personal disaster; now in Lily Wu, young, beautiful, and intelligent, yet driven by obsession to redeem the prestige of her family at any cost to herself. Thinking again of the complacent Mr. Char, I could guess at some of the means she had used to achieve her purpose. As old-fashioned and melodramatic as a Victorian novel.

Willing self-sacrifice on the altar of family honor! Filial devotion! I was on the point of some private lip curling. Then I reminded myself of Lily's background. Although we were of the same sex, I could not judge her entirely by standards which I or any other Occidental might have. Lily was the product of a culture countless generations older than mine, of a family whose traditions were as much a part of them as were their physical features, different from my own. I didn't have enough self-assurance—or arrogance, call it what you will—to assume automatically that a Chinese girl's concept of basic values was inferior to my own. I had to accept her definitions if I wanted mine to receive equal consideration.

With this little mental gymnastic accomplished I felt immeasurably relieved. I forgot distrust. From that moment I was Lily's partisan, whatever happened.

My decision must have been revealed in my face. Lily sighed deeply and gave me a smile so natural, so filled with relief, that I realized fully for the first time how great a strain she had been under. Acting a role occasionally with acquaintances is one thing; maintaining a constant, unnatural pretense with someone as close as a roommate is quite another.

"Let me introduce you to my family," she said, and at that I knew our relationship had entered a new phase. She went to her bureau and took the enlarged snapshot from a drawer, then sat on the bed beside me. I looked again at that small group, the gray-haired man with a benign face, the husky grinning boys, the tiny mother in Chinese dress.

"I took this snapshot shortly before I left for Hawaii," Lily told me. "We were very poor, and a cousin in Honolulu offered me a college education, so my parents sent me there. The day I took that picture was the last time we were all together."

"What are their names?"

"The tall boy, that's Gordon, the one who majored in psychology."

He looked older than Lily; he was almost twice her size. "Why didn't he come here to see Chadwick?" I asked. I'd been wondering, out of this family which had only one daughter, why a son didn't take on the mission which Lily was performing.

"Gordon was killed in Italy," Lily said quietly. After a moment she went on. "The one next to him is Eddie: he's taking his premedical at Stanford on the GI Bill. He is married, and his wife expects a child next month. The boy on the left of my father is Lincoln; he's still in high school. The little fellow is Johnny."

My question was answered.

"I want to tell you about my father," Lily went on. "He is an herbalist. He knows so many things which ordinary men do not know; he has studied all of his life. He is gentle, absent-minded, not like other men. My father is very wise. But he is not shrewd."

I knew what she meant. Mr. Char was shrewd. That was one of the reasons why he basked in air-conditioned luxury while Mr. Wu lived in a cheap little bungalow. The dead man had been shrewd, too, I remembered.

"Your father and Mr. Chadwick came from very different backgrounds. How did they happen to be friends?"

"They met in China. Mr. Chadwick was a tourist, and my father was studying with an old herbalist there. They happened to be together on a train which was attacked by bandits. My father saved Mr. Chadwick's life at risk of his own.

"There is a belief among my people that when a man rescues another from death he is responsible thereafter for the life he has preserved. My father is modern—he is American-born—but he respects many Chinese superstitions even though he may joke about them. He considered the other man his friend, and, although there was seldom public social contact between them, since my family rarely left the neighborhood in which we lived, Mr. Chadwick came often to our house. For us his embezzlement was a tragedy, since we lost everything we possessed. I was twelve years old when he was sentenced but I still remember vividly."

That made her two years younger than I. She looked eighteen, rather than twenty-five. But Chinese always look much younger than their actual ages. Women of other races would give fortunes to know that secret.

"Lily, what did the chop have to do with your father's losing—" That question was never finished.

Someone knocked on the door, and I ground my teeth with impatience. Our room was getting to be about as private as a hotel lobby. Lily admitted Louise, who was carrying a tray of cosmetics.

"I need company," she announced. "Evelyn's glooming out the window, Doris is still invisible. And there's a cop parked in the hall. I can't wander around the house talking to myself. Mind if I visit for a while?"

I minded very much. I hadn't found out all I wanted to know; there were still unanswered questions perplexing me. Lily assured Louise that we were delighted to see her. She held out the shagreen box. "Cigarette?"

Louise said no, thanks. "I can't smoke now," she explained. "Have to do my nails. By the way, Miss Wu, you seem to be the only other woman here who uses polish. You don't happen to have some Rosy Future, do you?"

"Please don't call me Miss Wu," Lily said, smiling. "It sounds too much like my college professors." She went to the dressing table and opened a drawer. She dropped the picture and the little box into it, and removed a case which contained several bottles. "I don't have that exact shade. Perhaps you can use one of these."

Louise set her tray on the floor in order to examine the nail polish. She held bottles under the lamp to compare colors with her bright nails, selected a shade, and began to remove polish before applying a new coat. I sighed with impatience as I realized that she intended to sit there until she finished her manicure.

Louise was very acute; at my sigh she raised her eyes quickly. "Am I interrupting anything? Just say so and I'll make myself scarce."

Lily gave me a warning glance and started to speak, but I answered first. The Chinese girl had much more on her mind than I; if she could conceal her feelings so gracefully I might at least try. "You're not intruding, Louise," I reassured her. "Lily and I were just reminiscing about Honolulu and wishing we were back in the sunshine."

Lily would know what I meant by that.

I looked at the tray Louise carried. It was made of plastic and packed with cosmetics. "Do you mind if I investigate?" I asked.

"Go ahead. That's the joy of my heart; it's designed to use in the bathtub," Louise said. "Just a moment." She reached for a small blue box and put it in the pocket of her sweater.

I picked up the tray, which was very light, designed with legs which unfolded so it would stand above the water level in a tub. There were several compartments, grooved to prevent bottles from sliding. In the center was a framed magnifying mirror which could be tilted at an angle. There was even a cigarette box and ashtray. The cosmetics fascinated me. Many jars, variously labeled: Dry Skin Cream, Wild Rose Emollient, Stimulating Lotion, Night Massage Oil, and so forth. I wanted to open them and sniff each one, but didn't dare. They came from a place called Lucien's on Fifth Avenue.

Lily and Louise were chattering away about the new long skirts, the nuisance of having to buy longer slips to match, the satisfaction of being able to find colored fabrics after years of drab war dyes, and other such feminine trivia. They used a fashion vocabulary which was completely foreign to me. I thought of my scanty wardrobe and my Plan. Part of that plan was a project I'd cherished for years: enrollment in one of those make-yourself-over courses at a famous salon.

I had to accept the fact that I wasn't going to have any latitude in choosing a New York residence for a while. But I might emulate some of the Oriental patience of my roommate and make the best of present difficulties. I could stop gyrating like a whirling dervish in a vacuum of frustrations and take one definite step toward that new life.

I made a mental note of the address of Lucien's before I set the tray back on the floor near Louise's feet.

Lily took the pins from her black hair and began brushing it with practiced strokes. Louise was manicuring her nails. I smoked leisurely, watching the two of them. We might have been three frivolous inmates of a girls' boarding school.

But Louise's fingers trembled as she applied nail polish; she had to stop frequently and steady herself. Lily's arm was turned so that the red stamp on her wrist was not visible. They were both agile liars—neither aware of what the other was concealing.

Louise stopped when she had finished one hand and waved it to dry the polish. She said with an air of complete honesty, "I don't know when I've been so nervous. The real reason I came in here was that I felt so jittery after what's happened. Evelyn is generally cheerful, but today she's way down in a black mood. Doris is still hiding in her room. I needed normal people to talk with, and now I feel better. You two are so new here that this business can't affect you."

Oh no?

She uncorked the bottle of polish and began on the other hand. "It'll be a relief to get out. After my dinner date I go to work. We're on the air tonight at eight, in case you want to listen." She mentioned the station and the program, which was a mystery serial. "Three nights a week," she added. "When you hear the voice of Alice, loyal wife of the daring super-detective—that's me."

While she went on chattering I glanced at the clock. It was still midafternoon. Pale yellow sunlight was slanting through our windows; it shone dazzlingly on the snow at the sills. I wanted out of this dark place, to move among ordinary people, to breathe an atmosphere not weighted with tragedy and fear. Lily and Louise might be able to sit and prattle indefinitely, playing their game of reciprocal deceit, but I'd had enough.

I put on my coat and hat and struggled into galoshes. I said goodbye to them and walked past the policeman in the hall, half expecting him to challenge me. He didn't; he just slumped in his chair, looking bored. There was no further sound of activity from the basement, so I decided that Captain Weber's men had finished their examination and had gone back to make their reports. I let myself out into the fresh cold of the street with a feeling of liberation.

Lucien's was a small shop with windows draped in white net and only the name in silver script on the glass. Expensive. A slim young man with waving red hair and dreamy blue eyes undulated toward me as I entered.

"Yes?" he lilted. "Can I serve you?"

"I'd like a shampoo and wave," I told him. "Also a manicure."

"Certainly. When would you like to come in?"

"Today. Now, if possible."

His brows rose with refined disapproval. "One moment, please. I will see whether there is any time available."

He bent over a large book on the reception desk, the pages of which, I noticed, were not filled with appointments. His voice registered surprise and pleasure. "You are fortunate! There has been a cancellation. Mr. Lucien himself can take you."

Dreamy Eyes ushered me toward a booth at the rear, holding aside its blue satin curtains as if I had been a visiting princess. Lucien himself was there, listening to music from a tiny silver radio. He switched off the radio as he rose to greet me, received my fur coat tenderly, and hung it up after a quick glance at the label. Then he turned around and inventoried my appearance with intense interest, which somehow I didn't mind at all.

"My dear," he said, "you appear to be very tense." He touched my brow delicately. "Those lines of strain! I would suggest, if you have time, a nice soothing massage before we work on your hair."

I found myself assenting obediently. He drew the curtains like a priest veiling the holy sacrament, whipped out a blue satin apron and tied it around me, urging me into a soft leather chair which tilted back. "Close your eyes, please," he murmured. "Just relax."

He smoothed fragrant cream on my face and began to work. His hands were amazingly deft yet gentle; by the time Lucien finished that massage I was relaxed. While he dried my hair by hand with warm towels and a brush Lucien and I chatted cozily. I liked him; he was as friendly and sympathetic as any girl I had ever known. Before I knew it I was telling him without embarrassment about my Plan. He became gratifyingly excited

"My dear Miss Cameron," he said, "I wish you would put yourself into my hands for one month, just four weeks. I could bring out potentialities of which you have never dreamed. For instance, you would be amazed at what I could do for you with proper hair styling. This year the short cut is fashionable, but I never advise following fashion unless it suits the personality. For you, definitely, the upsweep is indicated; your features are perfect for it."

He went on to explain why, talking of throat line, classic-gamine features, and so forth, while I absorbed it like a thirsty plant drinks water. I'd been wearing a scraggly shoulder-length bob with a conventional side part and forehead dip. I was as tired of it as I was bored with my outgrown personality. But I demurred at the radical changes he proposed.

Lucien warmed to persuasion. "You will not believe," he assured me, "what miracles can be done until you see for your-self." He produced a package from a table drawer. "Let me illustrate. This," he confided, "was one of my most challenging problems, a girl with multitudinous handicaps. We achieved a transformation, Miss Cameron, literally a transformation!"

He exhaled reminiscent admiration. "You never saw such willpower as this girl had! Her speech—a bullfrog, I assure you, sounds better than she did. And with the most ghastly Bronx accent! She studied voice, she took dancing lessons, she slaved. And with her features I, Lucien, worked a miracle."

He lowered his voice. "I took pictures as we progressed. She consented because of the discount. You should see her now. Not perfect yet, for she still has a serious orthodontic problem. But when we're finished…" He waved his hand toward infinity.

He spread four professional photographs before me. "See that hairline," he said, touching one of the prints. "Before the electrolysis that was. She suffered agonizing headaches after each treatment, but it was absolutely necessary. The poor girl looked like an orangutan."

She actually did. Her forehead was unusually low, which gave her face a stupid look. Thick, dark brows almost met over her nose, making her appear ill-tempered. The last picture showed her with thinned and shaped brows and a completely changed hairline. Her eyes had seemed unremarkable; now they were large. I turned to Lucien, puzzled.

"I can understand the electrolysis, but her eyes!"

He clapped his hands with discreet delight, then produced a small blue package. "This is the secret. I taught her, since she can not afford to come here often. Of course doing it oneself takes much longer."

The box contained a package of long, curving lashes, glue, and tweezers for applying them one hair at a time, scissors for trimming them after they were glued on. "You finish with the tiniest bit of mascara," Lucien purred, "and they absolutely defy detection!"

The bill for Lucien's ministrations was eighteen dollars. The cosmetics I purchased were another twenty-five. I removed money from my purse with fingers tipped in a glamorous deep rose shade which matched my carefully tinted mouth. I sailed out of Lucien's with my upswept coiffure held high. Clutched in my hand was the address of one of those "little" shops where I could get Bergdorf frocks at Macy prices. Lucien had told me what I might not have discovered for years, that New York women who dress smartly on limited budgets patronize such places.

I reached the shop at closing time, but the brisk little woman who owned it was delighted to stay and help me choose a wardrobe. She worried over my shoulder, but I assured her that the color of the bruise was worse than the discomfort. Lily must have used some of her father's herbs, I realized. I bought four dresses and arranged to return later for fittings. I left there wearing an aquamarine cashmere frock with cocoa suède belt, soft as a lover's sigh, and with lines...

On the way home after dinner I thought of those pictures Lucien had shown me. If that girl could start with such formidable handicaps and achieve a miracle, any woman could be attractive. Now I understood why Louise spent hours taking those ritualistic baths in the pink marble tub. She was putting on her wonderful eyelashes.

My feeling of exhilaration evaporated as my taxi passed Fourteenth Street and entered the Village. My spirits sank lower with each turn of the wheels, depression settled over me at thought of reentering that house, breathing that malign atmosphere. For a brief interlude I'd had welcome relief from pressure, and a good thing too.

The house was lighted; police cars were parked again at the curb. I paid the driver and started up the steps. Someone touched my arm, and I turned.

"Do you live here, miss?" The speaker was a stocky young man in a dirty camel's-hair overcoat. His round nose was red with cold.

"Yes, I do."

"What's your name?"

"Janice Cameron. Why do you ask? Who are you?"

He stomped his feet in the snow, and his breath smoked out. "I'm Hank Miller from the *Mirror*. Did they find the killer yet? Any new developments?"

I shrugged and started up the steps, but he followed like a persistent puppy. "Aw, be a good kid. I need a new lead for tomorrow's story." As I reached the landing he caught my arm. "Hey, I've got an idea. Why not buzz around to Number One Fifth with me and have a drink? I'd like to get a feature—'Beautiful Janice Cameron tells how it feels to live in a murder house.' Come on, baby."

"No, thanks," I pulled away.

For a moment I glowed at the "beautiful Janice Cameron." Then the rest of it registered. Murder house. Those ominous words echoed in my mind as I opened the door and went inside.

Chapter Thirteen

Everyone was in the living room except Louise and Bela. The same stolid policeman was watching, the same tension prevailed. Doris hadn't appeared for hours. She was here now, looking better than when I'd last seen her. Her color was bad, her skin was still tallowish, but the bitter expression in her face was gone; she seemed relieved.

She sat close to Henri. To my surprise that reserved individual had lost his poise; he kept biting his lips and glaring at the officer with open hostility. A chair was vacant near him, and I took it. At my curious scrutiny he muttered, "This is too much! This—this Gestapo! I thought when I came to America there would be no more of—"

The officer cleared his throat. "No whispering." Henri's muttering stopped.

I turned to Lily, who sat on my left. "What's this all about?"

She was wearing black velvet, with pearls in her ears; she was fragrant of Tabac Blond. The sable coat lay over the back of her chair; apparently she had also been out somewhere. She said in a low voice, "The police have discovered some kind of evidence. In a room next to that of the dead man they found—"

The policeman coughed and glared at us; Lily grew silent. I settled with a cigarette, looking around the room. Jarvis was slumped miserably on the window seat; he looked like a man waiting for the executioner's tap on his shoulder. Evelyn sat alone on the sofa, fingers twisting, eyes staring into space.

A figure appeared in the doorway, and we all glanced in that direction. It was Bela returning from his interview with Captain Weber. His bright eyes appraised my new appearance, which I had completely forgotten. He gave me a grin and a gesture signifying approval as he went to join Evelyn.

I was called next.

Captain Weber was sitting at the kitchen table, his assistant by his side with notebook open. Both men looked tired and in need of shaving.

"Sit down, please." Weber was surprisingly affable. I immediately wondered what he wanted from me.

"Yes, Captain. What would you like to know now?"

"I want to talk to you again about the night Mr. Chadwick was murdered."

"You mean the morning," I corrected sweetly. "It was nearly three o'clock when—"

"Of course. Now tell me again exactly what happened, every detail you can remember."

I told him—everything I chose to remember.

"You are positive it was a man's voice you heard answering Miss Sayre from the basement?"

"Yes. There was one thing I noticed at the time, which did not come clearly to me—remember we were all very sleepy—until the next day. Evelyn Sayre and I talked with Mr. Chadwick earlier in the evening, as you know. The man who spoke to her at three in the morning had a different voice."

He leaned toward me until I could smell the stale cigar odor which surrounded him like an aura. "How do you mean, different?"

I explained that, then said, "Do you mind telling me what has happened, Captain? Or are we not permitted to know?"

His lips drew back in a smile. "Certainly. There was somebody hiding in that storage room."

"What storage room? Remember I just moved in here."

"Next to the super's room. Somebody dug a hole in the wall and hid there, watching the man in the next room."

They had discovered the cigarette butts and pieces of beaverboard. I wondered what piece of furniture they'd been swept under, decided it wasn't important. No mention of fingerprints. Had they found the candy wrapper? Captain Weber didn't mention that either.

"We located Murphy, the former superintendent," he told me, "in a Brooklyn hospital. He says someone mailed him a hundred-dollar bill wrapped in blank paper and he went out to have a little nip. He's been drunk ever since."

"Mr. Chadwick might have done that in order to get the man's job."

"He only left Sing Sing yesterday. Nope. Somebody else helped Chadwick get into the house. The real-estate agency says he turned up asking for a job immediately after Miss Manning phoned them to hire another man. The timing was too good to be accidental."

"And you think the person who arranged to get him into the house waited until we'd all gone to bed, then went down there and tortured—" I stopped. "What would he do that for?"

"Money."

"But Mr. Chadwick hadn't any money. He was just out of prison."

"You've heard the story of his embezzlement?" I nodded. "There were rumors—there generally are in such cases—that some of the money was hidden in this house. Actually most of it was recovered, except about twenty thousand dollars not accounted for. Anyhow, the building was searched from basement to roof, and we know there was nothing in that rumor. But if some screwball had brooded over the case and was cracked enough to believe—" He shrugged.

"You mean someone who lives here? In this house?" When Weber didn't answer I went on. "But Evelyn was in the living-room working. No one could have reached the basement without her knowledge."

"That's what she claims. But there's something fishy about her story." The chair creaked as he leaned back and reached into his vest pocket.

"You're an intelligent girl, Miss Cameron, with respect for the law. Here's my phone number. I want you to keep your eyes open. If you hear or see anything the least unusual let me know right away."

His smile was flattering; it said that we understood each other, that there was mutual regard between us. I tried to look flustered and pleased as I took the card, and he nodded dismissal.

I started back toward the living room and stopped. Louise was just coming in the front door, escorted by an officer. Weber had sent to the radio station for her. I wanted to know what she would have to say, so I went to our room. They passed on their way to the kitchen, and when Louise's escort returned to the front of the house I opened the door slightly and stood against it.

"Sit down." There was a new note in Weber's voice now. "I want answers to some questions."

Sound of chairs scraping on linoleum. Then Weber snarled abruptly, "Your name is no more Kane than mine is Epstein. What is it—Carnera?"

I held my breath. Her answer came clear and steady. "You are close, Captain. My name is Louisa Canelli."

"Why did you change it? Afraid of the police?"

"Professional reasons. I'm an actress, as you know."

"But you're afraid of the police, Canelli, aren't you?"

Such a changed attitude from the one he had used with me! His voice grated like a key turning in a cell lock. "What are you afraid of? Ever been arrested?"

"No."

I leaned against the door, holding to it with both hands. I felt sorry for Louise. I hated Weber for his insulting tone. If he had spoken to me like that I should have wanted to throttle him. "Ever been fingerprinted? Don't lie now. We can find out easy enough." There was a pause. She answered in a low voice, "No, I've never been fingerprinted. But I've been shoved around plenty by the police when my brother was arrested. He's serving time now." "Where? Sing Sing?" "Yes."

Then he pounced on her fang and claw. Words erupted from him in a scorching torrent of bullying and accusation. The gist of it was that Louise knew criminal methods, she came from a family of criminals, therefore she must be concealing knowledge of the crime committed in this house. He wound up by suggesting that she had acted under direction of her brother or some of his gang. It sounded preposterous to me. But his technique probably was to accuse possible suspects of the very worst and so trick them into admitting the lesser evil in an attempt to defend themselves.

To all of this Louise answered steadily, no, no, no. She was still in control of herself when he told her to get her coat on again; she was going down town with him. For further questioning.

As chairs began to scrape back from the table I closed the door, feeling as tired as if I had undergone the same brutal grilling as Louise. Under my weariness was relief that I hadn't been tricked by Weber's phony geniality into telling him anything. If Louise were implicated they'd find it out anyway. And what they didn't know about Lily Wu they couldn't get out of me with red-hot needles.

To hell with them, I said to myself, as I crawled into bed and closed my eyes.

The following morning I discovered that being the soignée type wasn't so simple as Lucien had made it sound. I remembered how sleek I had looked when he finished arranging my coiffure, but could not re-create the effect myself. He had used some kind of lacquer, and it left my head with ends sticking out at all angles like a worn whisk broom. Nor would my hair comb in any direction other than up.

I would have asked Lily for help, but she had gone out. I had not heard her dressing; that was frustrating, too, because I wanted to hear the rest of the Chadwick-Wu story. I put on my new cashmere frock and went across the hall in my mules. Louise and Evelyn were drinking coffee in their room. Evelyn was dressed, while Louise sat with the pink robe around her, hugging a steaming cup. When I asked if she would help me comb my hair she said she'd be glad to.

"If you'll wait till I finish this pick-me-up." Her eyes looked hollow, with purplish circles under them, and her shoulders sagged. She caught my sympathetic glance and said, "I must look a wreck. Weber tried to give me the works last night. They kept me there for hours."

Evelyn came over and put her hand affectionately on Louise's arm. "Try to forget it, dear. It's all over now, and they can't do anything to you. Drink your coffee and you'll feel better."

Louise smiled gratitude at her. "Thanks, Evelyn. I'm lucky I drew you for a roommate."

While Louise drank I went to the window. The radiator there was comfortably hot; Bela was a conscientious furnace stoker. I appreciated his dependability when I looked out at the sullen gray sky, the earth covered with dirty snow. I turned my back on it and surveyed the room. This had once been the dining room, Evelyn had said. Mahogany paneling ran halfway to the ceiling; the balance of the wall was papered with a cheerful country scene. There were two dressing tables instead of the built-in one which Lily and I shared. Evelyn's was bare except for some old-fashioned tortoiseshell toilet accessories and a bottle of Yardley's Lavender. Louise's dresser was littered with bottles and jars, scattered hairpins, costume jewelry, and an overflowing ashtray.

There were also some little squares of red-and-gold-striped foil. I picked one up. "May I?"

"Go ahead, take it all. I seldom eat candy anyway; it's bad for my skin. Jarvis gave that to me."

Jarvis, of course. The murdered man had been his obsession. Jarvis was pleased to visualize Chadwick in prison while he lived comfortably in his former home. It might have been worth a hundred dollars to Jarvis to humiliate his enemy completely by installing him in the house as a servant.

Then to observe secretly, gloating as Chadwick sat despairing in his sordid quarters, inundated with bitter memories, to watch and plan for that final interview... My imagination could go no farther. I tossed the candy back on the dresser. Captain Weber had this evidence; let him follow it to its conclusion.

Chapter Fourteen

"**H**ere's your coffee, Janice." I roused from my unpleasant reverie and thanked Evelyn. I sat before Louise's dresser and drank coffee while she began to work on my hair.

"This is the way it's done," she said. "You part it from side to side on top and pin the front hair together—that goes up last. Then you part the back down the center, take half, and bring it up crossways—see?"

I watched in the mirror, remembering that interview I had overheard. Louise was a strangely contradictory person, a mixture in which very likely the old Louisa struggled often against the new determined Louise. With the transformation in her appearance, accomplished at such cost, there must have come a psychological change which was more than external. Terror of the police which had shaken her when they first entered the house might have been a signal reaction of the earlier, homelier, humbler girl who remembered painfully a time when she was unable to protect herself. Now she had reached a point where a different background and improved appearance served as a sort of armor. Louise had risen above so many serious handicaps; I hoped that she was not in real trouble now.

Finally I could restrain my interest no longer. "Louise," I said, "what did the police want with you? If you mind my asking, say so."

Evelyn knew. She set her cup down and moved as if to protect the younger woman. She sank into her chair again as Louise answered calmly, "I would have minded once. I don't now. They discovered that my family was Italian. And my brother is a criminal."

She inspected my head, inserted another hairpin. "It's funny," she said. "When I first moved in here I used to wake up sweating sometimes for fear someone might find out my real name and where I came from. Now that it's out I feel relieved. And if there's anybody who doesn't like it, they can go to hell."

She stepped back and admired her work. "There. You're glamorous again, Janice. After your hair's trained to the upsweep you won't need lacquer. Now if you'll move I'll get busy on myself."

She took my seat and began to comb her hair. "Yes," she went on, "I was terribly impressed to think I was living in what was once the home of an aristocratic family. I used to imagine how wonderful it must have been to live here when it was a real home."

She lit a cigarette and turned to Evelyn with a wry smile. "Remember you thought I was cynical, laughing at the hard-luck story Henri told us about Doris? Well, while she was enduring what she called a dreadful time, working as some-body's secretary and living in a clean, comfortable room, I was clerking in my father's stinking little cigar store for two dollars a week, keeping house for him and my brother in a Bronx slum."

Her nose wrinkled with disgust, as if she could still smell the effluvium of the place from which she had escaped.

"What a rathole!" she said. "Our kitchen window looked out on a light well; we never saw the sun. There were rags stuck in the broken glass in winter. I had no one to help me keep house; my mother died when we were kids. My old man never got over the Depression, when we were on relief for two years.

After that he couldn't think of anything but making money. He stood behind the counter of that store fifteen hours a day ever since I was ten and my brother was thirteen. As soon as I was old enough he enlarged the business and put me to work.

"I begged to go back to school. He always said that we were too poor, that he needed my help. I believed him—until I found out one day that he owned the tenement building we lived in, owned it clear, without even a mortgage—" She broke off and smashed her cigarette into shreds.

"I might have stayed even then, I guess, if I could have helped my brother. But nobody could do anything with Vito. At twenty-one he was running with a gang. I left when he was finally sent to prison. That's what got our pal Weber so excited yesterday. Most crimes are committed by habitual criminals; it's natural for police to work from that angle. Weber would have been delighted to prove something on me because of Vito's record. He even tried to force me to give my complete personal history from the time I left home. I refused. It's none of his business. Or anyone else's!"

Her mouth tightened. Louise was remembering. She wasn't going to talk about that period in her life. I didn't want to hear it.

"After a while," she continued in a lighter voice, "after I got the job I wanted and a room in this house, I wrote my father and told him where I lived. He never answered." The shrug which accompanied these words was eloquent.

"Yes," she went on reminiscently, "I was thrilled at having a room here; I'd never been in such a fine place before. I envied the lucky family that used to live here. Until I found out who they were and what they were really like. Now I've learned— there are lots of people worse off than I, even if they had governesses and fancy schools, or doting mothers with private incomes. So now I've got over being scared someone might find out my real name or the background I came from. And I feel a hundred percent better."

Evelyn said softly, "We're all hiding something. I'm still a little bit ashamed, I must confess, of coming from a farm. I know it's ridiculous. But I've been trying to sell that old place for months now just to get rid of my past."

She moved in her chair and sighed. "I'm glad you feel as you do, Louise; you'll be more comfortable with yourself from now on. I wish I could feel the same."

Louise turned quickly to her. "What's troubling you, Evelyn? You've been looking so terribly worried lately."

"I am worried. I feel very guilty—because I didn't tell Captain Weber the complete truth."

Louise laid down her comb and went over to put an arm around Evelyn's shoulders. "What crime did you commit? Something dreadful, no doubt."

Evelyn smiled and shook her white head. "It might have been serious." She looked as if she wanted to drop the subject, then said breathlessly, "I told the police I was in the living room working all the time, and that wasn't true. I mean—because I didn't work all the time. I—I dozed off for a little while. Anyone could have passed the door, and I might not have known it."

Louise laughed and tilted Evelyn's chin up with her hand. "Come on now," she teased. "Why not tell the whole truth and ease that tender conscience of yours? We love you. Nobody will think it so terrible as you expect. I've known for a long time anyhow. You were upstairs with Bela, weren't you?"

Evelyn's gray eyes widened, while scarlet crept up from her throat and suffused her face. "You knew?" she whispered.

"Of course. You can't deceive your own roommate. I'm in favor of the idea anyhow. It's time you had some love life if you're ever going to take the plunge." She lit another cigarette and blew a cloud of smoke through which she squinted at the other woman mischievously. "I've heard on good authority that after a female reaches maturity it's necessary. Stimulates certain glands and keeps her young."

Evelyn looked as if she didn't know whether to register gratification or shock at Louise's frankness. I suspected that behind such blushing confusion was a little bit of feminine complacency at being able to reveal that she was now initiated into what had long been a mystery.

The other two began to laugh, and for a while I joined them, then grew quite sober. The import of what Evelyn revealed had just come to me. She had not been watching the hallway; anyone from upstairs could have been in the basement.

I tried to sound casual as I asked, "Evelyn, how did it happen you appeared so quickly when Doris was fussing in my room? You must have come downstairs some time before that."

"Wasn't it lucky I did?" she said. "You remember after Bela left I came in here to get my work. You were asleep, Louise."

"I wasn't asleep," Louise corrected. "I had a headache and didn't feel like talking."

Louise might discuss intimate details of her family life or emotional problems, but she wouldn't explain those headaches. The things which Lucien told me were secrets a woman never reveals.

Evelyn was still recapitulating. "When I returned to the living room everyone had gone. That was after eleven. I went upstairs and—and stayed there until about one o'clock. When I came down again the fire looked so pleasant, with coals still glowing, that I sat on the sofa to watch it. I must have fallen asleep, for the next thing I remember is hearing Doris talking. You know the rest."

She looked hopefully first at me and then at Louise. "What I told the police was almost true. You don't think I should tell them everything, do you?"

"Don't tell them anything!" Louise was emphatic.

I felt uneasy. This was one thing which should not be concealed. "Evelyn," I said, "I think you ought to tell Captain Weber that you were asleep in the living room. You needn't mention that you were upstairs. But he should know the rest."

Louise started to protest, but Evelyn agreed uncomfortably that perhaps I was right. "I'll tell him," she promised.

I broke the awkward silence which followed by announcing with great animation that I had bought some new clothes. "I have to go for alterations this afternoon. How about having lunch with me, both of you? Let's go somewhere very swish and celebrate."

Both women became interested at mention of clothes, and Louise asked questions about design and fabric which showed that she was much more fashion conscious than I. When Evelyn regretted that she couldn't be with us because she had a class to teach, Louise said she'd love to go. She added, "But I'd like to see Jarvis first. I made a recording last night at the studio, and I want him to play it back for me. He won't let anyone touch his precious machine, so I have to ask him to do it when he's there."

"Is he at home now?"

"This is his day off."

"I'm not in a hurry," I said. "If you don't mind I'll come along and listen. I've never heard that kind of recording, and I'm interested."

That was true. But I was far more interested in the fat man, the man who ate candy wrapped in red and gold, the man who had a persecution complex. I wanted to take a closer, more careful look at him now. But only in the company of a third person. Jarvis was number-one candidate for murderer.

He admitted us with scant welcome. "Oh," he said, pulling the maroon flannel robe around him, "it's you. What do you want?"

When Louise told him the reason for our visit and showed him the record he grudgingly consented to play it for her, but not until the music on the machine was finished. "It's bad for the mechanism to stop an automatic player while it's in cycle," he explained, as half apology for his rudeness. He waved us to chairs and went back to his own by the window and picked up the big scrapbook he had been reading.

"What's this dreary music you're listening to?" Louise asked.

Jarvis lifted his eyes with a scowl. Probably he was of the cult which considers conversation during music a sacrilege. "'The Isle of the Dead,'" he said. "Koussevitzky's interpretation." He tapped the big black book. "Fitting accompaniment to this. I'm playing it for Chadwick while I refresh my memory with Mother's scrapbook."

He scrunched farther into his chair and reached for a chocolate from the box beside him. Jarvis seldom chewed; he gulped. As one creamy mess slid down his throat he automatically picked up another while he continued to read. I craned toward the record player and discovered with relief that the fast record was about to drop. That music was too macabre for my taste.

Louise looked at me with inquiry, and I raised a finger to indicate the number of records left. She nodded and picked up a copy of *Metronome* which lay by her chair. The ashtray there was filled with cigarettes and covered with encrustations of ash which indicated that it had probably not been washed since the day Jarvis acquired it. I remembered the cigarettes stubbed out on the little French table in the basement. I glanced around the room, trying to get a further impression of the man who lived in it. The only clean things were the record player, which had been carefully dusted, and rows and rows of record albums. In the adjoining bedroom an open closet door betrayed incredible confusion: shirts and underwear on the floor, trousers drooping from hooks instead of hangers, dirty socks. I wondered who changed his bed linen. If someone didn't do it for him the sheets were probably gray.

I glanced at Jarvis, disliking him more and more. This was the man who pushed a trunk on me; a lot he'd care if I got a fractured skull.

He sat slumped, his blubbery body filling the chair, the big book resting on his paunch. He was absorbed, and his lips moved as he read. The record played to a finish and began again. Jarvis, the music sensitive, didn't hear it. I watched him. He was staring at a page in the book, holding it closer to his eyes, as if by bringing it into sharper focus he could find that what he saw was an error of vision. His face grew white as I watched. He swallowed.

"Jarvis," I called, starting toward him. Curiosity blazed in me; I longed to snatch that scrapbook from his hands. He looked up blankly. "Your record's repeating."

"It is?" He cocked his head sidewise, listening. I reached the table and tried to see the page in front of him. He darted a sharp glance at me and deliberately turned the book so I could not see it. He folded a corner down in a big triangle, rubbing it hard. His finger left chocolate on the following page. He rose abruptly, clutching the book against him.

"You'll have to go now, Louise. I haven't time to play your record. Just remembered an appointment."

Louise was surprised. "All you need to do is put it on the turntable. We'll listen while you dress."

"No. I want you to leave!" His voice ascended the scale. He flung one fat hand toward us in a gesture that brushed us from his sight. "I haven't time; come back later. Will you get out?" The last was a scream.

We left in a hurry. All the way uptown I thought about it, wondering what thirteen-year-old news item could have excited him so. Jarvis hadn't looked at the clippings Henri brought, so it might have been among those. But I couldn't remember anything which should cause violent reaction in anyone other than Doris. Maybe we had not seen them all. Doris probably hadn't been such an assiduous clipping collector as Jarvis's mother; he said she used to cry over the scrapbook. Now it looked as if he were wallowing in the same emotional orgies. But this kind of brooding was worse, since so much time had passed. My puzzled thoughts were terminated by our arrival at the cafe where we had decided to have lunch.

When we were at our table I returned to the subject. "What do you think was wrong with Jarvis? Is he usually so hysterical?"

Louise made a sound of derision. "That's a polite word for it. He's always been peculiar in his own revolting way, but I've never seen him act completely nuts before."

"He needs a doctor," I said. "He's projecting himself completely into the past, wallowing in bitter memories."

Louise sniffed. "He and his bitter memories! I'm fed up with that stuff. Let's forget it for a change."

But I couldn't forget; Jarvis's hysteria seemed to have infected me. I thought of it all through lunch; it was in my mind while the seamstress at the dress shop stuck pins in my new frocks and discussed alterations. We had planned to see a movie, but now I didn't feel like going. Much as I detested the atmosphere of that house, something drew me back to it. Louise looked disappointed when I suggested going home, but I couldn't help it. No use inflicting her with my mood, my compulsion to return. I couldn't explain it myself.

It was late afternoon when we reached the Square; I could hardly wait to get the door opened. Yet once we were inside everything seemed normal. Doris and Henri were playing gin rummy on the window seat, Evelyn sat on the sofa with a block of writing paper and pencil.

Doris looked up at our entrance. "Hello. You're home early." I said some thing noncommittal; Louise didn't reply. She was cross, irritated with Jarvis for his rudeness, disappointed that my promise of a pleasant afternoon had been fraudulent.

"Where's everybody?" she asked.

Henri shrugged lack of information or interest; Evelyn was too absorbed to answer. When Doris asked if we'd like to play some bridge I looked at Louise, and she said we might as well. We set up a table and drew for partners. It was Henri and I against the two women. I expected an ordinary game of domestic bridge; to my surprise I found myself concentrating furiously, trying to keep pace with three experts.

The first time Henri made a psychic bid in spades I had a high honor count in that suit; I floundered, trying to rescue him from disaster. He got the bid at four no-trump and played smoothly and unhesitatingly to a little slam. After that I sat straight in my chair, absorbed in trying to keep up with his lightning mind.

We had changed partners for the second rubber before I became aware of music from upstairs; even then it registered only in the periphery of my brain. Doris bid and made a successful four hearts; we were vulnerable and struggling for the rubber. Lily came into the room and stood watching quietly; I hardly noticed her. I bid five clubs and Henri doubled; he was such a brilliant player that I grew tense with antagonism toward him, determined to make that bid. As I analyzed the dummy and planned my game I became aware that the music from Jarvis's room was growing louder. I played my hand to an ignominious defeat, and we were down eleven hundred points, vulnerable.

Brassy chords reverberated from upstairs, and it seemed to me that sound waves rushed into the room with almost physical force. I was very irritated. "Sorry, Doris," I said. "I should have made that bid. I know excuses are ridiculous, but I do wish Jarvis would choose something less nerve-racking for his concert."

Doris bit her lip and nodded. Bela had said she disliked Jarvis's music, but she refrained from complaining now, perhaps because of her resolve to win our good will. I turned to Lily and asked if she'd like to cut in, but she said no, and went over to the sofa.

We had to raise our voices during the next bidding to be heard over that awful music. Louise got the bid at three no trump; as Henri spread his hand for her the music stopped, and the quiet was wonderful relief. I let out a sigh, and Doris's shoulders relaxed.

Then the record began again. Louise muttered under her breath as she started to play the hand. It was almost impossible to think over that music.

Wagner. It would have been magnificent in a concert hall; in that small space it was overwhelming. Somber chords carried by the brasses, mounting to almost unbearable crescendo, then repeating, growing constantly more powerful.

I shall never enjoy Wagner again.

Finally Louise threw down her cards so hard that they scattered all over the floor. "Why doesn't someone remind that fat slob," she demanded in a shrill voice, "that other people live in this house besides him?"

As if in answer to her request we heard feet rushing down the third-floor stairs. Bela. He pounded at Jarvis's door and yelled, *"Will you turn that thing down?"* He descended the second flight and strode into our midst. Bela was distraught, and his voice shook with anger.

"I've been trying to work all afternoon; now that guy's driving me crazy. I'm painting something cheerful—Washington Square in the spring—and he plays the 'Liebestod'!"

The "Liebestod." Love-Death. Death again.

Henri had been picking up scattered cards. He laid them on the table and looked at Bela. "What did he say when you asked him to stop?"

"Didn't bother to answer. I doubt whether he heard me over that racket."

Bela pulled out a pipe and filled it with tobacco. His hand was shaking so that he couldn't hold a match steady to light it. He rammed the unlit pipe back into his pocket and announced furiously, "I'm going to stop that infernal noise if I have to wreck his goddamned machine!"

Henri rose and laid a hand on the other man's shoulder. "You had better let me go, Bela," he said. "You are too nervous; you'll provoke a quarrel. I'll talk to him."

He started up the stairs. His legs disappeared from sight, and music swelled louder as Jarvis's door was opened. In the room below we were tense, waiting for sounds of argument. We heard the music grind to a horrible scratching whine, then there was no more sound. Not even voices. Uneasiness crawled around the room as utter silence continued. We looked at one another; no one spoke.

Then Henri appeared halfway down the stairs. He leaned over the railing and called in a low voice. "Bela. Will you come up, please?"

Bela went. We waited again. Still no sound. When tension had become intolerable, Louise and I pushed back our chairs with one accord and started up the stairs.

Jarvis's door was ajar; we entered the room together. The two men were near the window, bending over the big armchair.

Something in maroon flannel huddled there, head lolling, feet sprawled, arms dangling.

Bela turned and saw us. "Get out!" he said.

"Wh-what's the matter?" Louise stammered. "Has he passed out?"

Henri raised a white face and looked at us with horror-filled eyes. His voice was a sick gasp as he said, "He is dead."

Chapter Fifteen

Police were in possession of the house again. Weary hours later we sat and waited our turn to be questioned, munching without appetite on sandwiches delivered from a delicatessen. Evelyn wouldn't eat; she wept instead, lying with her head on Bela's knee, shoulders shaking under the lavender smock. Lily sipped coffee in a big chair, pale and silent. Doris and Henri whispered to each other, holding hands on the love seat. Louise and I played an erratic game of gin rummy with the cards they had abandoned.

An officer appeared. "Miss Cameron, will you come up?"

I laid down cards and started. Louise rose. "You wait, miss," he told her.

"I will not!" she said, and her voice rose an octave. "We were in his room together this afternoon. We were the last ones to talk to him." She climbed the stairs by my side.

Captain Weber was in Jarvis's room. With him this time was a man named Goldstein from the district attorney's office. Another plainclothes stenographer waited with notebook in hand. Jarvis's body had been removed, but a chalk mark outlined the big chair where he had died, running down the front and over the rug to indicate the position of his feet; I turned my eyes away from that reminder.

The rest of the room was the same as when we had last been there except for the articles on the table next to Captain Weber. He sat in a corner near the record player contemplating the big scrapbook, a black leather diary, a wallet, a white envelope, and some slips of pink paper.

Weber said, "Miss Manning tells me that you girls visited Jarvis Lloyd this afternoon. Tell us what happened."

"We came up to play a recording Miss Kane had made," I said. "Jarvis was here, listening to music and reading that scrapbook. He was in a very despondent mood, and he became increasingly disturbed as he read the clippings. Finally he told us he didn't have time to play Miss Kane's record and asked us to leave."

"Asked us!" Louise put in. "He practically threw us out of this room!"

"Is that right, Miss Cameron?"

"Yes."

"What else did he say?"

"Nothing much. He was hysterical. When we didn't leave immediately, he screamed at us. I was curious about what he had been reading, but when I tried to see the page he turned down a corner of it and shut the book."

"Like this?" Weber opened the scrapbook to a turned-down corner; on the following page was a smear of chocolate. I bent over the newspaper photograph. It was a picture of Mrs. Lloyd, the mother who wept over the clippings, clinging to the hand of a plump, scared, much younger Jarvis. The heading said, Another Victim of Chadwick Greed. The text beneath it was an interview which I didn't read. The date was May 1936.

I said, "Yes, that's the page. I remember the chocolate mark he made when he turned it."

Weber and the man from the district attorney's office glanced at each other.

"How did Jarvis die?" I asked. "Did he kill himself?"

"He died of poison, probably self-administered. We don't know yet what it was. We found an empty bottle of scotch on the table by his chair and a glass with his prints on it." He picked up the leather book. "Has either of you ever seen him writing in this diary?"

We had not.

"It was hidden behind some record albums." He flipped the pages, weighed it in his hand. Mr. Goldstein spoke. "I am sure Doc McCarthy will say those entries were made by a man who was mentally deranged."

"Who is Dr. McCarthy?"

"The psychiatrist attached to our office."

"Was it Jarvis who killed Mr. Chadwick?" Louise asked.

"Looks like it. Miss Sayre finally admitted that she was asleep in the living room at the time the murder was being committed. Lloyd could have got past her easy enough. Simple to disguise his voice when he spoke to her from the basement. After you all went back to bed it was just as easy to walk upstairs again."

Mr. Goldstein asked, "Has either of you ever observed Lloyd acting—prior to today—in a peculiar manner?"

I said I didn't know him, but in the short time I'd been there his conduct had seemed to me to be very erratic. But I didn't know how far erratic behavior had to go to be considered insanity.

Weber turned to Louise. "You've lived here a long time. Tell us about Lloyd."

"Frankly, I thought he was just a self-centered boob who liked to whine about his troubles. Every night he came home complaining how miserable he was in his job. Somebody was always doing something spiteful to him. Then when Doris's father was killed he threw a fit, said it was a good thing the man was dead, that he deserved killing. Jarvis was drunk that day. But ever since then he acted as if something was on his mind. He sat and brooded. And he played the most awful music."

She mentioned "The Isle of the Dead" and what he had said about its fitness as accompaniment to reading the scrapbook. She told about the Wagner. Weber nodded, as if this were further confirmation of what he already knew. I had been looking at the articles on the table during Louise's statement. I asked curiously, "What are those pink things?"

Weber looked at the other man, and the latter said, "Might as well tell them. It'll be in the papers soon enough."

The detective picked up the pink papers. "These are Chadwick's pawn tickets. He pawned a diamond-and-platinum watch, a star sapphire ring, and a gold cigarette case for a total of six hundred dollars. We found them in his wallet, stuck behind those records. So, you see, the hundred Lloyd spent to get rid of the other super wasn't wasted. He got a good return on his investment. We haven't found the rest of the money; no doubt it'll turn up in a bank account somewhere."

"Then Jarvis really was the one who killed Mr. Chadwick?"

"Looks like it." Weber opened the envelope and removed a folded piece of paper. "We found this hidden with the diary and wallet. The handwriting is Chadwick's."

The note said, "Everything worked as planned. I am installed here. Come down to visit me when possible so I can thank you. C. C."

By the time we finished that session I was ready to drop. As soon as we were dismissed I went to our room. Lily was waiting for me. I started to unzip my dress, and she said, "Just a minute, Janice."

I sighed. "Now what?"

"I know you are very tired. This has been a great strain. But I think we would both sleep better if we felt completely secure." She held out a package which contained a new barrel-bolt lock. "I bought this today. We can install it ourselves now—if we have proper tools."

"Lily." I said waspishly, "please stop being so damned devious. What are you hinting at?"

"We need a hammer, a chisel, and—a screwdriver. I have a special screwdriver in mind."

"You mean the one we found in the dressing room?" I had completely forgotten it. "Isn't it around here somewhere?"

She laid the lock down. "You recall when I went to the basement just before the police arrived?"

"Of course."

"I locked the door and returned the key as I told you. I also left the screwdriver downstairs by the super's bed. I carried it in a handkerchief. Janice, I want to know whose fingerprints are on that screwdriver."

So she hadn't taken that attack on herself as lightly as she pretended. I zipped my dress up again. "Let's go."

There was an officer in the basement sitting under the glaring light with a pocket novel in his hands. He looked bored, glad to have visitors. I asked him how much longer he would be there, and he said he expected orders to leave soon. We discussed the murder and Jarvis's suicide, and Lily complimented him on the efficiency of the police. He tried not to stare too obviously at her exotic features as we talked.

Finally we worked conversation around to our newness there, our nervousness at living in a strange house where such terrible things had happened, and told him we wanted to put a lock on our door. He approved, and offered to help us find tools. In the empty room where Chadwick had died we found various things: a hammer, a chisel with a broken edge. The screwdriver was on a chair, and I picked it up.

"You don't want these any more, for fingerprints or anything?"

"No, miss. I guess you can take whatever you need. The lab boys tested everything."

"Even this?" I held up the screwdriver, looking impressed.

"Sure. It didn't have anything on it but Chadwick's prints. He must have puttered around here a little, trying to make like a real super."

He explained how to install the lock, and we thanked him and went back to our room. It took a bit of figuring, but we finally got started. We talked as we worked.

"It was Chadwick who hit you." My voice showed the surprise I felt. "Why?"

Lily was using the hammer and chisel to cut space on the doorframe for the lock. She marked the spot with pencil and chiseled carefully. She said, "It doesn't make sense, does it?"

"Maybe," I conjectured, "the realty office mentioned that our room was vacant. We weren't expected so soon, remember? He had just come to work here. He sneaked up to have a look at his dead wife's room, carrying that screwdriver so if anyone challenged him he could say he was making repairs. Then when you walked in he was so startled that he hit you without thinking and rushed out."

Lily's brows drew together slightly. "That could be the explan—" She broke off as someone knocked sharply on our door.

"Girls!" Doris's voice was strong with authority. "What are you doing in there?"

I opened the door, and she came in. "We heard the noise," she said. "What on earth are you hammering?"

She started toward the dressing room, but halted as Lily emerged with the hammer in her hand. I had been about to blurt that we were putting a lock on our door and had every right to do so; a glance at Lily's face kept me quiet. Concealment was automatic with Lily, I decided. She smiled pleasantly and said, "I was tightening some coat hooks which are loose. Did I disturb everyone?"

Doris became conciliatory. "Not really. I guess we're nervous after what's been happening here." She turned reluctantly; she wanted to see for herself what Lily was doing but didn't have quite enough nerve to force her way into the dressing room. She left after apologizing to us for the dreadful time we'd had since we became her tenants, commenting that now it was over we could relax and forget the past few days.

Lily made no comment. She went back to work and finally got the lock into place. "There," she said as it slipped into the barrel neatly. "We'll both feel more secure now."

"It's a little like locking the stable after the horse is gone, isn't it?" Apparently she didn't hear me; she was pulling her dress over her head. I was actually too tired to think clearly or to talk. I wanted to hear the rest of Lily's story but felt that I couldn't stay awake through the telling of it. We settled into our beds, and I tried to be polite and keep my heavy eyelids open when Lily spoke. "Tell me what happened in Jarvis's room today."

I repeated the story. Lily pondered. "I'd like very much to see that scrapbook."

"I saw it, Lily. A picture of Jarvis and his mother." I described the picture and news caption. "You know how emotional he was about his mother. Rereading that story might have been all he needed to work up a suicidal mood. With sound effects. All that morbid music he played. He said it was fitting, and I guess it was, after what he had done." I repeated the words slowly. "After what he had done! It's hard to imagine Jarvis being so cunning. I mean, writing to Chadwick in prison—that must have been how he contacted him—helping him to get a job here just so he could kill him in his own house."

"Jarvis had a persecution complex. He had been brooding for years. Besides, Chadwick's death was probably accidental, the result of his weak heart. Why would Jarvis torture him?"

"He wanted the money."

Lily sat up abruptly. "What money?"

"Captain Weber said that about twenty thousand was never recovered. Jarvis might have tried to force Chadwick to tell him where the money was."

She pulled up the blanket at the foot of her bed and lay back. "I do not see how he could have gone unobserved to the basement that night."

I told her then part of what Evelyn had confided earlier in the day. "She was asleep. Captain Weber must have given her hell for not admitting it before. I think that's why she was crying tonight."

"Probably. Good night, Janice."

"Good night."

I lay half awake, my thoughts drifting foggily from one conjecture to another. Jarvis's surveillance of Chadwick took place prior to our arrival at the house. When music was heard from his room everyone took for granted that he was there enjoying his own private concert, just as we had taken the same situation for granted today while Jarvis was actually dying. Easy to put enough records on the automatic player to last for an hour. When Jarvis looked out the window and saw us arriving he sneaked upstairs; time for that while Bela was showing us our room.

A man with his sick mind might have enjoyed spying on his enemy, working hatred to the pitch necessary for violence. Torturing, then, could have been part of his mental aberration. I recalled the way he had looked with horror at his hands the next morning when Louise suggested that someone stoke the furnace. Was Jarvis remembering how he had used those hands just a few hours before?

I got up to go to the bathroom and found myself washing my own hands vigorously. I took a drink of water and went back to bed, leaving the door to the dressing room ajar, forgetting the lock.

I was just floating over that final borderline into sleep when I heard a sound in the bathroom. It pulled me back as if jerked by wires. I waited for the click of the light, the gush of water. No such sounds. Instead, there were stealthy footsteps. The door to the bathroom opened. Someone entered our dressing room cautiously, a flashlight streaked across the carpet, clothes hangers rattled. Then the light and the intruder were gone, swiftly, without sound. Doris sneaking in, I thought, checking to see what damage we've done to her property. I hope she's satisfied.

Chapter Sixteen

Newspapers the next day told the story more completely than we had heard it from the police. Jarvis had died from an overdose of sodium amytol, probably washed down by the large quantities of liquor he drank. Tabloids drooled over the dramatic ending of the Chadwick case. One reporter wrote a lurid story with childhood pictures of Jarvis, an account of his musical talent, his frustration, his final act of vengeance and self-inflicted death. Another paper used drawings featuring Jarvis seated in the big chair, working up emotion with liquor and Wagner's music, swallowing barbiturates in macabre toasts: to his mother, to his wasted life, and to the man whose death he had caused.

Lily and I were reading, with papers scattered around us, when Evelyn and Louise came to visit. We evaded the subject at first. Louise complimented me on the hairdo which I had accomplished without help; I showed some new clothes and described others which would be ready soon. Lily moved around picking up papers; we all refrained from discussing the tragedy because of Evelyn's sensitivity.

Surprisingly it was Evelyn herself who first mentioned it. "Bela would like to buy Jarvis's radio-phonograph and the records if his family will sell them," she said. "Do you think that's ghoulish of him? He was wondering what a fair price would be."

"I should think half the list price would be fair," Louise said in a businesslike tone. "That isn't ghoulish of Bela. But I'll tell you what is. Do you know there have been people here already asking for Jarvis's room? As soon as they read of his death they came running."

I could understand that; I had recently been desperate for a place to live myself. I said, "Did Doris rent it?"

"No. Jarvis's relatives are coming from Kansas to get his things. As soon as they're out Doris intends to have the second floor remodeled for herself and Henri, so they can rent the rest of the house and still have privacy."

"She is a practical woman," Lily commented. "That is what one would expect her to do."

I'd had something on my mind for several hours. Now I spoke about it, to find relief. "You know," I said, "I felt uneasy all yesterday afternoon. While Louise and I were uptown I couldn't get Jarvis out of my mind. I know I'm not psychic or anything like that, but just the same I wish we had gone up to see him again when we came back."

Lily asked, "Didn't anyone see him?"

"Nobody," Evelyn told her. "We were all busy. I went to the library to do some research, Doris was at Gimbel's buying a black dress, Henri and Bela were working."

She looked at Lily, and the Chinese girl answered her unspoken question quietly. "I was visiting relatives down on Mott Street."

"And all that while," I said, "Jarvis was alone, getting drunk, stuffing himself with sleeping pills. Nobody knew or cared."

"I don't see how you could have gone back," Lily said, "if he had ordered you out of his room."

"Yet," Evelyn said sadly, "a word, a friendly gesture might have pulled Jarvis out of that terrible mood. But none of us went near him. I've thought of it often, not only about Jarvis, but others too. How frightfully alone one can be in a city like this—*especially* in a city like this—with people crowding from every side and no one really caring whether you live or die." Her eyes filled with tears. "None of us cared about Jarvis. Maybe the reason he complained so often was just to get a little bit of attention."

Louise said, "I keep remembering that crack I made about him yesterday. I wish I hadn't said it."

"You meant no harm, Louise," I consoled. "He *was* fat." I added silently that he was a slob too. I was still remembering with resentment the trunk which might have fractured my skull.

"I'm the one who should feel ashamed," Evelyn burst out. "If I had admitted to Captain Weber that I was—was not watching the hall all the time, he would have turned his attention on the men in the house. They would have searched Jarvis's room earlier, and found that evidence. Jarvis would have been arrested; he wouldn't be dead today. They'd have found him mentally unbalanced and put him in a hospital for treatment."

"Is that what Captain Weber said to you?" Lily asked. Evelyn nodded, dabbing at her overflowing eyes.

"Please," I said, "it's all over. There's nothing we can do now. Let's not talk about it any more."

"All right, Janice," Louise said. "You heard my life story yesterday; let's talk about you. What are you planning to do here in New York? Are you going to school, like Lily, or hunting for a job, or what?"

I answered, with modesty false as the eyelashes she wore, that I had written a novel which was going to be published in the fall. Evelyn and Louise made surprised exclamations, but Lily merely smiled. That little sibyl already knew; such information was undoubtedly part of the dossier she received about me, since the *Star-Bulletin* had carried a news item with my picture.

Local girl makes good. I remembered the congratulatory visit I'd had from Bob after that story came out, the faint overtone of regret and envy in his voice. The girl he jilted me for had promptly launched into Honolulu's social round, while he was stuck behind a *koa*-wood desk in her father's office. I realized with satisfaction that now, for the first time in four years, I could think of him without bitterness. He had gained thirty pounds and his hair was already receding. I had lost ten and mine was done in an upsweep.

As symbolism it was completely gratifying.

At that point Doris came to our room, carrying a manuscript in her hand. "Excuse me for intruding," she said, "but I wanted to tell you something. Captain Weber just left. His department considers the case closed; his men won't bother us any more. I thought you'd be glad to know."

"Won't you sit down?" Lily suggested politely.

"For just a moment." Doris sank into a chair, laying the typed pages carefully over her knees. "I should like to offer a suggestion. Henri and I thought that it might be pleasant if we could all have dinner together. We were planning a little party to celebrate our engagement, but of course this is not the time for a party."

Not a word of regret for Jarvis. He had been merely a bothersome tenant. Not a word about her dead father or his imminent burial. No doubt Doris felt like celebrating his death, instead of mourning. Chadwick dead meant thirty thousand dollars to her.

Louise brightened at the suggestion of dinner. "Thanks for the invitation. It sounds good to me. Where shall we eat?"

Doris's face showed a visible struggle between newly declared affability and habitual stinginess. The latter won. She said after a pause, "It might be better to eat here. It isn't so public; we can be more at ease, and there are so many of us. I'll provide whatever we need."

"The kitchen is no place for a party meal—there isn't room," Louise said. She added irritably, "And did you intend that Evelyn should cook for us, as she generally does?"

I perceived that such had been precisely Doris's intention. She opened her mouth to deny it when Evelyn spoke. "I have an idea. Let's ask Bela to suggest some quiet place where we can go, and each of us will pay his own check. Doris and Henri can provide cocktails first, and we'll have them here. I'll make the canapés."

Doris was still having an inner struggle. Finally she said, after heroic effort, "We'll take you all to dinner! Having cocktails here is a splendid idea and much cheaper. If you'll make a grocery list, Evelyn, I'll order whatever you need for canapés."

"I've got a date with Max tonight," Louise announced. "May I invite him?"

Doris gulped. "Why, of course."

Louise grinned wickedly at this victory. She said, "You're very generous, Doris. I'll tell him to bring some liquor."

"Maybe Henri can contribute something, too, although I know he's low on funds." Doris sighed, touching the papers she held. "Writing is such a strain, and he hasn't been able to take much time for outside work lately."

I remembered the hours of grinding drudgery I had spent writing a novel at night while I earned a living in the daytime at far more exhausting labor than reading manuscripts for a literary agency. I couldn't feel so sorry for Henri as Doris, who always got that dying-duck expression when she spoke of him.

"Poor Henri," she said. "He's been so dreadfully upset over the terrible things which have—"

"None of that, Doris!" Louise interrupted. "Let's all make a solemn agreement that for this day, at least, we won't mention death. Then perhaps we can enjoy our dinner."

We agreed.

She stood up and announced that she was going out on an errand and would return soon. "Is there anything I can get, Evelyn?"

Evelyn said she would make a grocery list and go to the store herself. They departed, discussing canapé makings, and Lily and I were alone. I switched on the little radio to a program of rhumba music and busied myself with straightening dresser drawers. It looked as if we were going to be able to settle down at last.

Lily brought the ironing board into our room and pressed some of her clothes. Her lingerie was exquisite, handmade and of heavy satin. Many of her slips were slit at the side to match her Chinese panel dresses. I thought of the simple student who lived at the Ramsey Residence not so long ago, the quiet, color-less girl who wore cotton dirndls and bobby socks. Lily had achieved quite a transformation, both in her wardrobe and in her mode of living.

I wondered what she and her "uncle" had talked about when they were together yesterday. Had she described to him how she obtained possession of the Wu chop and thanked him properly for his help? Would she move back to Mott Street as soon as the furor over the Chadwick case subsided? I wanted to ask a lot of questions, but they were all pertaining to the subject we had promised not to discuss. Plenty of time from now on, I decided, and put it out of my mind.

I killed time by taking a bath in the pink marble tub, slightly startled at seeing my reflection in the ceiling. I puttered with my new cosmetics, admiring the result. From time to time people passed in the hall, and I decided eventually that a good cure for the restlessness which was beginning to grow in me was some work therapy. I suggested to Lily that we help Evelyn in the kitchen. She had finished her ironing and was pressing one of my blouses as expertly as a professional.

"No kitchen work for me, thank you," she said. "I cannot cook, and I have no desire to learn."

"You can't cook, and I hate doing laundry," I joked. "We would make a good team." I realized as I said it that I would miss Lily very much after we parted company.

She dimpled at me. "We're a good team now. Tell Evelyn I'll help serve drinks if she needs me."

I wandered into the living room first. Louise was there, her hat and coat on a chair; she had evidently just returned. She was arranging red roses in a vase on the piano, and taking occa-sional sips from a cocktail glass as she worked.

"Max brought these roses," she said. "Wasn't that sweet of him?"

She indicated someone whom I had not noticed, a man who stepped forward from the window bench for introduction.

Max Bloom was a solid man, very blond, with a friendly smile. His eyes behind shell-rimmed glasses were a warm brown. "Here's a contribution for the bar," he said, holding out a bottle of White Horse.

"I'll take it to the bartender if you wish," I offered. "Louise, Lily says she'll help serve when she's needed."

"Okay; we'll set up bar on the card table. Bela's mixing drinks. Watch out for those cocktails he makes," she warned.

As I passed the door of Doris's room she called to me. "Janice, could you help for a minute?"

Her quarters were the smallest and meanest I had yet seen in the house, hardly large enough to accommodate her furniture. Two narrow windows overlooked the frozen garden below. There was no color, just the drab brown of broadloom-carpeted floor, the faded taupe of old-fashioned velvet drapes at her window. In the corner was an office desk with a typewriter on it.

Her dresser, that unfailing index to a woman's personality, was covered by a white linen scarf on which I noticed a bottle of My Sin perfume (new), some eye lotion with a glass cup, a jar of hormone skin cream, a silver-backed mirror, and a picture of Henri in a plastic frame. The family photograph she had removed from her father's bag was not in evidence.

Doris was wearing a black crepe dress which fastened down the back with dozens of small crepe-covered buttons. It collapsed dispiritedly over her flat bosom, but the white lace collar helped. I had started to button it for her, trying not to touch the pimples on her back, when Henri appeared.

"Let me do that," he said. Doris turned to him with shining eyes.

"I have some Courvoisier," he announced, holding out a bottle just as Max Bloom had done. "It was reposing in my room, waiting for an occasion. Now we shall enjoy it."

He tossed the bottle on Doris's narrow bed and began to button her dress with expert fingers. As he worked he bent and kissed her throat, and Doris shivered visibly. "On another occasion, *chèrie*," he murmured, "we shall have champagne."

I picked up the White Horse and backed out unnoticed.

Evelyn and Bela were in the kitchen. While Bela measured cocktail ingredients Evelyn mixed a cheese spread at the sink. Her checks were pink; she bustled around with the pretty authority of a woman who knows she performs an important domestic function. She knelt to open the oven door, and the fragrance of pastry filled the room. Evelyn rose and said, "A few more minutes and they'll be ready to serve."

My mouth had begun to water. "What are you baking?"

"Hot canapés. Some tiny rolls stuffed with meat."

"I'm sorry I asked!" I groaned. "I don't know whether I can last until they're ready."

"I've got something to fortify you," Bela said. He agitated a two-quart fruit jar, sniffed the concoction, and filled one of the cocktail glasses on the kitchen table.

"Try this," he urged. "Louise has already sampled the first one, so I need someone with a fresh taster. This is my own creation, the Budapest Buzz Bomb."

I accepted the glass and took a drink. One swallow collapsed me into the nearest chair. Bela beamed and blinked. "Potent, isn't it?"

"Potent!" I gasped, tears stinging my eyes. "I'm trying to decide which is the buzz and which is the bomb."

"Darling"—he flourished the mixture—"it works scientifically. First one buzzes gently and then—the explosion!"

"I'm still buzzing gently," Louise announced, coming into the kitchen. Her face was flushed, and her eyes were very bright. She picked up a glass. "Let's try the second version, Bela."

He filled the glass for her, Louise was prepared; she sat down before she drank.

Henri and Doris arrived, and Henri set his bottle on the drainboard. Bela poured cocktails for them and for Max, who appeared in the doorway and was introduced all around. Louise, I noticed, had already finished her second drink. She twirled the glass and drained the last drop in it. She set it down carefully and batted her long lashes with an expression of surprise.

"Hey, Bela," she said loudly, "this is a terrific mixture. I'm beginning to feel all unraveled."

My one drink had muddled me a bit, but Louise was tight. Evelyn sent her a look of reproach as she went to the stove to inspect her pastries again. Louise caught it. "Don't act so outraged," she said defensively. "I need this. In case you don't know it I feel lousy."

Every eye turned toward her. "I went to church today," she announced. "The first time in weeks. I lit a candle for Jarvis. You know why? I couldn't get him out of my mind, lying cold and stiff in the morgue while the rest of us enjoy ourselves."

Her voice rose, and she added melodramatically, "I went to say goodbye to him this afternoon. I can't forget how he looked—white as wax, lying there so lonely, with that big gold ring on his hand. The ring he was so proud of, remember? All he ever got—"

There was a loud crash. Evelyn was standing by the stove, the glass baking dish which had dropped from her nerveless fingers in a shattered mess at her feet.

She didn't see the broken glass or the ruined pastries. She stood staring at Louise, her face frozen in a rictus of horror, eyes wide and blank with shock. Then she became aware that we were all staring. She slumped into the nearest chair and dropped her head into her arms, shuddering.

Chapter Seventeen

Bela was at her side instantly. "What's the matter?" His voice shook with anxiety. "Evelyn! What's wrong?"

It seemed a long time before she raised her head. When she did, her normally candid expression was gone and her face was closed, secret. "I felt dizzy," she said dully. "I must have lost my balance."

She averted her eyes and looked at the floor. "See what I've done!" she wailed. She went on her knees and began picking up the mess. "I'm sorry." She spoke without raising her glance. "That was very clumsy of me."

"It doesn't matter, darling." Bela turned to Louise accusingly. "No wonder she's upset, the way you were raving! Let's have no more of such talk, Louise."

Louise looked sober now. "I'm an idiot," she admitted. "I should have kept my mouth shut. Especially when I was the one who suggested we all should forget this business for today."

Henri had gone to the sink. While this dialogue went on he opened the brandy bottle and poured liquor into a glass. He touched Evelyn's shoulder gently, and she looked up. "Please drink this. It will make you feel better. Someone else can clean the floor."

She rose and took it from him obediently, raised the glass to her lips. "Not in the kitchen, darling," Bela commanded. He steered her toward the door. "You go sit by the fire and relax. I'll finish here. Somebody take this stuff to the other room."

Max Bloom picked up the cocktail tray and glasses while the rest of us straggled after him toward the front of the house. Evelyn sat with her face averted, staring into the fire. She sipped the brandy Henri had given her and shuddered as it went down her throat. Max poured drinks for the rest of us and settled between Evelyn and Louise on the sofa, holding his cocktail. A few seconds later he sat erect suddenly, looking with amazement at the glass in his hand.

"What is this? A delayed-action bomb?"

Louise's laugh was self-conscious. "Bela will be glad to hear that, Max. If a walking distillery like you can feel the first drink, it's a success."

Lily came into the room then wearing lime-green crepe, her black hair twisted coronet fashion around her head, high-heeled green suède pumps on her small feet. Max's eyes widened; I heard him ask Louise if Lily were in show business. Louise shook her head. She was very subdued, but she brightened when he put an arm around her casually and murmured something in a low voice.

Bela arrived with a tray of canapés and asked for a drink. Max poured refills while Lily and Louise passed canapés. We chattered in determined gaiety, trying to ignore the tension following Evelyn's accident. In spite of our efforts conversation was erratic between awkward silences. Our eyes kept returning to the piano, reminder of Jarvis playing Debussy.

Finally Bela took his feet off the coffee table and said, "Let's go to Angelo's. I'm starving."

We all welcomed a chance to get out of the house.

The little café was in a basement. The warm interior smelled of garlic and tomato sauce and strong Italian coffee. Angelo, a tubby man with red cheeks, wore a white apron over his round belly. As we stumbled in, stamping snow off our feet and breathing warmth gratefully, he started toward the door with a perfunctory smile of welcome. Then he saw Bela.

He rushed forward, engulfed him in a huge embrace, and pounded enthusiastically on his back while they greeted each other simultaneously in Italian. Bela introduced us by waving a hand and declaring that we were all his dear friends and wanted a fine dinner to celebrate Doris and Henri's engagement. He added, grinning, that the engaged couple were our hosts.

Angelo hurried to push three wall tables together, brushing wrinkles from their red-checked cloths. There were only two other people in the room, a man and a girl in a corner with heads together, talking solemnly. Angelo produced breadsticks, chianti, and thick glasses. When he asked what we wanted to eat Bela suggested he bring us his best dinner, and he bustled back to the kitchen to give orders.

Bela picked up the wine bottle and began filling glasses. "Let's have a good Italian toast, Louise," he said. She hesitated, then raised her drink and murmured a toast which we all tried to repeat.

Max leaned forward. "So you're Italian, eh? What's your real name, sweetie? You've never told me."

Louise looked uncomfortable. "Surely you've seen the papers?"

"Nope. Never read anything but the *Racing Form* and *Variety.*"

"My name is Canelli," she told him. "Louisa Canelli."

"Suits you better than Kane. You shouldn't have changed it."

Relief suffused her face; she started to say something, then patted Max's hand instead. Bela demanded our approval of the murals he had done in the cafe—voluptuous barefooted women carrying baskets of grapes, dark-haired men making wine. The colors were bold, the people looked earthy and alive. He explained that he had once lived in Italy and had painted these scenes from memory. I liked them much better than the tired old cab horses.

Whether it was the wine or the atmosphere or her recent admission of identity to Max I didn't know, but Louise's mood changed. She relaxed, like a girl come home after long exile among strangers. She chattered with Angelo, evidently asking questions about his business, his family. I couldn't understand what they said, but his eyebrows, his shoulders, his waving hands indicated that the family was wonderful but business stank.

Louise explained. "The public doesn't seem to know he has opened this place."

Angelo shrugged. "Pretty soon I thinka they find me, maybe. Tonight we don' care. Is short life. Hava fun now."

He went to a battered piano and started to thump "Finiculi-Finiculà" with many wrong notes and much enthusiasm.

Max turned to Louise. "Can you sing?"

"A little."

"Why don't you join him?"

"Okay, I will."

She walked to the piano and asked a question, at which Angelo nodded and played soft chords. Louise began to sing Toselli's "Serenade." Her voice was contralto, surprisingly rich for a girl of such small stature. By the way she sang it was evident that she loved her language and the sentiment of the song. We applauded wildly when they finished.

The couple in the corner stopped talking to listen, and the man pantomimed a request for more wine. Our host went to the kitchen, stopping on the way to plug in a jukebox which contained nothing but folk music. He returned presently with more wine and a huge tray piled with food. As he served, he bellowed Italian songs in a hearty bass voice, insisting between solos that we must eat, we must drinka plenty, drinka plenty. More customers came down the stairs; they had heard music from the street and wandered in out of curiosity. Angelo welcomed them, his face pink with pleasure, moist dark eyes shining.

I glanced around our group. Henri and Doris sat close together holding hands. Evelyn's head had drooped on Bela's shoulder; she looked pale and subdued. Lily sat at the end of the table smoking and sipping wine; we exchanged slightly rueful smiles at our escortless state. Louise was singing softly to herself while Max Bloom watched her. His gaze was fixed, as if he were trying to listen to her voice and concentrate at the same time on some new, still nebulous idea which refused to materialize.

We drank a lot of Angelo's good red wine. The balance of the evening became a blur of laughter, music, and conversations where everyone talked at once and no one listened to what the other said. When a lively polka began, we danced. Presently I found myself hopping enthusiastically with a red-haired man I'd never met before and whom I've not seen since.

At two o'clock we went home, traveling in two taxis. By that time I was so groggy that I don't remember who rode with whom. My face felt hot, and I had begun to get an uncomfortable burning in my throat.

I remember that after we reached the house we separated and went to our rooms and that Lily and I undressed without speaking to each other. I didn't know whether she was as dizzy as I, because I saw her only through a haze. She moved in a sort of slow-motion effect, and after she got her dress over her head and her slippers kicked off onto the floor she murmured something under her breath and crawled into bed still wearing the rest of her clothes.

"Shame on you!" I said with a giggle. "You're drank! I mean, you're drunk!" She didn't seem to hear me. Maybe I hadn't said it aloud, but only thought it.

I told myself solemnly that I wasn't going to sleep in all my underwear like she was doing, and although the room swam around me, I managed to get into my nightgown. Then I discovered I was still wearing a girdle and my shoes and stockings. I couldn't kick my shoes off, and bent toward my feet.

That did it.

I managed to pull myself erect by holding onto the bed, then I staggered into the bathroom and was thoroughly, devastatingly sick. I had just enough sense left to wash my face with cold water, close the bathroom door and slip the lock into place, turn the key in the hall door, and open a window. Then I collapsed onto the bed.

I don't know how much later it was that I awakened with a feeling that my body was one lump of ice. I had been sleeping without covers, and frigid air from the open window was crawling around me. The light was still on, and I lay staring at the painted ceiling, my mouth thick and brown-tasting, my head throbbing as if someone were beating it with a mallet. Maybe this awful pounding awakened me, I thought dully.

Then I heard the sound.

It came from the dressing-room door. I managed to move my head enough to look in that direction. The knob was turning. The door creaked slightly, as if someone on the other side were trying to force it—someone who did not know about the new lock and thought the door was stuck.

I called cautiously to Lily. She didn't stir, although the light shone directly on her face. She lay limp as a doll, her eyes closed.

"Lily!" No response. "Wake up!" I whispered. "There's someone trying to get into our room!"

Lily lay inert as a corpse. I broke into a sweat which turned to ice along my ribs. I had taken for granted that she would respond when I called. I slipped from bed and shook her, gently at first, then as hard as I could. My shaking moved her light body, but she did not respond. I bent over her, listening to the slow heartbeat, the labored breath of unconsciousness. It was only then that I realized Lily would not awaken.

Fear rose to suffocate me, and my heart began to pound violently. I had been so certain of seeing her eyes open, of hearing her whispered response. No use counting on that now. I was alone—nobody to help, to share my panic. I got under the covers of my own bed and lay there trembling.

There was a sound from the other side of the door which led to the hall way. I sat up, clutching blankets, and stared as if I could will that door to petrify in its frame.

The knob began to turn. Slowly. Quietly. The door creaked. Then the key started to move from the lock with tiny jerks. I watched, choking with terror, as it gradually loosened and dropped to the carpeted floor without a sound other than a faint clink as it slipped from the lock.

Someone on the other side of that door was determined to enter our room. If he knew Lily was unconscious and I was helplessly alone he would come in. My only chance of keeping him out was to convince him that both Lily and I were awake. I switched on the radio.

As I waited for it to warm up I said loudly, "Hand me those cigarettes, will you, Lily?"

Music blared into the room, the most blessed sound I had ever heard. The Milkman's Matinee. I laughed hysterically and began to babble, praying that my voice would sound like that of a woman making remarks to another and getting answers. All the while my eyes never moved from that door.

I never did hear the footsteps retreating. But, although I watched until my eyeballs ached, the knob did not turn again. After a while I got enough courage to get up and brace a chair under the doorknob. I closed the window and went back to bed. Then I lay there, alternately sweating and shaking, listening to the Milkman's Matinee until welcome daylight streaked across the sky.

Chapter Eighteen

Eventually I slept, and when I awoke it was eleven o'clock. The radio was still on; what irritated me into consciousness was the insanely repetitious squawk of a commercial.

"Silkee, it's so smoooth! Silkee, it's so soooft! Silkee, it's so sooothing! Silkee for that Silkee skin! Buy a jar of Silkee today from your nearest—"

I switched it off and lay supine, my eyes turned toward the windows where I had watched daybreak appear some weary hours before. My head ached, there was a bitter taste in my mouth, and I slumped in dull misery. There was a strange feeling of motion somewhere; gradually my vision sharpened, and I perceived that the world outside was a mass of whirling white. Snow. It filled the air, huge feathery flakes fluttered past the window, shutting the house in like an animate, impenetrable curtain. I hated it. I wished I were a million miles away from this frigid world, from this house which had become loathsome as a prison.

My mind cleared then, as I remembered why the house was inimical. Not the house, really. Some human being in it was the enemy. Last night, while we were supposed to be enjoying the first pleasant companionship we had shared since Lily and I came to live here, someone put knockout drops in our cup of cheer. That was irony for you.

I tried to wet my dry lips with a dry tongue and closed my eyes to think better. That made the throbbing in my head more painful. I opened my eyes and stared at the window, at the snow which filled the world outside.

How were we drugged, and when? I went back over the evening. Lily had not taken a cocktail before dinner. She drank wine at Angelo's. Then it must have been put in the wine. There had been opportunity enough, since each of us left the table occasionally. Any person in our group could have done it.

So we came home and went innocently to bed, and if I had not upchucked my share I would have slept as heavily as Lily while our unknown visitor entered. Entered for what purpose? Lily's jewels? She kept them in an unlocked dressing case, and it would be easy for a thief to find them during the day when we were out. To attack Lily again? Not again, for the man who had previously attacked her was now dead. Some person wanted entrance to our room for a purpose which required longer than a few minutes to accomplish.

I sat up in bed and called Lily. No answer. I spoke several times, then went over and shook her as I had done hours before. She stirred and made a faint sound, but she did not waken. I opened the window and scooped a handful of snow from the ledge, wrapped it in a handkerchief, and laid it on her head. I bent over her.

"Lily! Wake up! Lily!"

"Yes?" Her heavy lids raised, fell. "What is it?" She opened her eyes, regarding me blankly. "My head." She was apologetic about it.

"Lily, listen to me. You've slept long enough. Wake up!" I shook her again. I knew how painful it must be, for my own head was aching abominably, but I kept on shaking.

My urgency penetrated and she said, her voice no longer blurred, "I'm awake. What is it?"

I leaned over her. "Someone drugged us last night." My voice was bitter. "Then they tried to get into our room."

She lay very still, and I could almost see awareness being summoned back by sheer effort of will. She brushed the wet handkerchief to the floor, raised on her elbow, and looked at me.

"So." She said it flatly. "Tell me."

I told her what had happened. When I finished she got out of bed, glancing down at the satin slip she wore with faint surprise. She stood looking around the room, her eyes resting briefly on the door with the chair propped under the knob, the key on the floor beneath it. She picked up the scarlet kimono, took a bottle from the dressing-table drawer, and headed for the bathroom. I followed.

We washed our faces with cold water, and I winced as I bent over the basin. Lily must have felt worse pain than I, but no sign of it showed on her stoic face. She poured some small white tablets from the bottle and swallowed two.

"What is that?"

"Benzedrine. You'd better take one, Janice. We'll need clear heads to day."

I swallowed one.

The bathroom was steamy and smelled of Louise's bath salts. That meant she was feeling all right or she wouldn't have had the energy to perform her morning ritual. Doris's and Evelyn's toothbrushes were wet. They were awake and active too.

Back in our room Lily voiced my previous thoughts. "We were the only ones who were drugged." She lit a cigarette, made a wry face at its taste, and put it out. She said, "It is fortunate that you were sick last night."

"I realize that. Lily, who wants to get in here? Do you know?"

She had been pacing the floor. Now she stopped, seated herself with feet tucked under, assuming, perhaps unconsciously, the pose of that unforgettable Kwan Yin who sits remote, aloof, eyes fixed on the lotus held in her upturned palm. Finally she said very slowly, "I believe I know who was at our door." Her dark eyes raised to meet mine. "The murderer."

"You mean that Jarvis didn't—" I broke off, realizing with something like relief that even while I made this token inquiry I wasn't actually surprised.

Lily continued thinking aloud. "When we discussed Jarvis's death we were both trying to convince ourselves; I felt certain he was incapable either of homicide or suicide, yet the evidence was so convincing that for a while I tried to accept it. Later I found it unacceptable."

"Then you believe Jarvis was murdered too. Who killed him?"

"The same one who tried to get into our room. It must have been either Henri or Bela. The day Jarvis died everyone else was out of the house for several hours, while the two men remained here. They have several things in common: both are Europeans and both had opportunity, yet neither has apparent motive."

"But, Lily, while we were all together here we heard Jarvis upstairs playing those records. The music began after we started our bridge game, and at that time Henri was across the table from me. He never left the room until he went up and found Jarvis's body. As for Bela—"

"Bela was on the third floor. He could have come quietly down the stairs during your game. I'm thinking of that. But none of this conjecture fits so far. It takes more than a few minutes for a person to die from an overdose of barbiturates. Their effect is slow, gradual, progressing from sleep to deep sleep, to coma, then death. Let's not go into that angle now. I'm convinced that Jarvis was murdered; how it was done I don't know."

"But you think one of these men killed Jarvis because he discovered something in that scrapbook."

"Yes. Jarvis was not subtle; he was incapable of disguising his feelings. He would have done such an impulsive thing as run direct to the guilty one to accuse him. Possibly even to congratulate him. Remember Jarvis hated the dead man and said he deserved to be killed."

I tried to imagine the scene: Jarvis almost uncontrollably excited, the other, quaking inside with rage and terror, outwardly calm. "Jarvis, promise me you won't say anything until you've heard the whole story. Let's have a couple of drinks while I tell you all about it."

Business of mixing highballs. Very strong for Jarvis, who gulped liquor. Potent with barbiturates for Jarvis, who must be silenced. The detailed, highly dramatized narration, illustrated with pawn tickets, a scribbled note, a wallet. Lengthy explanations for an audience growing inattentive, whose responses thickened as perception gradually dulled, whose eyes finally closed. Relief. The terrible relief. Then action. The evidence cunningly planted, the second glass removed. Fingerprints erased, Jarvis's limp hand pressed on the objects police were to find. The records selected carefully and stacked on the player. The stealthy exit, while Jarvis sat slumped in listening attitude. Not listening.

But the drug took some time to kill a man. Those records would have played for an hour, not longer. By that time Jarvis was unconscious; he could never have started the player mechanism. I made an exclamation.

"Lily, I know how the records could have been played! And with no one in the room!"

"Tell me."

"Have you ever seen a Radio Owl?" As she shook her head I went on excitedly. "I saw one once; you can buy them in record shops. It's a mechanism which works by electricity, and you can set it to turn on your radio or turn it off at a certain time. Those records could have been put on the machine hours ahead of time and the Owl set to turn them on just when we heard them begin. I'm pretty sure that if the automatic business works for radios it would also work for record players."

"Did Jarvis have one?"

"I don't know. I was in his room just a short while, and I don't remember seeing one. But whoever killed him could have had one, and removed it before we came in. Either Bela could have come down the stairs while the music was so loud and we were playing cards and taken the thing away—or even Henri could have removed it when he went up and found Jarvis dead."

What clever histrionics had followed that discovery, no doubt made even easier by release from prolonged strain. Was it Bela, whose hands trembled, whose voice shook with rage as he commanded a dead man to turn off his music? Or Henri, reluctant to go to Jarvis's room, who looked sick with shock at discovery of his body?

What had Jarvis discovered?

"Lily," I said, "I saw the page Jarvis marked. It was nothing but a picture of him and his mother."

"So you said before. That was one of the things which puzzled me. Think, Janice, of Jarvis's narcissistic nature. Don't you realize he must have looked at that particular picture many times? Why should he be suddenly excited at seeing it again?"

I digested this. Finally I said, "You may be right. But it fooled me. Even chocolate on the page."

"The murderer is clever. And careful. He found the scrapbook—of course Jarvis told him about it—turned down a different page, and marked it with chocolate. Now the police have reached the conclusion he intended them to reach, and the way is clear for him to act. Last night, the first night there was no police guard in the house, he tried again."

"Lily do you know what he wants?"

Her black eyes regarded me obliquely from a face pale as ivory. She was measuring me, calculating how much she dared tell. Then she said thought fully, "I think I know. I believe that the tortured man told him where to find it. Hidden here. Somewhere in this room."

She jumped to her feet. "Mr. Chadwick was in the dressing room. We'll start there. Let's get these clothes out."

After we piled our clothes on the two beds we started examining the walls, working from the door back toward the end of the narrow space, taking opposite sides. Each satin-covered rectangle was held in place by the frame of the wooden panel adjoining it. We pounded on the wood, pried around the frames. We found nothing until we reached the end of the room. On the bathroom side a panel which normally was covered by clothes hanging there sounded hollow.

"Get the screwdriver," Lily said.

I found it and handed it to her. She knelt and put the steel tip under the frame of the panel, prying gently. It opened like a small door, and we peered into the darkened space which was disclosed.

Someone entered the bathroom and turned a lavatory tap. We crouched, not daring to move. It seemed an hour before we heard water gurgling down pipes, then footsteps across the floor, and sound of the door closing.

Lily whispered, "There's a flashlight in the bureau drawer." When the beam of light was directed into that darkness we both leaned forward eagerly. This space had been left when the bathroom was installed to enable a plumber to reach the pipes of the pink marble tub. We saw copper pipes and dust, some dry crumbs of mortar and raw bricks which formed the wall of the hallway. The dust had not been disturbed. Lily reached inside and painstakingly felt every inch of space. She turned the light on every angle of that hidden compartment.

There was nothing more.

We exchanged a look of disappointment, then Lily shut the door and rose from her knees. We hung our clothes back without comment. For the first time since I had known her Lily made no effort to conceal emotion. She had been very tense during our search; now she flung herself face down on her bed in an attitude of utter dejection. For a moment I thought she was going to cry.

I sat on my bed opposite, feeling awkward, not knowing what to say to comfort her. I wanted a cigarette and some coffee, for, although the benzedrine had helped and I could move now without feeling that my veins were filled with lead, my head still ached.

Lily wasn't crying; she lay completely still. After a while I said, hoping to distract her, "It could be Bela. The night we arrived he took a long time answering the bell. He could have been the one who peered out the window."

I stopped and dug back in my memory. "But Doris said she and Henri had just started to work. That probably meant she had just gone up to his room. If he had been in the basement he might prefer not to answer the door. Either man had opportunity to get down to the furnace room that night, for Henri was alone and Evelyn admits she left Bela an hour before Doris awakened her. Maybe that's why she has looked so worried ever since then. Maybe Evelyn knows something she hasn't told. That could explain her peculiar behavior last night."

Lily raised her head. "What do you mean, Janice? She didn't act so strangely. She was depressed, of course, but Evelyn has been depressed for days."

"You weren't there, Lily. It was before you joined the party. We were in the kitchen, and Louise had had too much to drink, and she'd been jittery all day anyhow. She started talking about Jarvis—how she went to the morgue to say goodbye to him, and—"

Lily sat up straight. "And Evelyn reacted strangely to that?"

"She certainly did. She dropped a glass baking dish and it smashed on the floor. Then she threw a nervous fit."

Lily traced a pattern on the carpet with her slippered foot.

"Rather a delayed reaction to Jarvis's death, wasn't it? Or a second reaction, actually. She cried very hard when she heard of it the day before. Or had Evelyn been drinking too?"

"No. It was the way Louise said it, I guess. Remember we didn't see Jarvis close up as we saw the other man. So we couldn't visualize what he looked like. But Louise described him so graphically—she talked about how waxen he looked, lying on that slab in the morgue—" I stopped, hating to remember.

"Go on."

"Oh, she talked very sentimentally about that gold ring he wore—how pitiful it seemed to see him lying there with the ring on his hand, the only symbol of recognition he ever possessed."

Lily's foot stopped moving. She said quickly, "And at that point Evelyn dropped the dish?"

"Yes."

The Chinese girl stood up abruptly and went to the dressing room. "There's no time to waste. We must talk to Evelyn."

She shoved clothes aside impatiently until she found a pair of black flannel slacks and a blouse. I followed her example, dressing as quickly as I could. I had acquired some courage with benzedrine, but not enough that I intended to stay alone in that room for even five minutes unless someone tied me. When Lily opened the door I was right with her.

No one was in the kitchen. Coffee cups and toast crumbs indicated that someone had breakfasted there. We each drank a glass of milk from Evelyn's quart container. As we passed Doris's door we heard her typewriter. We went to the next door down the hall and knocked. Louise answered. When we entered we found her sitting in bed with a net on her hair, reading a magazine. I decided to let Lily do the talking. She had no chance for a while. Louise began to chatter immediately.

"Feeling better? Get rid of your hangover? Mine wasn't so bad as I deserved after those cocktails and all that wine. I'm glad you're here so I can spill my wonderful news. Max got the idea last night, and we threshed out part of the details by telephone first thing this morning."

I had never seen Louise so excited. "What news?" I asked.

She laid down her magazine and announced dramatically, "Max has figured out an angle that may get me to Hollywood!"

You can't, I thought. You're smart and determined, and you may have talent—but you can't. That's too much even for you to attempt.

Louise rattled on, practically reading my mind. "The only thing wrong now is my teeth, and I'm going to have them fixed right away."

"Fixed?" It takes years for good orthodontia.

"I'm getting these crooked uppers extracted and a permanent bridge made. I'm photogenic, you know, and Max says my voice records are swell, so once I get the teeth changed I'll be set."

She was actually delighted at the prospect of such torture. Electrolysis. Artificial eyelashes. Voice culture. Dancing lessons. Now false teeth. What willpower!

"Isn't it funny?" she said. "I might have beat my brains out for years as Louise Kane and never got a break. Just because Max found out my real name and that I speak good Italian—" She clasped her hands together like a child awed by his first Christmas tree.

"What does Italian have to do with it?"

"I'm going to work in an Italian picture. There's a little company in San Remo on the Riviera that's making pretty good films now, and they're being released here. Max can get me in because his cousin owns part of the company; Max has been handling local publicity for him. After I've done a couple of parts he's going to start giving me a buildup—new dramatic discovery, you know. Like Valli—did you see her in that film at the Roxy? Only I'm not going to use just one name. We've thought of a wonderful name for me. Fiore. Luisa Fiore—that means flower." She giggled. "Know where we got it? From Max's last name, Bloom. Isn't that terrific?"

Lily and I agreed that it was indeed. Louise waved her hands impatiently. "First I have to get these damned teeth out. That'll take a little time."

"I hope you don't have them out immediately," Lily said.

"Next week. Why?"

"I am giving a party tomorrow night and should be very disappointed if you could not come."

Louise looked interested. "What kind of party? I hope it's in Chinatown."

"It will be in Chinatown. Tomorrow is the eve of Chinese New Year. To my people it is a very important day. We entertain our friends at dinner while we wait for midnight and the Dragon."

This was the first I'd heard of any New Year party, and I concluded that Lily must have decided on this invitation very suddenly. I had not remembered the date of Chinese New Year, but I knew Chinese well enough to be aware that they entertain only family and closest friends on such an important occasion. Lily was making everyone in the house a close friend on very short notice.

"That sounds marvelous," Louise said. "Can I ask Max?"

"Please do." Lily glanced around the room, as if missing Louise's roommate for the first time. "Where is Evelyn? I should like to invite her also."

"She's at school. She'll be home about three. I'll tell her when she comes in."

We chattered for a while longer and then made our exit. We stopped at Doris's room to invite her, and Doris accepted, looking faintly dubious at mention of Chinatown. When we were alone again Lily dropped her languid pose and began to pace the floor. Such nervousness wasn't in character for her, and I found it contagious. After a while I said uneasily, "Don't worry so much, Lily. Evelyn will be home soon, and you can talk to her then."

Lily stopped in the center of the floor. "I hope so. I hope that nothing happens to her."

"What do you mean?"

She sighed. With an obvious effort to maintain patience she said, "Didn't it occur to you last night when Evelyn reacted so strongly to Louise's description of Jarvis?"

I chewed my new manicure, puzzled. "Didn't what occur to me?"

"Such reaction indicates one thing: it is possible that Evelyn knows the identity of the murderer."

Chapter Nineteen

"How could Evelyn know?" I asked.

"I'm guessing now," Lily admitted. "But it is possible that Evelyn caught a glimpse of the man she spoke with in the basement. Keep in mind that she is an artist, trained to observe and remember details of form and color of which the average observer is seldom even aware. At the time she talked to him she stood part of the way down the stairs, and presumably he was directly at her feet."

She sat in a chair and cupped her eyes with her palms.

"What are you doing?"

"Remembering the stairs." She was silent for a while. Then, "What part of him, or how much of him, could Evelyn have seen? It has something to do, possibly, with the ring Jarvis wore. His right hand. Big gold ring on his right hand. Now if he stood with that hand on the stair railing while he spoke to Evelyn..."

She uncovered her eyes and looked at me. "If Evelyn saw his hand, if she remembered suddenly that the hand she saw did not wear a ring, she would know that Jarvis was not the man she talked to. If she saw something else—" Lily shook her head impatiently. "Who was in the kitchen when Evelyn had the accident?"

I concentrated, trying to bring the scene back. "Why—all of us except you. Max stood in the doorway. Evelyn was at the stove. Bela was making cocktails. Henri and Doris were near the sink, and Louise sat at the table." I described the tableau as well as I could remember it.

"What was the general reaction?"

"Bela was worried over Evelyn and very annoyed with Louise. Doris stood and gaped. Henri gave Evelyn a drink. Then Bela shooed us all out of the kitchen and finished the canapés himself."

"That's a good description, but it doesn't tell much." She stood up, suddenly reaching a decision. "Janice, I'm going upstairs. Are you willing to do some snooping with me?"

"Of course."

We met Henri on the stairs. He was wearing a shabby topcoat, with a gray woolen scarf around his throat, and a gray hat. "Did you wish to see me?" he asked politely. Lily told him about the Chinese New Year party and said that she intended to invite Bela also.

"He is not here," Henri informed us. "The new superintendent came to work this morning, so Bela is celebrating his freedom by spending the day in art galleries. Some friend of his is having a show this week. Bela declared that he intended to walk from here up to Fifty-seventh Street."

"In this weather?" I was incredulous.

Henri pulled on gray woolen gloves which matched his scarf. "He is quite mad, that one. He said he has been confined too long here by the hunger of that furnace, and would escape today if he had to walk through a blizzard."

We didn't ask Henri where he was going, but he told us anyhow, looking pleased. He had a date with a magazine editor to discuss possible serialization of his book. He followed us as we turned back down the stairs. When he opened the front door a wave of frigid air rushed in, and he closed it hurriedly behind him. We watched his tall figure bending into the wind as he headed toward Fifth Avenue. Then we started up the stairs again.

We went to Bela's studio first. The door wasn't locked, but there was a chain lock on the inside, and we fastened that before we began to search the room. It was a mess. Bureau drawers opened with difficulty because of the manner in which their contents had been rammed into them. Two drawers contained articles of clothing: socks, shirts, underwear, handkerchiefs, all tossed together. The top drawer contained a miscegenation of articles: half empty tobacco sacks, crumpled letters, theater programs, a few sketches, three bank statements which had not been opened, silver coins, and a five-dollar bill. In the small drawer of a deal table we found a bunch of papers. I helped Lily look through them, feeling very guilty.

"Now I know what it's like to be a thief," I muttered.

Lily glanced sidewise at me. "Don't be silly. You know why this is necessary."

I knew. We were looking for evidence which would either indicate a guilty man or absolve him from suspicion.

We found a few things of interest. One was a clipping from a San Francisco newspaper, a picture of a fortyish blond woman in a silver-fox jacket stepping off a transcontinental plane. She had an enameled, predatory face.

Her name was Madeleine Baldwin-Ferris-Carlake-Palyi, the aluminum heiress, and she had just obtained a decree of divorce from Bela Palyi on grounds of desertion. The date was almost a year ago.

There was also an envelope stuffed with bills marked "please remit," "overdue," "final notice," and so forth. We didn't read them carefully. I knew Lily must be remembering, as I was, that Bela had bragged of the large amount of money he made from his work.

If he lied about one thing he would lie about another. I wondered if Evelyn knew about the blonde in silver fox.

We descended to the next floor very cautiously, because Louise was talking on the telephone at the foot of the lower stairs. Henri's door was also open; it was not the custom in this house to use locks. There was a key on the other side, and we turned it to guard against interruption. We worked very fast this time, and I found my heart going like a rusty clock as I searched.

Doris's fiancé lived in a manner which was a marked contrast to Bela's disordered existence. Every drawer was meticulously neat. I was surprised to discover that under his shabby outer garments Henri gratified sybaritic tastes. His underwear was of heavy silk in pastel shades, monogrammed H. L. His satin pajamas were custom tailored, also monogrammed. His ties and shirts and socks were few and of cheap materials. Puzzling and inconsistent. I thought of the expertness with which he had fastened Doris's dress, remembered his mouth pressed to her throat. Possibly Doris knew of this hidden dual nature of his and reveled in it. Maybe she had given him the fancy underwear and pajamas. Men love to give women expensive lingerie—why not the reverse?

His desk held a thick manuscript which had been written with a French typewriter equipped with the cedilla and necessary accent marks.

Les Maquis Sant Partout, par Alain Duvivier. The folder which contained it was stamped with the name of a literary agency on Madison Avenue, probably the office where Henri worked. I puzzled over this, and then decided that perhaps he thought in French, so he had to write in that language and then translate his own work. The name Duvivier might be a nom de plume. In the bottom drawer, under some copy paper, was a leather correspondence folder. When Lily opened it a passport spilled out.

Henri Ledoux, aged thirty-eight, born in Paris, and much more information which I did not try to translate. It was visaed for Portugal and South America, the usual route for many émigrés from France. Lily scanned it, studying every word. While she was reading I opened a soiled white envelope which was under the passport. I gasped as the contents slid into my hands, and could feel a warm red rising from my throat. Involuntarily I glanced around the room while I extended my find to Lily without a word.

The envelope contained a remarkable assortment of what I had often heard jokes about but had never seen—French pornographic post cards, all photographs of living models. In a few seconds I got an education which years of formal schooling had never given me. Lily's face was blank as she fanned the cards out; she examined their backs and then put them in the envelope and returned the leather folder and its contents to the drawer.

Another door in Henri's room led to a bathroom which he had evidently shared with Jarvis. The door to Jarvis's room was locked, but the key was in place; we turned it and went into Jarvis's sleeping quarters. Lily didn't stop to examine anything there; she went directly to the sitting room, and I followed. The scrapbook lay on the table by the window where I had last seen it. The book opened to a page which had a corner folded, and Lily looked briefly at the picture of Jarvis and his mother. Then she laid the book flat, started at the front, and turned pages slowly. About a third of the way through she stopped.

"A page has been torn from here."

I bent over the book and saw that where the pages were bound together there were some tiny shreds of paper, not noticeable in the binding unless one were looking for them. On the opened page, where Jarvis's finger might have touched, was a barely discernible indentation, running at an angle. His finger nail could have made just such a mark when he folded the corner of the missing page and ran a finger along the fold.

"But there's no chocolate mark," I said.

Lily held up the book, then laid it flat again and carefully removed one of the shreds of paper from the binding. It separated when it lay on the table; two pages had been torn out. "The chocolate-marked page was removed," Lily said.

The date of the marked page was April 16, 1936, the date before that was April 12, the one following was April 19. Some time, then, between April 12 and April 16, a news story had appeared which might point the finger to a murderer in this house. Lily and I looked at each other and nodded. She closed the book, and we retraced our steps. After we got out of Henri's room we fled to the lower floor.

I flopped into a chair in our room, panting for breath. When the pounding of my heart had subsided a little I said, "Lily, do you think we should call the police and tell them?"

"Tell them what?"

"Oh—" I gestured vaguely. That Bela didn't pay his bills? That he had been married to a rich woman who divorced him almost a year ago? That Henri wore silk underwear and collected erotic pictures? The prospect of revealing these intimate things about the two men made my face feel hot again. When it came to telling them to a man like Captain Weber I'd feel a fool and worse. But the scrapbook was something else. "At least we ought to tell Weber about the missing page," I suggested.

Lily answered with scorn. "Do you think he is the kind of person who will welcome that evidence from us? Perhaps he has already noted it. If he has not, how are you going to explain that we decided to search the rooms? That is equivalent to saying that you consider him incompetent."

"We could tell him everything that has happened," I said lamely, realizing, as I spoke, that confiding in Captain Weber was the last thing I felt like doing. I didn't want that hard, inquisitorial stare turned on me; I didn't relish the prospect of squirming under the kind of treatment he had given Louise. I looked at Lily. She was standing by the window, looking out at the snow which now drifted lazily past the glass. She turned around and said, "We can discuss the police later. Janice, please go and see whether Evelyn is home yet. I am worried about her."

Louise was lying across her bed with some sort of grayish beauty clay on her face. It was half dried. She said, a trifle crossly, that Evelyn wasn't home and had not called. I apologized for intruding and retreated to report this information to Lily

"What time is it?" Lily asked.

"Quarter of three. Lily, do you realize we haven't had any food? I'm not hungry, but I think we should eat something."

Lily nodded absently. She was putting on her galoshes. "I am going to that school to see Evelyn."

I reached for my own outer garments. "I'll go along. We can get a sandwich while we're out."

We trudged silently across Washington Square Park, which was deserted on this snowy day except for a few people huddled into heavy coats waiting for the Fifth Avenue bus at the end of the line. The settlement school where Evelyn taught was several blocks away. When we reached it the clock in the reception room said three. The warm building was noisy. Somewhere a piano was playing, children were singing in a nearby room, and from the small office near the entrance came the sound of a typewriter tapping rapidly. A pretty Black girl in blouse and skirt looked up from her desk as we entered. She had been transcribing a letter from the shorthand notebook beside her.

"How do you do?" she said pleasantly. "Can I help you?"

"We're friends of Evelyn Sayre," Lily said. "We stopped by to see if she's finished for the day."

The girl put her hand to her mouth in dismay. "Oh, I'm so sorry. She asked me to leave a message at her house, and I've been so busy that I forgot. Evelyn tried to call before she left, but the line was busy and she was in a hurry."

Louise, no doubt, discussing her wonderful future with Max.

"It doesn't matter," Lily said. "You can give us the message now."

"I have it somewhere." The girl rummaged among papers on her desk. "I know it's here, because I took the call. Evelyn was teaching a class when it came, and I wrote it down carefully because it was long-distance."

Long-distance? I began to get a sinking feeling. I glanced at Lily. She was watching the girl at the desk.

"Here it is!" the girl said with relief. "I knew I had it. A Mr. Hodges of the Valley Realty Company telephoned from Warwick. Some people who want to buy Evelyn's property are there, and he asked her to come up to Warwick this afternoon to discuss the inventory. Evelyn was to meet them at her house at four-thirty." She handed the paper to Lily and added, "Evelyn was so pleased. She's been trying to sell that old house for a long time."

"When did she leave?

"Right after she finished class—about two-thirty. She went directly to the bus station."

We thanked her, and Lily pocketed the note. We hurried down the street to the nearest public telephone. It was in a grimy little drugstore on the corner. While Lily dialed the operator I ordered hot chocolate for both of us. The apathetic proprietor set two steaming cups before me on the marble counter as Lily returned. We waited until he went back to the other side of the store, but I didn't need Lily's comment to confirm what I had already guessed.

"The Valley Realty Company is owned by a Mr. Johnson. There is no one named Hodges in his office."

The smell of hot chocolate was nauseating. I looked at my cup with revulsion. "What do we do now?" I asked in a low voice.

"We wait. I made another call. There will be a car here for us soon. Try to drink that, Janice. We're going to make a trip this afternoon."

She lifted her cup, and I followed her example, managing to swallow a few times. "Warwick is about fifty miles from here," Lily said between sips. "On the Greenwood Lake route. Evelyn may be halfway there now, since busses run frequently."

We both looked toward the street as a car crunched to a stop in front of the store, a black Kaiser sedan, sleek and powerful-looking. Lily slipped down from her stool, leaving me to pay the check. When I reached the car I found that the Chinese boy who had delivered it was sitting in the front seat talking to Lily. She beckoned to me, and I opened the door and slid in beside her. They went on talking; it was a furious argument in shrill, staccato Chinese of which I understood not one syllable. The boy glanced at me and said something to which Lily replied sharply. I gathered that he wanted to go with us and she was refusing.

Finally he shrugged and said surprisingly, "Okay, toots, have it your own way. But I still think you're nuts."

He reached into his overcoat pocket for a package which he laid in Lily's lap. "Here's what you asked for. Take care of yourself."

He got out of the car and said, his hand on the door, "I'll be in my office all afternoon, so call if you need me." He stalked away without a backward glance, overcoat flapping around his tall figure.

Lily moved into his seat behind the steering wheel and pressed the starter. The big car moved away from the curb. "Who is that boy?" I asked.

"He's not exactly a boy; he's a practicing attorney. That is my cousin Liu Char. His American name is Bill."

"Char? Then Mr. Char really is—"

"Yes, Janice. He really is my uncle. I didn't tell you before because you obviously enjoyed so much thinking of me as his mistress. Mr. Char's wife was my mother's sister. She is dead now. It is her fur coat and her jewelry which I wear."

I was so disconcerted that I said nothing. I settled down into the seat of the car, and the package on Lily's lap slid to the floor with a thump as I moved. "Pick it up for me, will you?" she asked, and I reached down obediently.

Lily didn't have to tell me what the package contained. I could feel the ominous, cold steel outline of the gun through the paper.

Chapter Twenty

We crawled through city traffic toward the ramp which led up to the West Side Highway. Lily drove effortlessly, shifting gears without hesitation, and she seemed deep in concentration. The sedan was warm, the windshield wipers clicked rhythmically, brushing away flakes of snow. We rolled along the deserted highway at fifty miles an hour, like a big black house on wheels.

It wasn't until we had crossed the George Washington Bridge and turned right on another highway that I said, "Don't you think at this point that we should have called the police?"

Lily answered without turning. "Because of a hunch? By the time we waited for them to arrive and made necessary explanations, persuaded them that we were right—it might be too late."

I didn't ask what it would be too late for. I preferred not to think about that. I said, "What will we do when we find Evelyn—if we find her?"

"Bring her back with us. Discover what she knows. If she saw something which identified the man to her we must persuade her to tell. She is in danger as long as she keeps that knowledge to herself."

"Why do you think she hasn't told anyone?"

"She would want to be absolutely certain first. That is the way her mind works. I'm guessing that she intended to verify her discovery when she returned from school today. But, you see, she has not returned."

We were in the country. That's the amazing thing about New York. You can drive off that crowded, supercivilized little island into unspoiled rural scenery in half an hour. A frozen river writhed along at the right of the highway, a mountain rose to the left. Roadside stands dotted the route, but most of them were closed, shuttered, and covered with snow. There was little traffic, and as we rode farther from the city houses dwindled in number and we saw fewer cars.

We turned left from the highway onto a mountain road. We traveled slowly over snow-covered asphalt hemmed in by ice-encrusted trees, climbing steadily, making torturous turns at which the big car sometimes skidded in a way which brought my heart into my throat. Just when I thought we would never reach the top we were there. Below us lay a valley dotted with houses. A huge lake glittered to the left, and mountains rose again in the background. We descended in second gear, passed the lake, turned right onto another mountain road, and began to climb again.

"What will we do when we get to Warwick?" I asked.

"Look for Evelyn. We will go to her house."

"Do you know where it is?"

"Yes. I have driven past it once before. Light a cigarette for me, will you?"

I pushed in the lighter, and while I waited for it to heat I reflected that of course Lily would know all about Evelyn's background. She had obtained information about my own house, a continent and an ocean distant from here. It takes money and time to get such accurate information. Well, Mr. Char had money. But why such infinite pains to find out all about the people in the Washington Square house? I asked this question of Lily aloud.

"It was necessary," she told me. "But you are exaggerating my efforts somewhat. I needed information only about the women in order to determine which could be induced to move so I could obtain a room there."

"How did you get the information?"

"Bill did that for me. I told you he is a lawyer; he works with the firm of Kelly and Ames as a junior partner. He hired some investigators. It wasn't difficult."

"Getting your family's chop back was a very serious project for you, wasn't it?"

"Yes," she said soberly. "I cannot exaggerate its seriousness or its importance to all of us. For one thing, my father can now resume his place in the community, reopen his business. He has been working for others since the Chadwick disaster. For years I have seen him struggling to clothe us properly, to educate us. But far worse than our poverty, our exile, has been the damage to his spirit. Loss of face is a tragic thing to a Chinese."

She stubbed out her cigarette in the ashtray on the dashboard. "This is Warwick."

We were on a road heading down toward a village deep in the valley. Once we were out of shelter of the mountain the wind blew in fierce, intermittent gusts against the windows, and the heavy car rocked occasionally, as if shaken by an invisible hand. We skirted the main street, driving through a residential section lined with huge old-fashioned houses set in vast snowy lawns like cakes on beds of icing.

We turned into a narrow country road at the end of the town, and Lily said, "We go about three miles farther." She leaned forward to peer through snow which blew furiously against the windshield. "You look for mailboxes. I must watch the road and the speedometer."

A black object, approaching very fast, loomed suddenly from around a curve. Lily swerved the heavy car to avoid a collision; the other car skidded, righted itself, and passed with a roar and a cloud of snow. We regained the middle of the road with difficulty and crawled on in second gear.

After two miles we stopped at each mailbox. I climbed out, lumbered through deep drifts, and brushed snow away to read the names painted on the sides of the metal boxes. Icy flakes blew inside my collar, my nose began to run, my eyes stung from the wind. Except for the one car which passed us there wasn't a sign of life, only smoke steaming horizontally from a few distant farm chimneys. Even the animals were under shelter in this bitter weather.

Getting out of the car for the sixth time I stumbled and fell against the box marked Sayre. It stood at the entrance to a narrow lane leading through a grove of birch trees. I beckoned to Lily, and she backed the sedan expertly and nosed it onto the lane. As we inched over the bumpy road we saw that another car had recently traversed the same route; at spots where snow had not yet blown over them tire tracks were visible.

Lily was gripping the wheel, leaning forward. She said, tersely, "Unwrap the gun."

I pulled at the paper with sodden gloves, and my teeth wanted to chatter. "I've never used a gun," I said.

"I have," she told me. "Ah, here it is."

I hadn't expected Evelyn's house to be so large. It rose before us in the fading light, an enormous square wooden building with storm-shuttered windows like closed eyes. Lily stopped the car, and we sat in the front seat, waiting.

Nothing happened. There was no sound other than the cracking of icy branches around us and an occasional whoosh of snow against the sedan doors. Lily took off her glove and slid her finger around the handle of the gun, moving the safety catch. "All right," she said.

I didn't want to get out. Neither did I want to stay there alone, giving a murderer opportunity to attack me. I slid across the front seat and under the steering wheel after Lily. She was bending over the road, brushing at surface snow with her left hand.

"Someone has been here recently, possibly the car which passed us. There are two sets of tracks, coming and going. Let's go to the house."

The porch was covered with drifted snow through which one set of footprints led to the front door. I followed Lily as closely as I could, my teeth by now clicking like a telegrapher's keys. The front door swung open at a touch, and we went inside.

We were in a narrow hall. Silence. Emptiness. Cold, bitter, and stale. Then a cracking sound in the next room. We stood rigid in our tracks and waited. The sound was repeated. We moved toward it on tiptoe. The sound came from the fireplace in the living room, where some burning sticks of wood were crumbling. As I saw them, the same anger rose in me which I had felt at sight of the scarred little table in the basement. The wood came from the legs and back of a delicately fashioned maple rocker, the seat of which lay forlorn and useless on the hearth by the fire still wearing the old-fashioned hooked wool cover which had been made for it. The paper for starting the fire had been obtained by tearing out pages from a beautiful old velvet-covered family Bible.

The last of the burning wood cracked and fell in red embers. Whoever destroyed the little chair and the Bible was no longer in the house. We searched it thoroughly from room to room, walking no longer with caution. My teeth had stopped chattering; I lost fear. Anger is a wonderful stimulant.

The house was empty.

We reached the kitchen last. The lock of the rear door was broken, and the door stood wide open. Snow powdered the floor like sugar; the air was so cold that it hadn't melted. We pushed the screen door and went outside, walking toward the barn, a huge empty building which looked as if it might collapse at the next strong gust of wind. Following Lily's gaze, I could see, discernible very faintly under top snow, a set of footprints. We traced them across the ground to the barn, then around the building to a deep gully which lay behind it. There the footprints stopped.

And that was where we found Evelyn.

She was lying in the gully behind the barn. Snow had already drifted over her so that at first glance the mound her body made might have been a rock or a shrub—except for the blue scarf which fluttered in the wind. In a very brief time she would have been completely covered by snow. We floundered down the slope, waist-deep in cold white drifts, to where she lay.

Her arms were bound to her sides, and her feet were tied. We got her out of there by dragging her up the steep incline, then I climbed into the rear of the sedan and pulled Evelyn's shoulders while Lily lifted her feet. As soon as she was inside the car Lily moved to the front and pressed the starter. We didn't talk; we were too breathless from our efforts, and there wasn't time. I fumbled with numb fingers at the rope which bound her ankles—it had been wound around her galoshes—and then untied the second rope which held her arms to her sides.

Lily said over her shoulder as we tore along that country road, "Is she alive?"

"Her heart's beating. Very faintly. Hurry, Lily!" I could hardly speak for the fury that was in me.

So clever! So easy! All he needed to do was tie her up, throw her into that ditch where she could scream her lungs out without hope until those lungs were paralyzed by ice. He could have come back the next day or the day following that to remove the bindings and leave her where she lay. The heavy material of her galoshes and coat would prevent rope marks. She might not have been found for weeks. By then all evidence of his presence would be obliterated by drifting snow; nothing would be found but a voiceless, frozen corpse.

Poor foolish Evelyn, some might say, wandered in back of her own house, fell down a hill, and knocked herself out, then froze to death in the snow. Wouldn't you think she'd have known better? Her epitaph.

It was dark when Lily and I finally left Warwick. We stopped in a diner where the jukebox was squawking so loudly that the dishes rattled. A couple of truck drivers at the counter stared at Lily while we ate quickly and in silence, then got out of there. We didn't begin to talk until we were headed back toward New York.

"Do you think she'll be all right?" I asked.

"I hope so. The doctor knows what he's doing."

We had left her in care of a Dr. Brown whose office was in one of the big old wooden mansions along the main street of the town. Fortunately he maintained a small private hospital upstairs, and his wife was a nurse. They took Evelyn in charge and were doing all that could be done for her.

We told them that Evelyn was my cousin, and when I gave her name, the doctor remembered the Sayre family from years ago. He was distressed to hear of her accident, and said that such things happened surprisingly often during winter months in the valley.

"Generally it's hunters, though," he said. "They stumble and sprain an ankle or break a leg. Had a couple one year who got lost in an ice storm not a hundred feet from their own house and wandered for two hours before they found a landmark."

Evelyn's head was badly bruised where she had "fallen" against a rock. I clenched my fists, thinking of that rock held in a human hand, slammed against her temple. There was no proof that she had been attacked, not the slightest evidence which wasn't already covered up.

We gave the doctor some money and told him we'd telephone that evening. I explained that I had to get home because my small child needed attention, and he accepted this fictional domestic necessity as a natural situation. He was too busy with immediate problems at that moment to ask many questions.

"She may be unconscious for some time," he told us. "Shock, you know, and the cold. Possibly concussion; we'll hope it is mild. What we must guard against now is pneumonia—she must be kept in bed, warm and very quiet."

"Please telephone me as soon as she is conscious," I said, and gave him the number. "Tell her not to worry, that Janice and Lily were here, and every thing is being taken care of. The property deal, I mean. She's anxious to sell the farm, you know; that's why she came out here today—to show it to a prospective buyer. I suppose he never showed up."

"Showed better judgment than she, poor woman," he declared, wagging his white head. "Now if you'll excuse me I've got work to do here, and I'm expecting a confinement call any hour."

The wind had begun to die down as we drove back through the valley over the lonely mountain road. The night had that crisp quality which indicated a drop in temperature. Variously colored neon signs glowed luridly around highway diners and stores, and through the lighted windows of houses one caught glimpses of people reading or moving around inside their warm, human-designed shelters. The bridge was a beautiful thing, its graceful arc outlined on the Hudson far below.

As we rolled along the parkway toward lower Manhattan I said, out of the weariness that had settled on me, "Lily, what next?"

"It is best that we do nothing, tell no one. We shall wait. See who asks the first question, makes the first move."

"Don't we even try to find out?"

"We won't have to. Let him worry and make exertions. He will do it soon enough. We could exhaust ourselves tonight checking to find who drove that car, where each of the men went today. But that will not be necessary. Wait and see. Wait quietly and conserve your energy."

Ordinarily I might not have been able to emulate this Oriental strategy, but now I agreed. I was so tired from lack of sleep, from letdown after our chase and getting Evelyn into safe hands, that I numbly agreed to everything Lily said. Evelyn was as well off as she could possibly be for the present. And tonight, when we went to bed, I intended to make certain no one entered our room. This time it would be possible to awaken Lily. And Lily had a gun.

She parked the car in front of a Fifth Avenue Longchamps, and we found a window table which looked out on the deserted street. While a waiter was bringing sandwiches and coffee Lily went to telephone and I improved my frostbitten appearance as well as I could. Bill Char arrived in a taxi as we were finishing our supper; we watched through the window as he seated himself under the steering wheel of the sedan to wait for us. When we came out he opened the rear door and we climbed in. He asked a few questions, and Lily answered briefly. She had not introduced us, and I couldn't understand their conversation, but at that point I was too tired to listen anyway. We rode home in style, chauffeur-driven, for the benefit of anyone looking out the windows of the house on Washington Square.

When we opened the door of that house it was as if nothing had ever happened. There had been no change. Doris and Henri sat on the sofa playing gin rummy while Louise watched. Bela was in the love seat with his feet stretched out, a sketch pad in his hands, doing a caricature of Louise. He had given her eyelashes two inches long. They looked like a peaceful and innocent group.

Louise spoke without breaking her pose. "Some more of our family home, at last."

I took off my coat. "Hello. Are we the last to come in?"

Bela signed his sketch and handed it to Louise. "No, dammit. Evelyn's out. That woman has gone traipsing to the country. A telegram just came from her saying she'll be away for a couple of days arranging to sell that farm of hers."

"Who on earth wants to buy country property at this time of year?" I put surprise into my tone.

"A shrewd operator," Doris contributed. "Someone who knows the place already and thinks it can be bought at a lower price now. Evelyn put it on the market last spring."

"What have you two girls been doing?" Bela's bright eyes took in our disheveled appearance, starting at the legs and working up. "Were you rolling in the snow?"

I almost gasped.

Lily answered smoothly, pulling off her gloves and slipping her coat from her shoulders. "Aren't we wrecks? We've been helping my uncle's two children build a snow man. The drifts were quite deep on Long Island."

"That's where you lived before you came here, isn't it?" Doris asked. She was remembering the uncle attached to the diplomatic service. "Where is his home?"

"Oyster Bay." Lily sat down and lit a cigarette.

Doris was still pursuing the diplomatic relative. "Will your uncle be at the Chinese New Year dinner?"

"Not for dinner unfortunately. They expect guests. But all of them will arrive in Chinatown before the Dragon appears."

"The Dragon?" Henri's interest in gin rummy waned. He laid down his cards and turned to us.

Lily blew smoke and swung her little foot as she explained. "At midnight, on the eve of our New Year, the Dragon comes out of his hiding place and dances in the streets. I shall not take the edge off your anticipation by describing him. You will meet him yourselves."

She rose and went toward the door, then turned, smiling. "I had to visit my uncle today to return something he had loaned to me." Her bright eyes regarded the group near the fire, and she included them all in the most amiable of smiles. "At Sun Nin Toy, our New Year, my people have a custom which many consider most commendable. We Chinese always pay all of our debts."

Lily held her large red alligator bag casually against her side as she spoke, but I knew it was heavy with the weight of the gun she carried. When we were undressing for bed I asked her, "Did you mean that tomorrow night you intend to pay a debt to someone in this house?"

Lily's beautiful face was set and stern. She answered in a velvet-soft voice which belied the steel determination which drove her, "In a way, yes. If possible I shall pay a very large and important debt, which has accumulated interest for many years. But before I can do that—I intend to collect one."

Chapter Twenty-One

I awakened with a start the following day to find Louise standing by my bed. "What is it?"

"You're wanted on the phone, Janice. I knocked, but you didn't hear me."

"Thanks. I'll be right there."

I looked at Lily's bed; it was neatly made; she was gone. My arms and legs ached as I stood up—muscle strain from my exertions of the day before. I pulled a robe around me and hurried down the hall. I picked up the telephone and heard Lily's voice.

"Janice?"

"Yes."

"Be careful how you answer." She spoke cautiously. "I'll talk. I called Warwick a short while ago, and the doctor says that Evelyn has only a slight concussion. But there is congestion in her chest, and her temperature is up. He is giving her penicillin and hopes to prevent pneumonia."

"Oh!" I gasped. Then I saw a shadow projected on the far wall. Someone at the head of the stairs, listening. I gripped the phone hard and went on talking, my eyes fixed on that shadow. "I'm delighted to hear that. Is there anything I can do to help?"

"Is someone listening?" Lily asked.

"Yes, of course," I said gaily. "Tell me all about it!"

"There is nothing we can do for Evelyn. Don't mention her name to anyone; let others ask questions if they wish. I shall not be home today, Janice."

"Where are you now?"

"At the public library."

I wanted to ask whether she had found the missing news item in the library newspaper files, but did not know how to word the question. Lily volunteered no information. Before I could say anything she went on: "This is what I want you to do. Stay in the house today; don't go anywhere alone. I'll send a car at nine tonight; bring everyone with you. Until then try to put this out of your mind and don't worry."

The shadow had not moved.

"Lily—" I stopped. "Anything else?"

"I'll tell you what you want to know tonight. Just be careful."

"All right. I'll let the others know." The shadow withdrew. "Goodbye. Don't work too hard." I put down the telephone.

I went to Louise's room first. She was sitting near the window with a mirror propped on the sill, plucking her eyebrows. "I'll call Max," she said when I told her about the car which would pick us up. "He'll be here before nine. Janice, what kind of clothes should I wear?"

"Your prettiest. This will be a real party."

I didn't tell her that ordinarily no one but family or intimate friends were invited to a Chinese house on such a night.

"What are you wearing?" She pursued that subject.

"I have that new sweater, you know, with sequins around the neck. And a long black skirt."

"Would you like me to do your hair again?"

"That would be a great help."

Doris was in her room typing. When I delivered Lily's message she asked, "What sort of place are we going to? I've never been in Chinatown."

"I've been there," I told her. "You are going to be surprised."

"Surprised at what?" Bela stood in the hall near the open door with an unhappy scowl on his face. I told him he would be surprised when he saw Mr. Char's apartment, and his scowl vanished, but he blinked continuously. He seemed very nervous.

"Evelyn ought to come home," he growled. "Has she called? I heard the phone ring a while ago."

I told him the call was from Lily. I added that I'd be in the house all day and would let him know the minute Evelyn telephoned. He started back to his studio and said he would tell Henri about the arrangements Lily had made for our transportation.

The day dragged endlessly. I was afraid to go out; Dr. Brown might call from Warwick. My new clothes arrived; I had forgotten them. I killed time by opening boxes and hanging things in the dressing room. I finished a crossword puzzle, then wrote a couple of letters to friends in Honolulu, telling them what a gay time I was having. It was a help to spend a couple of hours with Louise while she arranged my hair and chattered about her newly hatched career as an Italian actress.

By the time the car finally arrived for us I was so tense that my insides were churning. The driver was a wrinkled old fellow muffled to the eyebrows in a heavy coat who announced, "Missy send car. Thank you," and scuttled back down the steps to wait. We all crowded into the big car, and nobody said much on the way down to Mott Street except Bela, who sulked and muttered that he wished that Evelyn were with us. If he was putting on an act, it was a good one.

A bright lantern hung over the shabby doorway on Mott Street; similar lanterns shone over other entrances along the block. Doris hung back with little nervous exclamations as we started up the stairs. I gave her an impatient shove, and she began to climb reluctantly, while I herded the others ahead of me and followed. I remembered my own reluctance to enter this strange building, my surprise at the interior. The people who came with me this night were due to be even more amazed, for they had no previous acquaintanceship with the Orient.

A servant in black trousers and felt-soled slippers took our wraps in the red foyer, then opened the door to the next room. Mr. Char, dressed in a conventional dark business suit, waited for us in that beautiful room beyond the red door. Beside him stood Lily Wu.

She wore a Chinese panel dress of exquisite white lace threaded with gold. Her black hair was oiled, Oriental fashion, so that it lay glossy and smooth on her small head, fastened in a figure eight at the nape of her neck by gold pins encrusted with jade and pearls. From her ears swung pendants of jade, green as the greenest sea.

For a moment we stopped just inside the room. There were smothered exclamations from the men, gasps of surprise from Louise and Doris. Mr. Char seemed not to have heard them. He bowed graciously and said, "You honor this humble house. Please feel most welcome."

Lily's smile was dazzling. She turned to the table behind her and stepped forward, offering an octagon lacquered tray which held porcelain dishes containing candied melon, sesame cakes, watermelon seeds, citron, sugared ginger—this was the Yin-Yang of Life, sweet symbols of longevity, good-luck wishes for the year.

After we helped ourselves Lily led us across the peach-colored carpet into another room, still larger, where several young people sat at a round table. She introduced us to a dozen or more Chinese, using given names only: Eddie, Mary, George, and so on. We were offered tiny cups of liquor before we seated ourselves and food began to arrive. The Chinese were very gay. They played games which they taught us with much laughter; Rock, Scissors, Paper was one which quickly became popular. The men caught on fast, and presently, even vinegary Doris was laughing. Her eyes had widened at sight of so many jewels, such rich fabrics; in Doris's code material possessions indicated desirable personal qualities, and she forgave these people for being different from her in feature because of their wealth.

There was much good-natured laughter as Lily's guests tried to manage the ivory chopsticks at their plates; no one looked disapproving when finally hunger forced them to resort to forks and spoons. Bowls and dishes and platters of food kept arriving: shark's-fin soup, boned duck stuffed with water chestnuts and almonds and chicken and slivers of ham, pork with pineapple and paper-thin slices of carrot, beef and ginger, fried shrimp, beautiful pink lobster swimming in a heavenly sauce, chicken and almond hash, steamed whole fish covered with vegetables, and candied seaweed. Some of the dishes I recognized from past experience, others were strange, but all were delectable.

In between courses we had entertainment. Chinese musicians played, dancers in gorgeous costumes whirled and postured, swordsmen pantomimed a duel. Mr. Char moved from guest to guest like a dignified mandarin, drinking with each man at the table from cups thin as eggshell. Lily sat opposite me next to her tall young cousin Bill Char. I hadn't had a chance to speak to her except most casually. I watched our fellow inhabitants of the house.

Max used chopsticks expertly; he ate and drank with gusto. Louise tried to imitate him and failed with much laughter. A flush came into Doris's sallow cheeks; she began to lose her self-consciousness at being in such foreign surroundings, but she regarded each exotic dish with suspicion and merely pecked at the wonderful food. Bela looked glum and emptied his liquor cup as fast as it was filled, while Henri balanced chopsticks carefully in his thin fingers and seemed annoyed as he made repeated and futile efforts to capture different morsels.

I had never seen Lily so vivacious. She laughed often; she chattered incessantly. But she hardly touched the food before her.

We were spooning almond soup, the last delicious course, when a series of sharp reports sounded outside. Doris started and looked at Lily. "What on earth is that?"

Lily laid down her porcelain spoon. "The Dragon. It must be midnight."

"What Dragon?" Max Bloom asked.

Bill Char explained. "The Chinese Dragon comes out at midnight of the New Year, and we greet him with firecrackers." He grinned as a series of staccato explosions sounded in the street. "We can't watch from a balcony, as some of our neighbors do. Shall we go down to the street?"

Doris looked apprehensive, and Lily said, "Do not be alarmed. He is a very cheerful and harmless Dragon. But he likes us to welcome him when he passes our house."

We rose from the table and waited while servants brought our coats. Lily stood at the head of the stairs as we started down, wrapping a white chiffon scarf around her head. "There will be a crowd in the street, " she said. "In case we should become separated, we will meet here. After the Dragon returns to his temple our party really begins."

She must have found the missing news item. Did she know now which of these two men from the house was a murderer? There wasn't the slightest indication in her attitude toward either of them.

I wanted very much to talk to her, and I tried to linger, but Bela caught my hand and pulled me along with him. Bill Char was escorting Doris, while Henri and Louise and Max were already down the stairs. Mott Street was filled with people when we reached it. Bright flares flickered, throwing red lights on the faces around us. Merry Chinese milled from all sides, rushed from every building, laughing and calling to one another. I had been trying all evening to catch Lily's eye, but without success. Now, I thought, we can talk safely in this crowd. I slipped away from Bela and ducked into a doorway, waiting for Lily's white-wrapped head to emerge from the house.

When she finally appeared we were separated by a dozen chattering, shoving people. I started pushing my way through to her, watching the white scarf ahead of me, the dark fur of her coat to which a few snowflakes were clinging. Firecrackers exploded in the gutter; someone screamed, others laughed with delight.

Then the Dragon appeared, dancing and cavorting, and a thousand firecrackers popped in his path. The crowd pressed forward, calling greetings to the Dragon as he bowed in all directions, leaped into the air, coquetted with pretty girls and children who squealed with joy at his antics. He was a gorgeous figure, animated by the living men who carried his long, writhing body and performed the acrobatics which made the beast seem astonishingly real, a huge creature with flapping ears and cavernous mouth, glowing red eyes and a long tail glittering with tinsel and colored glass. Dancers stepped proudly ahead of him clad in ancient Chinese costume, while drums beat incessantly and cymbals reverberated in the crisp night air.

I watched for a moment, caught in the hypnotism of the scene, then turned to the crowd again. The white scarf was farther away now. I moved to the rear of the crowd, close to the shop windows of Mott Street, and made my way slowly toward the white-wrapped head I sought. Finally I reached her. She was clutching the arm of a laughing Chinese boy.

"Lily," I called urgently.

The white chiffon-swathed head turned for a fraction of a second, then the girl ducked into the crowd and vanished, while I stood gaping. Lily's sable coat, Lily's white scarf, a pretty Chinese face. To a casual observer she might look like Lily Wu. But she was not.

I turned back toward the pressing crowd and was immediately engulfed in a mass of people; not one familiar face among them. As I let myself be jostled I began to reflect; if I had been unable to find Lily I might not have been suspicious. But the fact that she had instructed another girl to masquerade in her clothes made it obvious to me that she had chosen to disappear.

I knew where she had gone. I struggled slowly through packed human beings while firecrackers sputtered, cymbals crashed, and the chattering mob grew more dense. It took a long time before I could finally reach the next corner. In contrast to Mott Street there was nothing to see but a deserted thoroughfare and darkened shops. A block beyond was the Bowery. I hurried toward it, looking for a taxi.

The house in Washington Square stood black and silent. I let myself in as quietly as I could and stood for a moment with every sense alert. There was complete darkness inside except for a narrow crack of light at the end of the hall.

It shone from the door of our room.

I stood uncertainly for a moment, straining for sounds. Utter stillness. Had I forgotten to turn out the light when I left for Chinatown? I couldn't remember. I took off my shoes and started on tiptoe down the hall.

The door to our room was slightly ajar. I pushed, and it swung inward. Standing on the threshold, I peered into our room. It was exactly as I had left it: my robe flung over a chair, satin mules on the carpet. I waited for interminable minutes, every muscle straining with effort to stand motionless. No sound. No movement. I stepped inside.

Something fell with brutal force on the back of my head, and I pitched forward into nothingness.

Chapter Twenty-Two

I heard sounds before I opened my eyes. Scratching and scraping. Hammering of steel against stone. Rattle as of gravel dropping onto wood.

My head ached badly, worse than ever before in my life. Nausea writhed inside me. It took effort, superhuman effort, to open my eyes. I concentrated, raised heavy lids, and closed them as I saw gray mist streaked with black. I tried again. The gray mist dissolved, the black moved. A man's figure, crouched at the end of the closet, bent toward the little door. I stared and blinked the blurring away. A moan burst from me.

The figure turned, rose. He came toward me, smiling.

"So you're awake now!" he said. "Happy New Year, my dear."

Henri. Smiling. Gleeful. There never had been such malevolent glee on a face. I must have tried to shrink back, for I began to slip, found I could not right myself, and fell sideways. I was bound, wrists tied behind me, ankles fastened together with a pair of nylons.

"Here, let me help you," he said. He reached, jerking me upright by the shoulder of my sweater. The pain was dreadful in my head. He shoved me back against the frame of the door.

"Don't start to scream," he said, "or I shall have to put you to sleep again. That would be a shame, for you would not be able to share this very gratifying moment with me. One minute, please, while I finish this little job."

He went back to the end of the room and knelt by the small opened door. He picked up a chisel and hammer and began to pound. He was chiseling mortar out from between bricks of the wall. As he worked, he talked.

"I've waited years for this," he said. "I've had difficulties. Money, distance, the damned war. And at last, after all my careful planning, that greedy old thief, my former estimable employer, objected to telling me where he hid the money. He wanted it for himself."

"You knew Chadwick?" I gasped. "But you couldn't—you're—"

"A pitiful French refugee? Let me introduce myself, Miss Cameron. Henry Longmire, former secretary to the great financier. He had made fine plans; a long voyage to a place where he could live in comfort for the rest of his rotten life—Ah, you're not comfortable, are you?"

I had begun to slide down again and could not help myself He came to me, caught my hair, and pulled me upright. "There, chèrie. Better?" A chuckle. "I hope you're enjoying this as much as I."

I bit my lip to stifle an outcry of pain. I wouldn't give this monster the satisfaction of hearing me moan again. I said between gritted teeth, "I am interested."

He returned to the corner. "Splendid. I'm delighted to have such an attentive confidante. Clever of you, guessing I would take this chance to return to the house. Of course you knew I wanted very much to get in here after hearing me at your door last night. Only you didn't anticipate that I would wait for you to follow me, did you?"

"No." There was a wound at the back of my skull which touched agonizingly at the sharp wood of the doorframe. I turned sideways, and waves of pain dizzied me. In spite of myself my eyes closed for an instant.

"Ah, headache? Never mind; it won't last long. Where was I?"

"Waiting here for me."

"Oh yes. After waiting thirteen long years for him to show me his little cache another short wait didn't matter. It has been a strain at times, but worth it. And now I can talk freely to someone at last. Because you, of course, will never tell."

He was going to kill me.

He went back to his hammering and scraping. My head was now at an angle, eyes turned toward our room. Something white moved in the hall beyond the door. I stared, held my breath. My heart began to pound in hard, irregular thumps.

Lily stepped into the room; she held a gun in her hand. Relief flooded me, leaving me faint. Lily pantomimed that I should go on talking.

I spoke to him. "What do you mean—I shall never tell?"

"Ah, at last! Here it comes!" A brick dropped out of the wall, and he hammered again. He answered, as he pounded. "Because you are going to have a regrettable accident, my dear. Very easy to arrange. I shall simply break your pretty neck like this"—he made a twisting gesture with the hammer—"between my two hands. Then I'll toss you down the front steps. An accident," he repeated with another chuckle, "like poor stupid Evelyn had."

I forced a laugh, a weak and hysterical sound. "But Evelyn is not dead."

Lily took a few steps nearer.

The pounding stopped. He turned toward me, his eyes glittering. "What did you say?"

"Evelyn is alive and safe. I drove to Warwick and found her yesterday a few minutes after you left. Remember the black sedan you passed on the road? Evelyn is safely hidden, and when she recovers—"

He strode toward me swiftly. "Where is she?"

His hand clutched my hair again and jerked me upright. He began to bump my head against the door frame, so that waves of red-hot agony flowed through me. Obscenities erupted from him, pouring out in rhythm with that cruel punishing hand. I moaned, and tried desperately to keep hold on consciousness.

He said, "You will tell me, you know. It might as well be now as later." He slapped me hard.

I slipped sideways toward the bedroom, and he moved around to pull me erect again, presenting his back to Lily. As he leaned over me she rushed forward. There was a dull sound when the butt of the gun smashed against his temple. He dropped heavily across my legs.

Lily stooped, and as she did so he stirred. She deliberately raised the gun again and struck once more.

He didn't move again.

She rolled him off my legs and started to untie my ankles. Her hands were shaking so that she couldn't manage the knots.

"My wrists, Lily," I said. She fumbled on the dressing table for a pair of cuticle scissors and cut the stockings which bound my wrists behind me. My arms fell to my sides.

"Can you do the rest?" she asked.

"I think so." I was so weak that I could hardly speak.

She laid a gentle hand on my shoulder. Tears were in her eyes. "I'm sorry, Janice, that you had to take such a beating. I couldn't shoot; he was too close to you."

"It's all right."

Lily went to the end of the closet and knelt before the opening. She used the hammer to pull at loosened bricks in the wall. We hadn't looked far enough the first time; we hadn't thought of a false wall. Three bricks dropped with a rattle of mortar. She reached into the dark aperture and removed a long, narrow metal box, the sort used in safe-deposit vaults. It was not locked. When she opened it there was money inside; she poured out packages of paper bills. Five-hundred-dollar bills in neat bundles.

Six hundred and twenty-two thousand dollars.

"Since we couldn't find this," Lily said, "I had to let him show us where it was. I was sure it was here, you see, after he tried to get into this room."

She was putting money in little piles on the floor as she talked. In careful stacks, a hundred thousand dollars to each one. She began to murmur to her self. "Mr. Hong. Mr. Kuo. Mr. Tsiu. And Mr. Lau—my honorable father's real-estate holdings. Mr. Chang—the last of our cash and our home. Mr. Wei—our bonds and securities. It's all here. He didn't have time to touch any of it!" She looked at me then, a strange little figure in her white lace dress, her face pale, her hair disarranged, her eyes shining with triumph. "It's all here!" she said again. She disregarded the twenty-two thousand.

When I could get my breath I said, "So that's what Chadwick came back for!"

"Yes. This is why he was in the dressing room. Checking to be sure his hiding place had not been disturbed."

"But I thought the money he stole was recovered."

Lily looked at the packages of bank notes on the floor. "This was not. This money he borrowed with the Wu chop. It was a secret transaction, never entered on the books of the firm. Charles Chadwick obtained this money five days before his arrest. No one in his office knew about it except himself—and possibly his secretary." She indicated the unconscious man on the floor.

"You knew that?"

"Since yesterday. I discovered it from old newspaper files. Henry Longmire sailed for Europe immediately after his employer was sentenced. He has never been heard of since."

"But, Lily, I still don't understand—"

She wasn't listening to me. Lily was carefully arranging a scene. She wiped the hammer with paper tissues and folded the lax fingers of Henry Longmire around the handle, then tossed it into the corner. She put the twenty two thousand dollars back into the metal box, polished her fingerprints from its surface, then, holding it with tissues, pressed the hand of the murderer around it and dropped the box beside him. It opened as it fell so that money was almost spilling from it.

She went into the other room with the rest of the money, to the bureau where the Laughing Buddha sat. She turned him upside down and stuffed his blue porcelain body with packages of five-hundred-dollar bills. When she finished, Lo-Han was worth his original price and six hundred thousand dollars more. She set him back on his teakwood stand. She patted his fat belly.

"Are you going to keep that money?" I demanded stupidly.

Lily turned to me. Her face was serene as some wise and dispassionate goddess of antiquity. "I am going to give the money to my father. It is rightfully his."

"Lily," I said again, "I don't understand."

She laid her hand on my arm, looking at me with a steady gaze. "You will hear the entire story later. Trust me, Janice."

I looked into her face. There are times when we must push our chips in blindly if we are betting on human values. If I could not trust this girl, I could never trust anyone again. My answer was in my eyes.

She smiled briefly and nodded. "This is what I want you to do now," she said in a brisk voice. "I shall go and call Captain Weber. I'll tell him I came to the house and found you tied up and unconscious, with this man just in the act of removing the box of money. I hit him with the gun, untied you, and found you could not be revived, then ran to call the police."

"But—"

"Don't worry. Henri never knew how much money was in the box, because he never saw it. The police will be so glad to find the real murderer and the missing twenty-two thousand that they won't ask too many questions."

She touched the man on the floor with her foot. "He never knew who hit him or what happened after that, so he can't tell. We can prove his identity from the newspaper photographs in the file. And eventually he will talk, be sure of that."

I lay back on the floor then, with a deep, exhausted sigh, and closed my eyes. It wasn't going to be difficult to stay there a while longer.

So Lily went to phone the police, and that is how they found me. And everything else happened just as she had predicted that it would.

Chapter Twenty-Three

The police finally departed that night, taking the murderer and the money with them. A doctor came and attended to me, and I was in bed, glad to be there. I refused sedatives, asking merely to be left alone so I could sleep. Lily undressed and climbed into the bed adjacent to mine.

This time I didn't have to ask questions. As soon as she was settled under the covers she began to talk.

"You remember I told you that Charles Chadwick came to our house and took the Wu chop from my father's desk?"

"I remember."

"Perhaps it is difficult for you to understand how important his chop is to a Chinese. My father's seal was his recognized legal signature, on record at the bank, valid as his own writing on any check or business document. His associates respected it as they respected his spoken word. Merchants and other residents of Chinatown knew of the friendship between Chadwick and my father and that my father had invested money with the loan association.

"Charles Chadwick came to our home and stole the chop at a time when my father was in China on business. He then went to six different men who were my father's friends with a letter which he had signed with the Wu chop, supposedly a request from my father. He borrowed a hundred thousand dollars from each. He knew that his firm was going to be investigated, and this was double insurance against the time when he served his sentence and regained his freedom."

"What happened then?"

"By the time my father returned from China, Chadwick was in prison and the case was closed. Since the money had been borrowed from his friends on his chop, the only way he could save face, preserve his own honor, was to repay what was borrowed. To some Occidentals this may seem a strange way of reasoning, but there are many cases on record where men other than Chinese have felt the same about personal integrity.

"You see, Janice, my father considered it his fault that his friends had been defrauded. If he had not made an error of judgment in friendship with a dishonest man they would not have been victimized. So he had to repay their losses. He sold everything he possessed to raise the necessary money; he even sold his business. Then he moved his family out to California, since he felt that he could no longer face the community. He has been working for another herbalist since that time at a very small salary."

"You said something about your home, Lily. Is that by any chance the house Mr. Char is living in?"

"Yes. He bought it from Mr. Chang to hold against the time when we would be able to return to New York. He and Bill have helped me through all of this. It was Mr. Ames, from Bill Char's law firm, who called on Chadwick in prison to ask what he had done with the chop. He was informed that we could buy it back, at a very big price, when Chadwick had served his sentence."

Her voice was beginning to sound tired. "Is there anything else you wish to know?"

"What did your father say to those men when he returned their money?"

"He told them he had discovered the Chadwick investment was unwise and was returning the loan. That's all. Of course they knew the truth; Chadwick was in Sing Sing by then—but no one mentioned it. Each of those men involved would have done the same thing in my father's place."

"What if Henry Longmire tells all this to the police?"

She sighed wearily. "I am taking a chance on that. Since the whole procedure was conducted so secretly by Chadwick, I am hoping that the other man did not know the details of it. In case he should tell the police I will produce the money and we'll have to go through a lot of red tape to get it back. I can prove all of this, of course. But it will be infinitely better if there is no publicity. Then my family can come home."

"You mean they can return to New York?"

"Yes. I hope so." Lily yawned. "I shall telephone Los Angeles tomorrow." She turned out the light.

There were so many other things I wanted to say: that I'd like to meet her parents and her brothers, that I hoped we would be friends for a long time, that I was glad I had been able to help a little. I looked at Lily—her eyes were closed. I slid down under my blankets and went to sleep.

Some time later, on a peaceful evening, we sat again in the living room of the house in Washington Square around a bright fire. Our group was smaller now, for several of our original number were gone.

Jarvis, of course, we would never see again.

Doris had fled to a sanitarium from which she refused to emerge. Her testimony at the proper time might be given by deposition, with consent of the district attorney.

Her lover was in prison awaiting his trial, with its certain verdict. It had not taken long, nor had it been difficult for the police to get a confession from him; at the end he seemed almost relieved to reach the finish of his long, nerve-racking masquerade.

We lounged in the living room with cigarettes and drinks in our hands, comfortably relaxed, each of us able at last to trust those companions who were left.

Louise was the only petulant one; she regretted the delay which postponed her important dental work. Max Bloom, whom we suspected had become more to Louise than merely her agent, said cheerfully, "Stop grumbling, sweetie. You're damned lucky you didn't get those teeth knocked out for you—or your head cracked open."

His eyes rested on Evelyn, thinner and more pale after her illness, but fast recovering now that Bela had brought her home. She wore pink rosebuds pinned to the shoulder of her blue velvet dress. And she sat very close to Bela, her gaze seldom wandering from the gold circle on her left hand. The California divorce decree of Madeleine Baldwin-Ferris-Carlake-Palyi had become final two days after our eventful Chinese New Year, and Bela lost no time in making an honest woman out of Evelyn.

"I couldn't resist it after I saw that farm of hers," he said with a grin. "We're going to move to the country and remodel the house. Maybe we'll open a home for indigent artists, eh, Madame Palyi?" He kissed the hand he was holding.

Soft pink crept into Evelyn's pale cheeks. "Bela's going to paint. That's most important."

Louise, the practical, asked, "What will you use for money?"

"Oh, I've got about ten thousand in the bank. Maybe more, I don't know. Evelyn's going to straighten things out for me. Aren't you, darling?"

"He hasn't opened a bank statement or paid a bill for months!" she said with fond reproach.

It looked as if the birds and flowers were going to be neglected for a while; Evelyn had another creative job to do.

"Bela," I said, "I've often wondered, why did you dislike Henri so much? Did you know who he really was?"

"You mean Henry? No, I didn't know who he was, but I knew his type; I saw enough of them when I lived in Paris. I suspected that he might not be French, but if he wanted to put on an act to impress Doris, that wasn't my worry. What really annoyed me was that I saw his manuscript, the one he stole from Alain Duvivier. Duvivier is dead, and his sister sent the script to the agency where our phony Frenchman worked."

"He was going to get the translation published as his own story?"

"I don't know. If he had, I might have written to someone I knew in Paris to put the Duvivier family wise. But I doubt whether Longmire would have carried it that far. He needed a front to make a hit with Doris, that was all."

"He knew who she was?"

"Of course. When he worked as Chadwick's secretary he used to mail checks to Switzerland for Doris's tuition."

Lily had been sitting in a big chair, listening tranquilly. She said now, "Tell us the story, Max; you've talked to the newspapermen. Let's put the pieces together."

Max cleared his throat, not at all reluctant to take the center of the stage for a while. "Well, you know the early part of it—Chadwick's investment company and so forth. Longmire went to work as his personal secretary about a year before the thing fell apart. He was a very shrewd guy; it wasn't long before he began to smell something in the works, and he ferreted it out bit by bit. He knew about the safe-deposit box in Florida, and Chadwick gave him five thousand dollars—in advance—to get out of town after the trial and keep his mouth shut. No percentage for Longmire in telling—he wouldn't get anything."

"The money in the house here—" Louise began, and Max nodded at her. "I was coming to that. Chadwick decided at the last minute to take out double insurance. He had just finished remodeling the lower floor for his wife. He stuck that money inside the wall and did a secret little job of masonry just as protection in case anything went wrong. Remember, he didn't expect to get such a stiff sentence. The law isn't too strict with embezzlers, especially when they know the right people. Remember the Benson case? He got only three years."

"But Chadwick was tried by the wrong judge," I said, remembering the comment of the news columnist.

"Yeah. And investigators found the major part of the dough in Florida. All he had left was the little cache here."

Lily said casually, "It was not very much money."

I looked carefully into my highball glass and said nothing.

Max laughed. "Maybe not to you, sweetie. Your family is obviously well heeled."

"It's a lot to me," Louise declared.

"Twenty-two thousand is plenty of dough to anybody that's flat broke," Max went on. "So Longmire went to Paris and played around until war broke out. He stayed in Europe then in preference to being drafted for the American army. He was one of those odd-job boys—hung around bars where rich tourists congregated and picked up a living from showing the hot spots, pimped a little, sold phony art, and so forth. When things got too hot in France he bought himself a passport and some identification papers—you could buy anything in Europe then if you had money—and went to Lisbon.

"As soon as it was safe he returned to New York with a French identity. That was when he made contact with Chadwick in Sing Sing. Doris had never gone near her father; the old boy was lonely and sick, and it wasn't hard for Longmire to persuade him that he had one loyal friend. He moved into the house, made a play for Doris, and arranged for her father to work here as super. He told the police he never meant to kill the man, that he was merely 'persuading' him to tell where the money was hidden. We know all the rest."

"What was it that Jarvis discovered?" Bela asked.

"The only news photo of Longmire on record. A quick shot of Chadwick walking up the courthouse steps with his secretary. Longmire looked different then; he was thirteen years younger and clean-shaven. Jarvis recognized him just the same."

"I still don't know how he killed Jarvis. Gave him sleeping pills, yes, but how did he manage it?" Louise asked.

"He told police that Jarvis came to his room with the scrapbook and said he had guessed the truth. Henry persuaded Jarvis to sit down with a bottle and listen to his story. As soon as Jarvis had a stiff enough shot inside him, so he wouldn't detect a funny taste, Longmire dissolved amytol in his next drinks. Jarvis went to sleep and never woke up."

"But the records—if Jarvis was unconscious, how did they start to play all by themselves?"

"He used an electric timer to start the machine. There are various kinds on the market. Jarvis had one which he brought home from the music store to try out and never used, and Henry knew about it. When he went up to 'discover' the body he unplugged the thing and tossed it out the window into the snow. He picked it up next day and got rid of it."

"Poor Jarvis," Louise said. Then she giggled. "Weber's face was certainly red, wasn't it? Having two girls catch a murderer for him."

"He was not so obtuse as he wanted us to think," Lily reminded her. "His men were looking over newspaper files; they would have come to the right conclusion eventually. He wanted the murderer to feel safe."

"While he went ahead and tried to kill the rest of us!" Evelyn was indignant at that memory.

"If you hadn't been such a dope, my dear," Bela reminded her.

"You're right," she admitted. "I was fairly certain that the man I spoke to in the basement must be Henri when Louise mentioned Jarvis's ring. I remembered then that I saw his hand on the railing while we talked, and he wasn't wearing a ring. I knew, of course, that it couldn't be Bela, because—" She floundered, and flushed into silence.

"Because you left me sleeping so soundly that night after your embraces," he said complacently. "Don't be embarrassed; go on with your story."

Evelyn's hands fluttered, and her wedding ring caught the light of the fire. "As I said, I thought it must be Henri. But I wanted to be sure. I don't know how I expected to make certain of his identity, but to me it seemed horrible to accuse a man of murder without first—" She faltered, then went on more steadily. "When I received that message about my house I was actually relieved. It postponed something which I dreaded. I never dreamed, of course, that a Frenchman would know my former home, that he would be inside the house, waiting for me. He drove to Warwick in a rented car. It looked like any other car, standing there. But when I stepped into the house—"

Bela muttered something deep in his throat and captured her hand again.

Max turned toward me. "How did you know, Janice?"

I shrugged. "It was really accidental. The night of the party I happened to see him break away from the crowd and hurry around a corner. I was curious, and followed. He was too clever for me; he heard me come in and waited behind the door."

The others looked at Lily. She smiled modestly. "There was no brilliant thinking on my part," she said. "When my cousin Bill Char asked me why my roommate had taken off in pursuit of that Frenchman, I began to worry, and then I followed her. I had trouble getting a taxi, and arrived too late to save her from being hurt. You all know the rest."

She still felt unhappy about the experience I had had.

Louise rose and mixed herself another drink from the bottle on the piano bench. "Thank God that's over. Now we know everything."

This time I looked at Lily and smiled.

She said, "Will you excuse us? My parents arrived yesterday, and they haven't seen Janice for a long time. We are expected to join them for dinner."

"Where to now?" I asked as we started. "Mott Street?"

"Yes. My family has taken possession of our house again."

They were waiting for us beyond the red door of welcome: Mr. Wu, gray-haired, scholarly, and benign, dressed in rich robes of dark blue; his tiny wife, who wore violet-colored silk, with the gold pins in her hair which denoted that she had borne four sons; a grinning younger brother, Johnny Wu. The other boys would remain in California for a while, Lincoln to finish his sophomore year of high school, Eddie to continue his medical studies at Stanford.

We did not speak of events already in the past. We drank fragrant tea. We discussed the unusually cold weather New York had suffered, and we talked about Hawaii.

Mr. Wu said, "You wish to return to Honolulu?"

I answered, over the lost feeling which took possession of me at the thought, "Not now. I don't know where I want to go. The house in Washington Square—" I couldn't finish. What I did not want to say was that now, surrounded by Lily's family with their affection and warmth, I felt lonelier than I cared to acknowledge.

Mrs. Wu rose from her chair and said in a tinkling voice from which the lilt of Oriental speech would never be lost, "Let us show you something."

She led me toward the rear of the house and opened a door. "Enter, please." It was the kind of room one dreams about, if possessed of sufficient imagination to conceive such dreams. Walls of palest green, color of tender new moss. A low bed spread with green-and-gold brocaded satin. A teakwood dressing table covered with toilet fittings of crystal. A soft Chinese carpet of delicate rose. I drew a deep breath.

Mr. Wu smiled and was silent. Mrs. Wu watched me with bright black eyes. Johnny Wu had not the polite reserve of his elders. He grabbed me and pulled me inside. "This is for you," he said. "Lily says you haven't got any mother or father. So you can be part of our family from now on." He turned to his parents. "Right?" The elders bowed.

Lily moved to my side. Her eyes were sparkling with laughter. "No more housing shortage," she said. "This is yours; no one else will ever use it. My room is next door."

Then somewhere in the house a gong chimed softly. My new foster sister took my hand and said, "Welcome to your home, Janice. Come now. Let us go in to dinner."